I0700587

EMPIRE OF GLASS AND STONE

BROOKE CLONTS

SECOND
STAR PRESS

Praise for Brooke Clonts'
Empire of Glass and Stone

"Rich world building, mysticism, complex family histories, chemistry— EMPIRE OF GLASS AND STONE *has it all. You'll love Yakua's intensity and her fierce transformation."*

—Jenna Evans Welch, New York Times bestselling author of *Love & Gelato*

"Set in a world the gods long-ago abandoned, EMPIRE OF GLASS AND STONE *crosses the razor edge of hidden magic, political intrigue, terrifying customs, and a single chance to make things right. Yakua Roca, the unstoppable female lead, learns what one will do for power, and another for love. A triumphant debut YA Fantasy novel!"*

—A.K. Wilder, bestselling author of *Crown of Bones*

Copyright © 2021 by Brooke Clonts

All rights reserved.

No part of this publication may be reproduced, distributed, or transmitted in any form or by any means, including photocopying, recording, or other electronic or mechanical methods, without the prior written permission of the publisher, except as permitted by U.S. copyright law. For permission requests, contact Second Star Press, LLC.

The story, all names, characters, and incidents portrayed in this production are fictitious. No identification with actual persons (living or deceased), places, buildings, and products is intended or should be inferred.

Book cover by Ben Dougal

Illustrations by Ben Dougal

Map by Brooke Clonts

Map art paintbrush pack from @mapeffects

Content edit by Fiona McLaren

Line edit by Sharon Stogner with Devil In The Details Editing

First Ed. edits by Kelley Riegert, Karie Crawford, and Katherine Petersen

Sensitivity Read by Stacey Parshall Jensen @SParshallJensen

Character art by Alice Maria Power

Ebook ISBN 9798985171907

Paperback ISBN 9798985171914

Hardback ISBN 9798985171921

Audiobook ISBN 9798985171938

Library Of Congress Number 2021923249

Second Edition January 2024

Notes from the author: This book contains graphic violence, human sacrifice, death on screen, demons, and man-eating stone giants. Only read if you are safe to do so.

To the women I've worked with.

THE KINGDOMS OF
HALLJA
KICHKA MOUNTAINS
SKARAG
ISU
FRIGEL MOUNTAIN
ISUL URQU
JASPA
FRIGELLES
RAINBOW SAND
HELILA SEA
THALAS
DUNES OF CHIRA
SISTER ISLA
OF HOLYA A
CHIRA
ISLAND OF MIRA

MINES OF HLOS
KIA MOUNTAINS
KIANI BAY
JOCO
JOCALYNA SEA
AYU RIVER
PARIA
COCHAS
PHACHA CLAN
QORI MOUNTAINS

CHAPTER ONE

MY MOTHER SET THE POLITICS of this kingdom ablaze when she rose through its ranks, but all that's remembered of her is the fear she left behind, hammered into our family name.

Roca.

I peer from inside our hut, lurking behind the tapestries hanging on our stone walls, and watch the messenger give a bundle of strings and beads, our culture's way of formal communication, to my father.

As my father enters our home, I keep out of sight, fighting the urge to reach out and force the beads from his fingers so I can discover the truth for myself. But I've learned that acting like my mother gives my father cause for a strong rebuke and a quick dismissal.

When the neighboring emperor, known across the kingdoms of Hallja for his cruelty, dispatched an army and stationed them on our border, our clan feared they would lay siege to our kingdom at least, though the emperor has been stationed there for months with no visible movement. No one has attacked and relations between the king and the emperor have continued behind closed doors, with few rumors to suggest what's being discussed.

We keep waiting for something to happen, some piece of news to gather forces to fight or to flee.

Neither has happened.

I step away from the door, pressing closer to the stones on the wall. My breath adds moisture to the air, my body a taut string as I wait for him to tell us the news the messenger brought.

My father scans the room, and my sisters stand from where they sit. My stepmother leans against the wall by the window. We are all waiting to hear the news.

"Stellya, Zarrill, Naya, and Yakua. Come, I have news," he says.

He calls for me too.

I emerge so he can see me. With all of us present, he gestures for us to come by the hearth, where he sits with his legs folded on a patterned rug I weaved myself.

I survey his face, noting that the stress lines have eased. His bushy mustache doesn't twitch but settles comfortably over his thin lips, his long hair brushing the tops of his shoulders in frizzy waves.

The formal message doesn't cause him stress. Does this mean the emperor left?

My stepmother hovers at the edge of the room, her fingers looping through the holes of her long braid. It's not unusual for her to remain quiet when the family gathers, but her usual sweet smile is vacant from the soft curves of her face.

My deceased mother would have commanded the room had she been here. She'd demand my father speak at once.

"Well?" my sister, Zarrill, asks, her voice dripping with impatience. Her dress droops from bony shoulders, the colors faded, the tassels worn thin. "What is it?"

"We received a messenger from the King of Cochas," he says in his deep voice that resonates. "His son just returned from traveling and is of marrying age. The king has invited the realm to a festival in his son's honor. They intend to formally announce each young lady who comes."

That's all?

My father looks at my sisters and his eyes almost sparkle at this pleasant turn of events rather than the grim news we anticipated. However, my brain struggles to comprehend how the kingdom plans a festival with an army on our border.

He doesn't look at me. Not because he doesn't love me or care for me in the same way he does for my sisters, but because I have a different heritage than they do. If I went to the festival, it would cause a stir, and not in a good way.

My younger sister, Naya, is my half-sister. Zarrill is my stepsister. I'm the only one born from my deceased mother. My father knows that if I join my sisters at the festival, it'll be a reminder to the clans of their association with me and the Roca name.

Though long dead, neither our clan nor the clans along the western cliffs have forgotten my mother's strange methods of worship. Or that she had powers of manipulation that she employed whenever she wanted to climb social ladders.

In the end, it got her killed.

While my father refuses to accept it and pretends otherwise, I inherited my mother's powers.

Zarrill rubs her arm, her lips pinched. "I guess that sounds fun."

The knowledge of the army and its impending threat bothers me, but my brain chews over the idea of the festival and the opportunities it could bring. If we are on the brink of war, it's more important than ever for our family to not be on the cusp of extreme poverty.

Marriage opportunities could come from this festival. If we want to rise in social status, marriage is the quickest way to do so. Though no one in our family has any real hope of establishing such alliances, perhaps I could use my powers to change that.

"Will we get new dresses?" Naya asks. She's barefoot, her feet so dirty, I'm surprised my father hasn't made her wash them. She'd worn through her last pair of shoes weeks ago.

My father's expression becomes strained.

He repaired a hole in his fishing boat last week and won't have the coin for such expenditures.

"I'll make you one," I say, keeping my voice even. "I'll make you both one."

I also plan to make one for myself, whether my father wants me to go or not.

My father nods his thanks and a wide smile splits Naya's eager cheeks. She rushes to me, her feet leaving dust on the rugs. "Thank you," she says as she squeezes me tight.

At her contact, my power swells, her emotion rolling over me in waves. I push her back. Emotion is a heavy thing, and I like it in manageable doses.

Instead, I push my brain back to considering the logic of our current situation and the upcoming festival.

If the King of Cochas invited the entire realm, including my family, to meet him, rather than push his son to marry into the Huya clan, or the wealthy class, perhaps it means the King of Cochas cannot find a worthy girl among his peers. Instead, he has extended his sphere to the other clans for reasons of his own.

But why worry about that now?

"What of the emperor?" my other sister, Zarrill, asks. She stares at my father with a furrowed brow, refusing to accept that the emperor's threat can be so easily tossed aside. She, like Naya, has the wavy hair of her mother, characteristic of most descendants of Ma Cochira, as well as a sharp, shrewd nose that came from her deceased father.

My father meets her gaze and I watch the two of them.

The emperor raised rock giants with powers that haven't been seen since the days of the gods and created an army that demolished the northern half of Chira. They say he forces his enemies to eat the hearts of their leaders. Maybe those stories are myths, maybe not, but Zarrill is right.

If I were the King of Cochas, I wouldn't be throwing parties with the emperor at our doorstep.

I hope that if the king is throwing a festival, it means he found a way to smooth the conflicts, but Zarrill's unhappy question cast shadows over Naya's smile.

I snatch Naya's hand and squeeze it.

Regardless of the war's outcome, I have my family to worry about. If the emperor invades, we're poor, and will likely be among the first to starve. If the emperor leaves without a fight, we're still poor.

The corner of my Father's mouth hitches down. "You're right, Zarrill. The emperor's plans to unite the kingdoms are ill-founded. The realms were always meant to be separate, and we should never forget the danger he could impose. But I'd like to hope the reason they haven't attacked is because they have no plans to. As small as we are, Cochas is a formidable kingdom. You don't tangle with a fisherman's hooks." A slow smile grows on his face, like the first rays of the sun in the morning, but he catches my eyes and cocks his head.

"You look even more stoic than usual, Yakua. What's bothering you?" he asks.

I take a deep breath. If he asks the question, I'll give him a truthful answer.

"You don't think this is smoke, father?" I ask. "To catch us off guard?"

He shakes his head. "The king would never do such a thing to his own subjects."

If a king has a viscous and powerful emperor on his border that he didn't think he could win, what lengths would he undergo to keep his head? On the other hand, if the king planned to betray his kingdom, there are better ways than throwing a festival. It's not like having the emperor attack while we're dancing makes a difference when the emperor commands stone giants the size of mountains. Offerings of easy warfare wouldn't be attractive to the emperor, nor necessary if the king gave up his throne.

Perhaps my father is right, and the king only wishes to cheer his subjects up.

I want to believe everything is fine, and that all I need to worry about is what dress I need to wear. Whether I should allow myself to relax or not, preparing for the festival is something I can do.

My father meets my stepmother's gaze, his bright expression a promise that relaxes the fine wrinkles of his forehead, which have deepened over the weeks. Even with the stress of war on the horizon, he smiles more with my mother gone.

My stepmother nods, her chest expanding with relief.

With my father's speech over, I head to the market to find Naya shoes. She can't go to the festival barefoot, and I need dye and thread for the dresses. While my income as a schoolmistress isn't much, since I'm young at eighteen years of age and still considered inexperienced, it's enough to buy the essentials.

A line of tents forms the market by the docks. Boats bob on the water as merchants sell wares in the shade of their shops. The slap of dozens of fish hitting the bottoms of merchant baskets brings the familiar briny stench of the sea. I stride past each of them as the sand swallows the green grass.

Pushing a tent flap aside, I step into the shoe shop of one of my old classmates, though we've not been long out of school ourselves. My memories of him shine with sandcastles, swimming in the surf, and childish laughter. I can always count on Sunqu to cheer me up when I need it, and I need it often. He never turns me away.

He stitches soles at a worktable, wearing a ragged tunic and a simple loincloth. Glancing up, he grins as I enter, his golden-brown hair hanging in his face. "Yakua," he says in a warm, welcoming voice, "you're not here to scare away my customers, are you?"

He's teasing, but I can't find it in me to smile.

The strong earthy smell of leather replaces the fishy scent from outside as the curtain swings shut behind me. Rows of molded leather hang from sticks wedged into the gaps of the stone walls. Knives, bottles of liquid, and straps are strewn across the worktable.

"I'm here to buy Naya shoes," I say. "Do you have any simple ones in her size?"

"No, but I can make a pair." He tilts his head, a question in his eyes. "For the festival then?"

Word spreads fast. "Yes."

His smile dims, as if hoping to be wrong. "I've had dozens of orders just in the last hour for the festival, so to say I'm busy would be an understatement. But fear not, I'll fit Naya in." He leans over his table and threads a tiny needle through a shaft of stiff leather.

The way he turns his back toward me indicates I should leave, but something about the festival bothers him, and I can't go without knowing what.

"Are you going to the festival?" I ask.

"Maybe," he says. "Why?"

I study his relaxed stance, which almost covers up the rigid way he holds his needle. Sunqu is an artist and has been for as long as I've known him. Even the sandcastles we made as children looked more like grand palaces for kings than something the ocean could sweep into nothingness before our next trip to the beach.

"You think it's odd that the king is throwing a festival when we're on the brink of war? And you hate how happy everyone is about it."

He looks over his shoulder at me. "Don't say that like it's a ridiculous statement of fact. Yes, it bothers me. I suppose people should be allowed this chance at frivolity after years of tension and rumors of war, but it doesn't sit right. The king might be an excessive, sometimes senseless person, but he doesn't invite peasants to his festivals. There's no political reason to do it. I can't wrap my head around it."

He's right.

Dread trickles down my back, like cold water.

I take a deep breath, absorbing the emotion, letting it fill me because dread makes me alive in a way I can't explain. Then I let the feeling go as I usually do, and dismiss it, my power trickling to nothing, seeping into the dirt.

Sunqu might be right, and he might not be. When neither of us are kings, what can we do? Except continue in the hopes that we can better our little lives in the meager way they can be bettered.

Sunqu spent several years at the capital of Cochas in an apprenticeship. When our schoolmaster discovered Sunqu's talents, he sent him to the king to hone his craft, which was a great honor for one so young. Not only did Sunqu study hard, but he also developed a close relationship with the royals. The king loved Sunqu's work so much that the king brought him into his fortress to be trained by the masters.

No one understands why Sunqu returned, not even me, though I suspect he returned for his father after his mother died. However, if anyone knows the king of Cochas, or has the most reason to be confused at this strange turn of events, it's Sunqu.

"Did you ever meet the prince?" I ask, keeping my tone neutral.

"No," he says. "The prince traveled to the other kingdoms to establish political connections. It's something they do to maintain peace and to form engagements with princesses in the other kingdoms."

"Maybe he wants something different?"

Sunqu raises an eyebrow. "Do you really believe that?"

"No."

Still, I can hope. Either way, I'm going. While I never use my powers out of fear the clans might discover I have them, this is the one time when I must. I have to find a way to pull my family out of poverty, even it means manipulating people the way my mother did.

I'll be smarter, more careful.

Sunqu finishes stitching the soles of the shoes he's working on and sets them down. "But you still want to go?"

He stares at me so long I'm forced to fill the stale air or drown in it.

"Yes."

"I suppose there will be noblemen, priests, and the like."

Priests?

If I married a priest of Ma Cochira, our patron goddess of the sea, I might prod the clans of our village to forget that my mother worshipped the goddess of death. What better way is there for a family to show piety than to count a priest among our numbers?

The local priest is called Darhi.

No one will forget what my mother did, but perhaps I can drag the Roca name out of the ashes. I can do it through Darhi the priest. He's a decent enough sort of man.

"What is it?" Sunqu asks. "You're calculating something, I can tell. Was it something I said?"

As much as I like and respect Sunqu, I don't need to explain myself to him. I'm here for the shoes, which means my task is done, my order in place. It's time to go.

"You're very talented," I say, backing toward the curtained door. "You're bigger than this place, you know. If I had your talent, I'd chase the world." It sounds very grand, but I mean every word. "Please pass the word on to your father that your service is wonderful, as always."

Sunqu bows with a fist over his heart and returns to his shoe repair.

I hurry past lines of tents to find sheared wool, my small bag of coins tinkling in the pocket of my dress as I go.

Zarrill's and Sunqu's apprehension is too glaringly real, but I'd rather bury that fear beneath the things I can control. If our kingdom survives, it's not too late for Zarrill and Naya to lead full lives.

If they have superior skills like Sunqu, I want the schoolmaster to offer them apprenticeships. If they decide to marry, I want it to be possible. I want the best for them. And if it's not too much, I hope things will improve for me too.

CHAPTER TWO

I TWIST A THREAD OF YARN and stretch it over my loom as Naya ducks inside the drapes hung around my personal space.

Excitement oozes from her wide hazel eyes as she crouches beside me. "Is this my new dress?" Innocent and young, with knotted hair around her face and a small chin, she gets excited about the littlest things and will watch me weave for hours, enamored by the bright colors and complex patterns.

I pull on a blue thread and motion to the curves I'm forming. "I'm weaving tales of water in honor of Ma Cochira." The patron goddess of Cochas.

She leans closer. "It's beautiful."

After spinning, dying, and warping the sheared wool I spent my last month's earnings on, this dress might be my finest creation yet, though I'm hoping Sunqu will come through and make shoes that will match Naya's dress well.

Naya shuffles and mud crumbles off her heels. The grime beneath her toenails could feed worms.

I wrinkle my nose. The shoes couldn't come soon enough, but I wish I could do more for Naya.

As for me, my regular sandals will have to do. I don't have enough money to buy more than one pair of shoes. In fact, I don't have enough to buy the wool I need for three dresses, just two.

I'll go with what I have. It'll be enough.

"Have you started on yours?" comes a voice I recognize.

Zarrill leans against a wood beam near the entryway and crosses her arms. Her wavy hair is a few shades lighter than Naya's.

She couldn't have listened long. I would have noticed her there even from behind the fishing nets my father hangs from the ceiling. The dim lighting saps the contours from her face and extracts all color from the rugs beneath her feet.

Clearly, she knows I intend to come, but is she unhappy about it?

I shake the fabric of Naya's dress. "No," I say, but I don't look at her.

"Why not? Did you not have enough money?"

I look up, searching her face for emotions that might lie hidden in crevices but don't answer. Nothing in her expression gives her thoughts away.

"I'll buy your wool, Yakua," Zarrill says.

I purse my lips, swallowing a lump that wants to work its way up my throat. I'm grateful that Zarrill's dress is already finished and folded in the corner. I'm too narrow and tall to wear hers, so she can't offer to give it back.

With the festival only a few cycles of the sun away, I'll be stretched to finish my dress in so short a time, so as kind as her offer is, I shake my head. "No, Zarrill. Don't waste your money."

Zarrill grimaces as Naya scampers toward me and throws her arms around my neck. "You two are the best sisters I could ever ask for," she says. "This is so exciting. I must tell mama."

I pry her fingers from my skin where her gratitude hit me like tidal waves and pat her curly-haired head. "Thanks, Naya."

I'm glad she's happy, but I examine the soft pink half-moons beneath my nails, so they don't see how uncomfortable their overflowing gratitude makes me. After years of being scorned, I don't know how to react when I'm treated any other way. Though my immediate family treats me with kindness, a lurking uncertainty questions if I deserve it.

The room quiets as Naya leaves, but Zarrill waits, her large lips pursed. We're both eighteen. She came into my family from her mother's previous marriage, while Naya was born from my father and Zarrill's mother twelve years ago when my father and stepmother joined themselves together.

Zarrill meets my gaze. "You know it doesn't matter to us who your mother was, don't you?"

I return to Naya's dress and tighten my threads, knotting the row I made. "I know," I say. It's not what Zarrill thinks that matters, though. It's not Zarrill who controls our lives, but the people around us.

With every interaction, our family is left further behind, and I can't sit idly by and watch my father do nothing. While I loved my mother, and cherish my memories of her, the shame of her choices is mine to respond to.

The mustiness of our schoolhouse doesn't affect the brightness of my students' upturned faces as they sit with their legs folded over the dirt floor, shadowed from the sun by the gardens outside. Their eyes fasten on my face.

"Who remembers how our kingdom began? Anyone?" I scan their faces and little Oci's hand pops up. She has an answer for everything, just as I had as a child, and she's one of the few who has warmed up enough to me and my personality to answer.

I haven't been a teacher long. The schoolmaster couldn't find anyone else who would accept the meager wages the school had to offer, and no one else would hire me. To me, these wages are everything.

Pointing to her, I say, "Yes, Oci."

Her curls bounce as her mouth spreads into a bright smile. "We were once ruthless and leaderless clans in the north, as apt to kill each other as to band together. We were closer to the giants Mirchira created at the beginning of the world than to the intelligent humans we are now. So the gods emerged from the sea and sailed to..." Her brow furrows.

"Kiani Bay," I offer.

The children always struggle to remember that name, though it's just north of us.

Her face brightens. I used to sit at that same desk and answer questions in the self-assured way she does.

"To begin their line of descendants," she continues, "They led twelve demigods and their tribes south to the Kichka mountains to create the kingdoms we have now. Though the blood of the gods has thinned since that time, Ma Cochira's blood is still strong in the stones and in the people of Cochas."

She knew the story word for word, just as every member of Cochas was expected to. I could have hugged her, if hugging was my thing, but I clap my hands instead. "Perfect! Next class, we'll memorize the crop schedules in the stars." I pride myself on that subject more than any other. My stepmother knows the positions of the stars by heart, but I always like to think the stars have more to say than just how soon we should plant our food.

My students stand one by one and file out the door as I intercept Oci and give her a quick squeeze. "You did well."

She clings to the patterned fabric of my dress. "Thank you, Ma Yakua." Oci gives me a shallow bow, her hand in a fist over her heart. "Are you going to the festival?"

"I am."

"You'll look beautiful. I wish I were old enough."

"One day you will be."

Her classmate, Mayu, waves to her from outside. She spends most of her time with him—her own Sunqu. In those days, my life revolved around memorizing faster than Sunqu and teasing him when I succeeded, enjoying how much it bothered him. For how often he pestered me, I had to return the favor.

Letting go of my hand, Oci skips after him, until a woman appears in the door and stops her. She bends to give Oci a hug and looks up, her eyes narrowing as she catches sight of me.

"Come on, Oci, walk fast. Hopefully, the schoolmaster finds a better teacher soon."

Oci's mother doesn't like me and reminds me often, but she can be the teacher herself if she chooses. The schoolmaster would happily pass the job to her if she so much as breathes a word of interest.

I watch them go with dry eyes and a drier heart. Though the hurt of a thousand words over a dozen years never fades, the scars healed with new scars.

Young Mayu angles his head as they withdraw, showing the patterns in the close shave of his hair. I can only hope the clan's hatred for me doesn't transfer to him and Oci.

Retreating further into the schoolhouse so the other parents don't see me lurking, I wait until they've all left before I start for home. My little school squats on top of a hillside full of grass, gardens, and a few meager trees. Following the gullies in the hills, I start toward the beaches with the market, with my home in the hills beyond it, but change direction and head for the ocean cliffs instead.

The trees scatter sunlight as I hike through the jungle. While the hike to the cliffs isn't far, the sun mounts the highest cloud in the sky as I arrive.

Climbing to the top of the tallest ridge, I let my toes creep over the edge. Little rocks tumble down an elegant waterfall and splash into the churning blue below—a canvas that stretches for miles until it meets the horizon. Salty air fills my lungs, and the strain of the previous few hours melts from my shoulders.

Most people would be afraid standing this high above the water, but the fear that afflicts others fills me with joy as my power feeds on the energy the emotion yields, pumping through my blood.

My mother explained my powers to me once as a child as she sat on the other side of my sleeping skin, holding both my hands tight in hers. "Did you know you have two spirits inside you? An animation spirit and a creation spirit. Everything has spirits, Yakua, and each god can control them in different ways."

"What can Ma Cochira control?" I asked her.

"The animation spirit, limited to water. She is the goddess of the sea."

"Do I animate water too?"

My mother patted the top of my hand. "No, child—just emotion. But emotion is a powerful thing."

The nostalgia of that memory overwhelms me, and I blink, rocking forward on my toes. Wind kisses my cheeks, caresses my fingers, and it's like she's here beside me, whispering words I don't understand.

I can live in this sacred spot, high above the splash of the sea, and a quiet journey away from the upturned noses of my clan.

Marriage to a priest can't be so terrible, can it?

It can't be worse than this.

"You don't have to jump," Sunqu's voice comes from behind.

I don't turn around. "And if I want to?"

"If you insist on diving to your death, might I suggest you ask someone to accompany you? So you don't drown without anyone present to help?"

While I came to be alone, I don't mind Sunqu's presence. "You're welcome to join me, though I don't usually take it kindly when I'm followed."

Sunqu chuckles while staying several feet from the edge. He's terrified of heights and never gets any closer. "Criminals get thrown off cliffs as punishment. It's not meant to be a pastime," he often states. Instead of repeating his usual discourse, however, he says, "I'm not following you. Or at least that wasn't my intention. I saw you turn from town and come this way and thought you might be upset."

This time, I turn to face him. "I'm not upset." And I fold my arms to prove it.

He shrugs. "I see that, but if you don't mind, I'll hang out down there where it's safe and make sure you get home in one piece. Your father will thank me. Someone must check on you."

He clambers down the cliffs to the lower rocks, close to an ingress where the water forms a natural pool. The pool shines an unnatural turquoise, the sand smooth and tawny.

While I don't expect to need his help, his concern comforts me. It's nice to have to have someone care.

Turning back to the cliff's edge, I kick into a handstand, shifting my weight between my palms until I let myself fall, tucking my legs into a ball. As I somersault through the air, I sense when I'm upright again, unwind, and let the wind sweep over my arms and shoulders until the water slaps my clasped palms and I drop into it. My breath catches, the cold sucking me in. Bubbles tickle my skin, popping as I swim to the surface where I wipe water from my eyes.

As I swim around the waterfall, Sunqu's figure scrambles down the last rock. I wade through the shallows, my dress sticking to my legs where I've tied the extra fabric. Meanwhile, he strides down the shoreline, a strange glint in the gold rings around his irises.

"If you planned to rescue me, you would have been too late," I say. "You're as slow as Naya. If I hurt myself, I'd already be swept away."

He rakes a hand through his hair. "What do you want from me, Yakua? I'll never keep up with you."

At least he admits to my superiority.

My mouth twitches. "I knew you admired me."

He leans over his crossed legs and picks up a pebble. "I'm glad. I was starting to wonder if you didn't know."

Sitting where the water knocks against the sand, he skips stones over the rippling surface.

I jab a finger into the pebbles, so round and smooth they might have been polished by the gods. Rather than speak, I enjoy the silence, and he doesn't interrupt.

At last, he holds his hands up, examining how his fingers have started to prune. "How long do you plan to stay?"

I'd forgotten he has shoes to finish before the festival, which begins with an early hike tomorrow morning.

"You need to get back to your store?"

"Eventually, yes. But my father will handle the orders until I return."

Sunqu's father mourned the loss of his wife, Sunqu's mother, so much that he fell into a depression that nearly lost him his business as well as his health, pushing Sunqu to hurry his return home from his apprenticeship.

Now that Sunqu has returned from the capital, he devotes all his time and energy to his father and his business. While I'm flattered he cares about my safety, I don't like taking up more of his time than is my due.

"I don't want to keep your father waiting."

He's fortunate to have the reputation he has. No one meets with the Sua family without loving them immediately.

Sunqu exhales slowly. "They can wait as long as they need to. Finish what you came here to do and take as long as you need. Just ignore me. I can sit and watch. You're adequate entertainment."

I lift my chin. "Adequate?"

"I can't give you too many compliments."

Shaking my head, I return to the water until it laps at my sides. But I can't let his statement go without one last quip. "Fine, you can have your entertainment. But next time you follow me, I expect you to jump too."

"Keep your expectations as high as you like," he says, "but you won't see me jump from any cliff of my own volition. I'll happily forgo that crown. I've no reason to impress anyone, so I'll keep my bones intact. Thank you."

"Liar," I say. "We all have someone we're trying to impress."

At that, he looks away.

After a few more dives, I stride out of the water and Sunqu smiles as I step past him, but my own words stick in my thoughts, and I hardly spare him a glance.

Whether it's suitors or salespeople, the world is full of people trying to impress and influence others. Sunqu does it every day in his trade. As a child, watching Naya look to my father for approval when she took her first steps, I learned this truth. We all want to be praised and accepted.

It's a lonely world when you're not.

CHAPTER THREE

BEFORE THE SUN'S FIRST RAYS can touch the clouds the morning of the festival, crickets chirrup at the moon. I braid my hair, don my cleanest dress, and shake Zarrill and Naya from their bed skins.

They groan and roll over.

"The sun's about to rise." When I muss Naya's hair, she covers her face with her hands. "We need to be at the temple."

Zarrill shoots up. "Is the sun up already?"

"It will be soon."

She tosses aside her blankets. "Why didn't you wake us?"

"What do you think I'm doing? Come on, I'll help you get ready." I pass them the dresses I made, absorbing their expressions as the sleepiness clears from their umber eyes. While they've seen me work on the dresses, they haven't seen them finished.

Zarrill's face breaks into a smile and Naya stops rubbing her face.

"They're gorgeous. I love the patterns," Zarrill says.

While anyone with money might say they're simple squares strung together, it took me many long hours by candlelight. Fortunately, the dresses turned out better than expected. Both of them have patterned rows of blue, green, and yellow, though I gave Naya's more yellow than Zarrill's to match her vibrant personality. Naya's dress has flowers and the blades of grass that grows on the cliffs. On Zarrill's dress, I weaved in serpentine sea monsters riding smooth waves.

Naya's eyes go round. "Will you do my hair so I look like you, Yakua?" She twirls and poses, impersonating me with a scowl on her face.

"I don't look like that," I say.

Zarrill picks up her dress like she's lifting a bouquet, though she peeks at Naya as she straightens. "You do," she says. "But we love you for it."

I scowl, though I don't argue. It's not like I have any reflective surface to look at to prove she's wrong, though one hand instinctively reaches up to touch my forehead, checking to see if my nose flares the way Naya's did.

Naya rushes to grab her hairbrush and returns with her dress on, smoothing the tiny stripes—a red and orange pattern, modeled after the sun. I brush the coarse strands of her hair, so they lay in smooth waves, like the ocean's surface. I'm the only descendant of Ma Cochira who didn't inherit the wavy hair.

My mother used to braid my hair tight every night before bed, so it curled like this in the morning. The other girls in our clan all had beautiful waves like Naya's. *People like you more when you look like them*, my mother told me. *They're more likely to trust you.*

While no one mentions my unique hair, it makes me sad to think there might be one more reason to consider me an outsider.

I used to twist my hair around my fingers and hold it until my arm ached, but it never curled.

Zarrill fastens individual strands of her own hair in an elaborate bun as I lay Naya's brush aside. I fluff my own hair, but it refuses to cooperate and lays limp as a beaten rug, so I toss my things into my bag instead.

Sliding my mother's heirloom necklace out from beneath my blankets, I shift the offering shells beside it so they chink as they roll onto the rugs. Zarrill leans over me and stays my hand.

"Yakua, I know how much that necklace means to you, but you should leave it. It might get stolen in an open tent."

I never go anywhere beyond our village without it.

My hand twitches as I brush the emerald with one finger. She's right. I can't leave it unsupervised with my bags, but I can't leave it behind either. The gold and silver clank in my fingers as I fasten it around my neck instead, cover it with my dress, and strap my bed mat onto my pack.

I'll just have to be careful no one sees the necklace. The silver snakes are symbols of Heliray, the goddess of death, and they would raise questions I don't want to answer.

My father tried to abandon the necklace in a river once. I hid behind a bush as he tossed it into the murky depths of the churning water. The metal snakes and skulls gleamed beneath the surface alongside a single emerald. My mother wore it every day before she died. When I look at it, I can see her standing over me with the necklace coiled around her neck. She'd brush the hair from my eyes. "Yakua," she would say, "you're my daughter and we don't let anyone tell us what to do."

I hoped one day my father might want to remember my mother and go looking for it.

He never did.

The necklace warms my skin, almost comforting.

"Yakua?" Sunqu's voice comes from outside the door, and I trip over the sleeping skins in my hurry across the rugs to see him.

Pushing past curtains to where tiny dots of light pepper the sky, the moon highlights Sunqu's cheekbones. He stands beneath the stone arch of our home with a box in his hands, which he holds out to me.

I meet his eyes as I accept the box with hesitant hands.

"For you," he says.

For me?

"You mean Naya," I say, turning to beckon her over.

He stops me by putting his hand over mine, still resting on the lid.

"No," he repeats. "I brought hers, as you requested, but these are for you." Quickly removing his hand, he gently prods the small box with his index finger.

He knows not to touch me too long. I would love an accurate read of his thoughts and emotions since he's never allowed me to do it before. But it's an invasion of his privacy and his trust, and I know better than to try.

"Please," he says.

I'm not sure what he means by this strange behavior.

While I'm loathe to tear my gaze from his, I'm also curious.

Sliding off the lid, a set of shoes gleam, made of a material I haven't seen before. They are white as milk, with little blue designs. "What are these?" My voice comes out hushed, almost reverent. "Shoes?"

No one ever gives me gifts.

"Glass shoes." He studies my face. "They're for the festival. If you get compliments, will you tell everyone who made them? I hoped everyone would see and want the shoes."

"Oh." My elation fades. "Did my sisters ask you to make them?" They might have if they thought my sandals wouldn't do. Or if they wanted to repay me for the dresses.

Or he simply wants to broadcast his wares and I'm scavenging for another reason.

"They didn't, but I thought you might benefit from them." He waits, his arms stiff at his sides. Seeing him so awkward surprises me and I half-expect him to explain the reason, though he makes no move to do so.

I can support him in his business ventures. Besides, my hands refuse to budge. I couldn't pry my fingers off the glistening glass if I wanted to.

A smile glimmers to life on Sunqu's face when he notices how tightly I'm holding them. "I'm glad you like them. Just remember to tread lightly. They're not meant for heavy wear." He meets my eyes again. "Before you left my shop, you told me I'm capable of more, and you were right. I've been given opportunities few here have received and I have connections with the King I haven't taken advantage of. This is me trying."

After holding my gaze for half a breath, he turns, his footsteps light and quick as he retreats down the stones that lead up our hill, past the tiers of my stepmother's lush garden, and into the trees.

While I don't want him to go, I'm too excited to open the box again to call him back. Lifting the lid, the slippers glimmer in the dark. As I try them on, the glass sides slide against my ankles until my foot settles into a comfortable mold at the bottom, and I'm surprised he knew my size without measuring. I point my foot and the shoes sparkle.

Rocks clink down the stone stairs as Zarrill catches up to me, holding Naya's hand. She gestures at my feet. "I see Sunqu made you a pair too."

"Do you like yours?" I ask.

Zarrill wears the same sandals she wears every day, though she holds a new box in her hands. "How could I not?" she says.

Little Naya's feet glisten in a pair of white slippers with painted yellow flowers. Not just white slippers, but white glass slippers. A small box like mine and Zarrill's rests in her hands.

He exceeded my expectations when he made shoes for all three of us, and my gratitude wedges in my throat before I clear it.

"I'd suggest keeping your sandals on until we get there," I tell Zarrill and Naya as Naya prances around, a wide smile squishing her cheeks. "You'll ruin them if you wear them now."

Zarrill walks ahead. "I already told Naya that. She won't listen."

Naya's shoes clatter against the rocks as she skips behind Zarrill toward the jungle path where grassy hills clash against dense trees and jagged mountains. "I'm not taking mine off. They're the most beautiful things I've ever owned."

Shaking her head, a small smirk plays on Zarrill's lips.

An image of the shoes scratched or chipped shoves into my thoughts. I replace my own glass slippers with sandals, stuff the shoes into the box, and trudge after my sisters.

"Yakua, wait."

Turning at the sound of my stepmother's voice, I wait for her to say whatever she has to say. She stands on her toes in front of her garden, one arm raised, her braided hair swinging across her back.

"Have fun and be safe," she says. "Look after my girls, will you?"

I bow my head, touching my hand to my chest, over my heart. "Of course, Stellya."

Her girls, because I'm not one of them.

Turning to the mountain, as I search for the temple on the cliff-side we should be hiking toward. A stone path cuts between the trees and veers upward, the sun shining brighter over the peaks.

Up there, on those mountaintops, the bitterness of my mother's memory will ebb and our lives will improve with just one festival. One song. One priest.

CHAPTER FOUR

MY LUNGS STRUGGLE TO expand as I take another step up the mountain trail. The town shrinks in the distance, nestled in the trees that separate our homes from the cliffs that drop into the ocean. The sky brightens enough that the dew on the overhanging leaves catch the soft light of the rising sun while birds twitter songs.

A branch cracks and Naya slumps against a rock. "My feet hurt so bad. I can't go on." She yanks off her slippers, tosses her bags, and massages the bottoms of her heels.

We did warn her.

Zarrill looks over her shoulder at us and grimaces.

"Climb onto my back," I say.

I can't give her my shoes and go barefoot when there are poisonous snakes in the brush, but I can carry her the rest of the way. My knees threaten to collapse as I add her bags to mine and then the weight of her frail body. Straining to put one foot in front of the other, I move, first across a bridge, then around the mountainside, up the boulders, and through a shallow river until the pain in my soles of my feet go numb. Zarrill hikes ahead but pauses to take both our bags when I stumble.

As I walk, I meet a series of stones wedged into a steep hill, leading straight up to the foot of the temple. Gripping Naya's legs until she flinches, I stumble up the incline. The hill flattens to a vast grass area and Zarrill drops our bags in a pile at the edge of the steep terrain, and hurries to join the assembled gathering.

Splayed lines of young men and women from the clans kneel before the rock pyramid temple I'd glimpsed at the foot of the mountain, Zarrill now among them, her face pressed to the grass as mountain deer graze beside her. I drop Naya, kneel, and swap my shoes for the glass ones.

The grass stretches out on a massive tier with a drop-off that leads down into the mountain's jungle and finally to a river in the distance. On the other side, warriors hoist a golden throne through the kneeling crowd. They climb the stone steps of the temple and lower the throne beneath the rising sun. This sacred place offered a godlike view of Ma Cochira's dominion on one side and the mountain on the other. Even the King of Cochas visits this temple often with his High Priest, though they rarely frequent our village below.

The King of Cochas stands, clothed in a red cape, feather earrings, and a matching belt. Gold bracelets clasp his wrists and ankles—a statement of his wealth and power.

He raises his arms. "Welcome to our celebration of Isul and Ma Cochira and, especially, the return of my son to the kingdom of Cochas. Let the festivities begin." He sits upon his throne as his servants lift and carry him to his tent at the edge of the open grass.

On the far side, near the jungle, musicians beat their drums. Flutes play and panpipes resonate as servants emerge from the trees with trays piled with fruit, meat, and corn.

My father said music keeps our souls alive as well as the souls of the animals we sacrifice. But Isul and Ma Cochira must not be hungry because the King of Cochas brought no deer for a ceremony. I don't mind. Fewer formalities leave more time for food and conversation, though I'd rather not be seen by the masses.

As Zarrill and Naya walk, I fall behind them, allowing their forms to cover my face.

Zarrill rolls her eyes but humors me as I walk both of them to the grass area that swells with dancers, scanning the crowd for Darhi's balding hair.

"They don't know who you are," Zarrill explains, misunderstanding my reason for scanning the crowd the way I do. She pulls on my arm as we stand at the edge of the grass. "It looks like there are people here from other villages."

"They'll find out I'm here soon enough," I say under my breath.

People like to talk, and I'm always an interesting subject.

But where is Darhi? I don't see him, and the idea that he might not have come unsettles me. What do I do if he's not here? Go home?

While I'm not sure how good my chances are with Darhi, he's unmarried and only a few years older. And if my mother could elbow her way into the upper class, I should at least be able to use my powers to prod the feelings of one person.

In case he doesn't show, I should keep an eye out for someone else.

A man with a stern expression approaches, the dark spots on his brow and cheeks revealing his age. He wears a tunic embroidered with gold, with gold tassels. "Excuse me." He bows. "I'm High Priest and brother to the King of Cochas. May I have your names?"

High priest? That's a station higher than Darhi.

I eye him closer than before. He doesn't wear a traditional engagement shoe, with a symbol of his wife's family name and arms, which means he is unmarried, though his skin is wrinkled from years of too much sun. His fingers are long and thin, not fine, though I see no evidence of hard work and toil. His hands bear none of the scars Sunqu's have.

The age difference isn't ideal, and something about his eyes unsettles me.

Can I convince myself to love such a man?

My heart revolts at the thought.

I open my mouth but Zarrill cuts in. "Zarrill Lamar." She points to Naya. "And my little sister, Naya Lamar." She pauses. "And Yakua."

He looks at me, waiting for a short pause before prodding me into speaking. "Yakua Lamar?"

"Roca," I correct him. "My name is Yakua Roca."

His eyes fix on me, and his stare makes even Naya shift.

I lick my lips. "It's nice to meet you." My words are kind, but my voice carries a stiff coldness, though I'm stiff and cold with everyone I meet, outside of my sisters and Sunqu.

The High Priest bows again and offers his hand. "Will you spare an old man a dance?" He speaks slowly, enunciating each word so I'm not sure if he's trying to sound proper, or if he worries I'm incapable of understanding him.

I hesitate, though I have no reason to refuse a man of his station. As I accept his hand, his fingers flex, exposing blue lines that crisscross over the back of his hand beneath transparent skin. "Of course."

Zarrill takes Naya by the hand and tugs her into the crowd.

As he smiles with yellowed teeth and grasps my fingers, I scan the dancers, unwilling to part from them. Somehow, I've secured a dance with the High Priest without using my power to accomplish it.

Now that I've done it, I'm not sure I like it.

The musicians play a slower song and I stumble over the change in tempo. The High Priest doesn't smile but watches me so vigilantly

I'm decidedly not flattered. It's a look that holds too much meaning, like he's expecting me to do something, to try something. Like he's waiting for something to happen.

I should speak to him, but men of his rank probably talk of loftier things than weaving, teaching, and cliff jumping, but I can't think of what those things might be. Family of the King of Cochas don't mingle with the fishermen clans of the coast.

The High Priest's hand tightens on my back. "Your mother was a mystic, yes?"

My body tenses with wariness at the change in topic. My mother is a subject I know never to broach.

"Did she teach you to worship the gods?" he asks. "Did she teach you her craft as well?"

Slowing my steps so I lag behind the music, my heart accelerates. I look up at his eyes as he gazes down at me, his head tilted with an eagerness that shouldn't be there. He wants to harass me, just as the clans in our village do. Even my own clan, the Lamuna clan, does. "What do you mean?" My voice is sharp, but not as cutting as it should be.

He tilts his head. "I didn't mean to upset you." He chews his lip. "I like your slippers. Where did you get them?"

Being a mystic isn't bad if you worship the right gods. He might be curious, and I overanalyzed his questions. But if he has heard of my mother, he knows the rumors about her too.

"A man named Sunqu in my village." Frost creeps into my voice. "His father owns a shoe shop."

"What are they made of?"

"Glass." I twirl with the rest of the dancers and take a deep breath as I step away, the air fresher with space between us.

"I've not heard of glass before, but it's a stunning material—as beautiful as you."

He recovers well.

"I'm not sure I can compare but thank you."

He shuffles his feet as he misses a step. "Do you like your village?"

Do I like my village with the majesty of staggering cliffs, and unforgiving fields of corn marching across the landscape broken by the humble schoolhouse where I teach children I love? My village, where I weave hope into dresses on my loom, where Naya and I crouch on top of our house and watch the blue lines of the ocean disappear into the horizon, where the air always smells like salt.

I don't just like my village. I love it, but the High Priest won't appreciate the patchwork shacks and shoeless children, not when he comes from a palace that borders the sea with nobles clothed in gold. "I like my village very much," I say.

But I don't like him.

The song trills to a close and the High Priest bows. "Please do me the honor of another dance. I'd love to hear more about you and your village but excuse me until then. I must announce you first." He straightens, turning to part ways.

"Wait." I stop him with a hand. "Announce me? To whom?" If he announces me, it'll expose my presence here.

He smiles. "To the king." Striding toward the tent of the King of Cochas, he ducks beneath the tent flap.

I'm stunned. Does he do this for every girl who comes to the festival? At least he'll announce my name in private, and, hopefully, my name will bleed into countless others. Trying to comfort myself with this, I push the concern to the back of my head until I have reason to resurrect it.

If the High Priest plans to announce me to the king, will he announce me to the prince too? I haven't seen or heard news of the prince, though I thought this festival was for him.

As long as I can stay without my sisters and I getting harassed, I don't care if the king and prince hide away in tents.

My chest hurts as I watch Naya and Zarrill dance without partners, but they smile as if they don't notice. Zarrill, like me, is old enough to have suitors but hasn't had one, and I suspect the fault lies with me.

I join them and twirl to the flutes, my dress swinging at my ankles. My shoes hold, white as ever, though sweat tingles on my forehead and drips down my cheeks and back.

A young woman I recognize, but can't place, stops Naya. "Where did you get those?" Her eyes follow Naya's small feet, her nose twitching. She has soft porcelain skin and a sharp chin, her dress sweeping out behind her in tassels that crisscross. I memorize the pattern for later, in case I have to make a dress again, though I try not to compare my own worn, plain dress to hers.

Naya bends over and takes one of her shoes off so the woman can see it. "Our shoe store. The owner's son, Sunqu, made them, and they're sturdier than my sandals." The brightness of Naya's smile catches fire and warms the woman's already bright features. "Aren't they beautiful?"

"They are!" Her eyes linger on the shoes as she moves on into the crowd. Several more dancers replace her in a circle around us and Naya laughs as I clutch her hands and dance at her side.

As fun as dancing is, I must make the most of my time here. I have to change our lives.

"Have you seen the prince yet?" Naya yells over the noise.

The prince returned from a quest to learn the customs of other kingdoms, gather experiences away from home, and strengthen treaties. I haven't met him in person, but on the rare occasions I saw the royal family, they always wore red belts and capes. Scanning the crowd for red, I find too much of it, none of them a cape.

"I'm sorry, Naya," Zarrill says. "I don't think he came. But if he did, I imagine he'd look for someone a couple feet taller." She muses Naya's hair and Naya sticks out her bottom lip.

"He was supposed to be here."

My swaying slows at her disappointment. None of us have seen the royal family outside of the King before, but I can't change that. Not even if I found myself a dozen Darhis to introduce us to the upper class. Unless the people or persons I find happen to be the High Priest and brother to the King, who does have a keen eye for me, for whatever reason.

I crane my neck and search for the High Priest's robes, but he hasn't returned, though he promised a second dance.

The sun sets behind a mountain peak, the vivid red and pink rays of light hitting the sides of the temple and trailing across the ocean's horizon.

Naya wipes sweat from her brow. "I think I'm done dancing for today. Can we get food?"

My stomach has been rumbling for hours.

Zarrill's head bobs up and down. "Yes, please."

We make our way to the lowest garden tier and squat in the grass. Zarrill and Naya's faces burn red as dyed cloth, dripping with sweat, and I'm sure mine looks the same. Despite the heat, the dresses I made complement them well and radiate color even as a dim twilight snatches the sky.

As we settle, a young man in the crisp lines of a servant's uniform approaches with water bowls on a tray, his long black hair combed back and fastened at the base of his neck.

Naya beams at me, and then at the servant. "Thanks, Sunqu," she says as she reaches for a bowl.

The smile that touches Sunqu's lips brightens when he hands Naya her water and his eyes find mine. "You're welcome," he says, though he's looking at me and not at her.

"You're a servant here?" I ask.

The boy who scoffed at the idea of having a festival with peasants and the threat of war on our borders is working for the King of Cochas at the same festival he sneered at. I suppose money makes hypocrites of the best men.

"I thought I could reforge my connections with the King." He points at my shoes. "For those. I just have to figure out how to gain admittance into his royal tent." His smile fades to a grimace as he regards the fabric structure across the grass field.

He took what I said seriously then. I hope it works out for him.

I fold my legs and pat the grass beside me. "The shoes are lovely. We've had lots of compliments. Will you sit with us?"

His eyes flick to where my hand rests on the grass, but his mouth purses with regret. "Thank you, but I have work to do. They'll be angry with me if I don't go back." He bows, balances his tray on his hand, and hurries across the grassy tiers toward the servants' tent.

Naya waves at his back. "Yakua, why does he always leave when you come?"

I bite my lip to stifle a retort. Why does everyone leave when I come?

No, Sunqu doesn't lie about such things. He truly does have work to do, and I can't keep him from it. Still sitting, I sway my torso to the music, hoping the tempo will push any questioning thoughts to the back of my head, but it doesn't.

Where are the prince and High Priest? Where is the king? And why haven't they emerged from their tent yet?

What if Sunqu's right, and I should be worried about something strange going on?

Unable to handle the flurry of questions with no answers, I leave to get water and return to find several young men surrounding Naya and Zarrill in the same spot on the grass.

I hesitate, glasses of water still in my hands, and turn around. They're doing better at making friends and connections without me there. It's better if I go.

As I walk away, Zarrill detaches herself from the party. "The bugs are awful." She glances over her shoulder at Naya, who laughs and twirls her hair as she flirts with a handsome boy her age. "Naya is having fun, though."

"They're talking to her," I say in amazement. It's a stupid statement. Of course, they are, but I have to force my jaw to close.

Zarrill sighs. "They're from the villages south." She says it like it explains everything. "I'm going to dance to a few songs." Then she strides off.

I stand at the edge of the party, uncertain if I should sit or set up our tent and settle down for the night. Naya beams in the dress I made her, but she's too young—barely old enough to attend. The boys fawning over her can't know her age or relation to me.

Everyone loves Naya. If she met a man, no one would suspect her of coercion, though even I can't resist her sweet smiles and innocent requests. After all, I made her the dress she wore. At twelve years old, she's too young to worry about marriage now. If she does want to meet men and bring them home, something has to change. Spouses like my stepmother, who look past reputation, are rare.

"She's beautiful."

I jump at Sunqu's voice and follow his gaze to my sister, pride swelling in my chest. "I thought you had to work."

"I'm done for the night." He gestures to his clothes, which are no longer his previous servant's uniform, but a simple sleeveless tunic that shows the lines of his arms and shoulders.

I face Naya again. "The dress makes her shine, doesn't it?"

Sunqu's face lightens when Naya laughs at something someone said. "Or she makes the dress shine."

He winks when I meet his words with a glare. "Don't get in a huff," he says. "The dress is pretty."

He's the only person I will let harass me this way.

Punching him on the arm like I did when we were kids, I say, "Fine. They're both beautiful."

"They are." His smile wanes. "So are you."

The compliment triggers a blush, but I squeeze his arm once and let go. It's my way of telling him "thank you" for the compliment without expressing it in words. He simply continues to gaze at Naya and her admirers. I'm grateful to Sunqu for knowing when a compliment is best served.

As the laughter of my sister continues to echo against the mountainside, he peers sidelong at me. "Naya has a lot to be thankful for. It was kind of you to make her that dress. It's obvious she loves it."

"Her life should be full of things she loves."

He extends his hand, palm up, and holds it there for several seconds. "Would you like to dance? As friends?"

I stare at his hand and then at his face to detect any teasing, but his smile is genuine. Does he not care to be seen with me?

"Are you sure?" I ask.

"I am."

"And you want to touch me?"

He pulls out a set of leather gloves I recognize from his workbench. "They're ugly," he says with an apologetic look, "but they'll work."

I nod, hiding the hurt that comes from knowing my best friend doesn't want to touch me.

As I place my hand in his, his touch, even gloved, sends my heart into a gallop, and I take a deep breath to steady myself. I haven't done a lot of dancing.

He leads me to the grass by the temple, where hundreds of other dancers pivot to the notes of a flute. As we join the line, his hand presses against my waist.

Wet blades of grass brush my ankles and their fresh scent mixes with the musky smell of leather as Sunqu moves inches away, one hand clenched at his side. Perhaps he doesn't want to dance after all. I know Sunqu's body language so well, I can tell when he's barely enduring. I refuse to meet his gaze as the dancers in the line step forward.

When I spin, Sunqu stands aloof, an arm's length away. As I sway, stepping toward him, he stumbles, and his cheeks darken to a deep magenta. Then our eyes meet, and the tension falls from my shoulders. I drag him toward me by the waist of his tunic. "You're worse than I am. Is it possible?"

He gives me a tight smile. "I thought I knew this one better. Give me a moment. I'm a little distracted." His movements smooth and he doesn't stumble again. Not the sure steps of a prince or even a priest, but not an embarrassment, either. At least he can lead.

When he looks up again, he gives a start, and his shocked expression startles me into pulling away. "What?" I demand.

"You're smiling," he says.

"So?"

"You never smile. You're like the queen of not smiling."

My father warns it's half the reason people don't like me, and another reason people struggled with my mother, though my mother learned to smile when expected.

Rolling my eyes, I take his hands and pull him into another spin.

As the song ends, I don't want this time with Sunqu to end, so I check the position of the stars and drag Sunqu to the cliffs that overlook the ocean.

He resists as I tug him toward the edge.

"There's no way you would survive that fall." He inches backward; his eyes wide as he gazes out into the empty void that drops off over the side of the cliffs.

"Stop being weird."

"I don't care what you say. I'm not getting close to that edge."

"I'm not jumping. Just look." I point to the reflection of the moon on the water. "Do you see her?"

He pauses, but his gaze doesn't move from his feet. "See who?"

A snakelike body leaves ripples of silver in the water as tiny horns emerge from the waves. I can only imagine the scales that glitter over the black depths of the sea.

I whisper her name. "Mungacu." They say she took the place of the sea goddess when the gods disappeared by helping lost sailors find their way to shore. But during bad storms, she eats them instead. My father avoids her when he sets sail on his fishing boat. He says she's just as likely to hurt you as to help, but I glimpse her occasionally from above and yearn to see her at the edge of my father's boat when I join his expeditions.

"The sea serpent?" Sunqu stiffens as I yank him toward me, closer to the edge than ever before, his eyes and lips round. "Is that really her?"

"It is."

He gazes out at the dark waves far below. "I've never seen her."

Mungacu's body coils and her scales shimmer as she leaps from the water and dives back in.

Sunqu's eyes glint as he grins.

No one spends as much time on the cliffs as I do, looking out over the oceanscape, so no one spots Mungacu as often. She appears around this time every evening and blends into the waves as if made of water herself.

A contented quiet settles between us, reminding me of times Sunqu took me out on the water in his much-loved little boat. Once, he rowed us to the stone arches that jutted out of a bay where young people cut their names into the rock with a stone. I jumped from the boat to climb, and he fell into the water when the boat rocked. As he shook the water from his hair, I scratched our names just above the waterline, where the waves would slowly erase their superficial outlines. That was a long time ago.

"Why did you come here?" Sunqu asks without looking at me. "Why come to this festival, knowing most of the people here don't like you?"

Do I tell him the truth? He's my best friend. I should be able to tell him anything.

I sigh. "I hoped to find myself a priest to marry, but he didn't come."

His brow furrows. As close as we are, I sense a chasm opening between us. Though I can't pinpoint the reason for it, I want to fasten it shut.

"Was it worth it to come?" I ask, brushing his forearm with a finger to sense his emotions—just this once. But his eyes narrow and he rips his arm away. "To the cliff, I mean."

"Don't. Yakua, please have enough respect for me not to do that."

I withdraw my hand and force my gaze back to the Mungacu.

He's known me so long, he must suspect what I can do, and when I'm trying to do it, without me telling him, but how? Am I so transparent?

Sunqu stands on stiff legs and stalks toward the lines of dancers. As he leaves, emptiness spreads. Outside of my sisters, he's all I have. And with my father ignoring the possibility of me inheriting my powers, Sunqu is the only person who knows I have them.

"I'm sorry," I whisper, but he can't hear me.

Just beyond Sunqu, outside the expanse of grass, the High Priest and one other man stand with their backs to the slope of the mountain, their eyes on me. As I catch sight of them, a shiver runs up my spine. I meet the High Priest's gaze and he turns away.

He hasn't asked me for another dance, but he also doesn't act like he will either.

I stand and follow Sunqu while the High Priest continues his conversation with his friend and doesn't glance my way again. Breathing a sigh of relief, I leave them behind. At least he intends to leave me alone.

CHAPTER FIVE

ARRILL STUMBLES OUT OF BED as the third day brings twittering birds and ribbons of light. Even Naya struggles to maintain the skip in her step as she walks to her pile of clothes in the corner. I push open our tent door and head toward the grassy plateau, Zarrill and Naya's sandals flapping against their heels behind me.

I'm wearing my glass shoes.

The King of Cochas's tent squats on the fringe, where an early crowd continues its merriment. Tireless musicians play and servants bring never-ending piles of food. While the ocean stretches to the end of the world in one direction, jungles capture the earth's colors in the other. And beyond the grass, vines hide grazing deer. I'll miss this place when we return to our village, as well as these final memories with my sisters. Even if I didn't accomplish what I came to do, I'll think of another way to meet Darhi.

A hand touches my arm and I spin to face the High Priest, his mouth spreading into a smile. "Are you enjoying yourself?"

"I am."

A chill radiates up my arm from where he touches me.

"Would you like to dance again?"

"Of course." I bow my head, my fist over my heart, and take his hand, trying to maintain a show of kindness. While I remind myself that I came to marry a priest, and here he is, as if the gods willed it, a dominant piece of me revolts at the idea of maintaining any kind of relationship with him, even a friendly one. "My sisters are asking if the prince is coming to dance. They're wearing their glass shoes today and they want him to see them."

"He'll come if he cares to." The priest looks off into the distance and shifts his weight from one foot to the other. Then he blinks and meets my eyes. Rubbing his arm, he gives a quick shake of his head. "I'm sorry, but you've reminded me of something I need to do. I'll be back."

He leaves me in a whirlwind of twirling dancers. I try to pinpoint what might have made the High Priest leave so fast, but nothing comes to mind. I sway once, twice, and then stop as my solitary shuffle draws eyes. Slowly, I leave the vast grass area as the sun creeps high into the sky.

My stomach growls and my energy seeps into the soil, as if Ma Hlocha, goddess of the earth, has sucked it into the green trees and moss that layers the jungle floor. I creep into the shade where the scent of meat and smoke summons me.

Sunqu sets a tray of food over the fire, but no longer wears servants' robes like the days before. Instead, he wears colored robes and an off-white tunic that gapes around his neck. As he tosses spices over fish, I wait until he looks up.

"Why are you cooking?" I ask.

He grimaces. "I asked for this job instead. It pays better, and I hated carrying trays."

"Already?"

He flips the fish over. "It didn't take me long to see that I'm as qualified as anyone else here, so why not? It helps when you already know etiquette and you're exceptional at your job."

"Or the previous chef was terrible," I tease.

His mouth twists into a grin. "That or I'm good at pretending to know more than I do. Although flipping a fish isn't too difficult."

I wave his statement away. "Did you know I danced with the High Priest twice? I honestly don't know why he's so interested—"

A hand touches my elbow and cuts me off. I turn to see the High Priest smiling down at me.

Horror and mortification jolts through me, and I freeze.

"Is this your friend, Yakua? The one who made your shoes?" He appraises Sunqu with a gleam in his eye.

I blink as my brain stutters to life, and I hope the High Priest doesn't think I was bragging about dancing with him.

Sunqu's eyes dart between us and his voice halts between each word. "Yes, I made them."

The High Priest's smile persists as if someone plastered it on his face. "Yakua called the material 'glass.' Can you make more?"

Sunqu nods several times, a trail of black smoke curling into the air above the fish. He must have forgotten he was in the middle of cooking. "I can make as many as you wish."

Gesturing toward the King's tent, the High Priest says, "Come with me, young man. The King of Cochas wishes to speak to you. If you're the same son of the shoemaker who worked at the palace over a year ago, then I believe you're already acquainted."

Sunqu sways in place. "My name is Sunqu. And yes, High Priest. Most certainly." A smile steals over his features.

I should be happy for Sunqu, but it'll be like the years before. They'll take him off to the palace and I won't see him again.

I grip the High Priest's arm without meaning to as Sunqu steps forward and all my desire for Sunqu to stay flows out of me. The feeling drains me so completely that terror shoots through my heart, filling me in turn with a burst of energy as bright as the sun.

I've never used my power without meaning to.

It might be nothing, except that the High Priest's face snaps to mine, and his eyes light up with bizarre triumph.

This is bad. Really bad. But it could go unnoticed if the High Priest doesn't speak of it to anyone. He might not know what happened himself. He got a confusing shot of jumbled emotions, that's all. I didn't mean to send them to him.

As I retract my arm, a small smile splits the High Priest's face and my hopes fade. He knows exactly what happened. Very few people in the kingdoms still have powers from the days of the gods. In fact, I don't know a single person who does.

But can he recognize power?

Lifting a single finger, he speaks, almost in a purr. "I will come back for you."

He shakes himself from my grip, resting a hand on Sunqu's shoulder. "I have quite the package of important news to deliver. If you'll excuse us. Come, Sunqu."

Black smoke continues to swirl into the air from the forgotten fish as they walk side by side to the tent. If Sunqu receives recognition, it's well-deserved. But what will the High Priest do with me when he returns? I'm not sure I want to know.

I take several deep breaths to steady myself and use a stick to toss the burnt fish on the grass where it smolders until the dew kills the last heated sparks.

Everything will be fine. I just have to convince the High Priest he imagined the whole thing. I'll use my power one last time and send him the doubt he needs.

Someone prods my shoulder and I turn to find Izhi, my clan cousin. She wears a yellow dress, the closest to gold she can afford, with dangling earrings. One eyebrow arches high in her usual expression of dislike. "What are you doing here?"

I really don't want to talk to her right now. I sigh and then motion to my sisters as they dance together.

Her upper lip curls. "You obviously couldn't afford a new dress." She looks me up and down. "But I like the shoes."

I raise my chin. "Sunqu made them."

Her lips twist. "Ah yes, he must have felt sorry for you."

Heat creeps up my neck, but I simply stare back at her, meeting her gaze with feigned indifference. While people aren't kind to me, they're also scared of me. After a few long minutes, she begins to fidget and then tosses her long strands of hair over her shoulder as she hurries into the crowd of dancers.

Still, her comments sting with truth. I strip off my shoes, trudging across the grass to toss my things into my bag in our tent. Naya and Zarrill can take down the tent without my help.

If the priest knows who I am and what I can do, and intends to return for me, I can't stay a moment longer.

I sling my bag over my shoulders and face the trail, my back to the cliffs and ocean. The stars quiver as they move across the sky overhead.

I'll have to make the hike alone, though my father won't approve of me traveling at night in the mountains. Rather than find my sisters in the throng of dancers, I leave a short message on Zarrill's bed skins.

Clutching my slippers to my chest, my feet ache and every part of me weighs so heavy I might sink into the ground, even without the weight of my pack. Rather than let the emotions drag me down, I bottle them and send them outward, releasing them like I would if I intended to influence someone else. Rather than channel the feelings into someone's skin through their emotional strings, I fling the icky feelings into the ground.

It doesn't change that I feel them, but it helps me see past it.

The temperature drops as the night deepens.

I take my first step forward but stop as screams erupt from a line of people standing at the edge of the overlook. My heart plummets to my toes as two women a few feet away point to the village below, where dark shapes, almost as tall as the mountain, approach our huts.

Boulders crumble beneath the giant's feet, still audible over the music and dancing. Fires flare at the edge of the village. I'm not there amidst the smoke, but the sight of it swirling in gray streaks against the black of night closes my throat. The rumors I heard about the emperor's giants make them out to be terrifying, but I didn't imagine them so big.

Cold air seeps into my skin, down to my toes. Just as we have all dreaded, the emperor of Isul Urqu has moved on Cochas at last.

CHAPTER SIX

SEVERAL OF THE REMAINING partygoers cower behind trees, but I can't join them.

I might never see my father again.

My father is down in those ruins, alongside the rest of my clan. Naya and Zarrill will hear of the danger soon enough. Up in the mountain, above the giants, they'll be safe. But the rest of our family isn't.

My lungs refuse to expand as I stumble over stones down the mountainside. My knees twinge with each jarring step, but the pain in my joints doesn't compare to the awful tightness in my chest and heart.

As I pass the vines that curl around the rocks, the growing darkness deepens the colors until they fade to black. Still, I run. My feet pound into the dirt and my heart hammers as I fight for air, my throat hollow and dry. The ground shakes and I trip. I push myself upright, ignoring the trickle of blood down my shins, and shove my way through the trees.

It takes far too long, hours at least, to traverse what I hiked before the festival, even at a run. The shaking fades and the dirt stills as I break out of the jungle, sprinting past the first ruined hut. Smoke hovers in the air and rubble mars the landscape, but the giants have gone.

When I scan the trees and mountains, I don't see them. They've either retreated north to the border or have continued to the villages south. Or they've crossed the river to the Qori Mountains and the capital. Wherever they've gone, I hope it's far from here, though I pity anyone who lies in their path.

Tears warm my cheeks as I climb the hilltop that used to be my home. Only the arch of our door remains with its billowing curtain.

"Father?"

Broken plants in the garden bed sway eerily in the breeze as I search the hillside.

I stumble into what remains of our ruined home to where my quarters once were, shoving aside stones and ripping my sleeping skins out of the mud, but can find no sign that anyone died—or survived.

I must find them.

My powers surge, a mixture of strength and adrenaline pumping through me.

Leaping to my feet, I turn toward the market, where the rest of the village would surely meet once the danger has passed. I freeze as the High Priest stalks over the battered rugs and broken stones, flanked by guards. My stepmother, my sisters, and my father are tied up and dragged like cattle behind him.

Relief makes my knees tremble, but the feeling quickly evaporates. They shouldn't be tied up. People don't tie up those they wish to help or protect. The High Priest won't be in league with the giants unless he betrayed his brother, our King. He certainly won't need an escort of armed guards to visit the destroyed home of a poor fisherman.

I must have missed something. Since I'm too far to touch any-one, especially anyone of consequence, I try to read the scene, but only fear swells from my family. There's enough there that when I breathe in, my chest expands with it. Energy surges into my heart, but as I breathe out, exhaustion drags at my shoulders and the energy fades as fast as it came.

While I could give them compassion, ease their fears, or redirect their anger, I can't use my power in front of an audience. If I do, not only could it escalate the situation if the High Priest perceived what I intend to do, but my father would never forgive me. Nor do I know the full extent of my powers, having hid them for as long as I've been alive.

Either way, I shouldn't need to manipulate the High Priest. We are both Cochean. Our enemies left, didn't they? Or perhaps I have enemies everywhere I look.

Struggling to stay upright, I fight to keep the exertion out of my face. I haven't felt this much fear before and have never felt the full weight of not using my power so acutely.

My father stares past me, over my shoulder, his face pale and stretched, as if he wishes he could run into the mountains or jump out into the sea rather than be dragged through the remains of his house amidst humid heat and stifling smoke with a cadre of soldiers glaring at his daughter.

People are dying. Homes have been demolished. Why does the High Priest bother to come here? It's not like my family has powers like mine. No one does, not for centuries—especially not in Cochas. It's often said that the blood and power of the gods dimmed in recent generations, or vanished entirely. But no matter how persuasive I can be if I choose, I didn't bring the giants here. Not even my mother was that capable.

My knuckles twinge as I grip my shirt where my mother's necklace bunches beneath the fabric. "Has the world gone to Uru Hlocha?"

Wrinkles deepen around the High Priest's eyes, and he motions to his guards. They let my family go and each of them falls to their knees.

The High Priest meets my gaze. "You would do well to sit too, Yakua."

"Only if you explain what you're doing here, and why you tied up my family."

The High Priest tilts his head. "I will. I promise."

I have no reason to believe him, but I bite my lip and lower myself to the ground.

Tears drip down my stepmother's cheeks as she kneels beside my father. One hand strokes the stones beside her knees. Even Zarrill's eyes water.

The High Priest motions to his guards and they form a half-circle behind me.

"Yakua Roca," the High Priest begins in a solemn voice, "you have been accused of conspiring with the Emperor of Isul Urqu to overthrow the King of Cochas and have been called to stand trial before the King of Cochas for treason. You are to leave your possessions behind."

I stare, the accusation resounding in my head, my shock making his statement a jumble of words without coherence.

Conspiring?

While the people of my clan have hurled many insults over the years, questioned my integrity, and ignored me, I never expected conspiracy to make the list. This is a whole new level of ridiculous.

Especially since I know little of the emperor, except that he overtakes neighboring kingdoms with frightening speed, and that he perched his army on our border months ago.

I haven't spoken to him. Never even thought to. During the short moments I planned my engagement to a priest, I didn't have conspiring with a conquering emperor in mind.

My brain scrambles to understand what experiences at the festival led the High Priest to this ludicrous idea, but I can't think of a single word I said, or action I made that would allude to this.

"It's not true."

I search Zarrill's face for a sign she might know an explanation, but her expression matches my father's—horror mixed with resignation. My stepmother teeters and Naya stares with wide eyes. If someone pushed my stepmother over, she might shatter. Two guards grab my arms. I want to throw them off, to scream, but I simply sit there, too astounded to react.

No one stands to defend me.

Tugging against their hold, my voice pitches higher. "I didn't do anything wrong."

The guards tighten their grip, and I wince at the pain.

Thumping his ceremonial staff against the stones on the floor, The High Priest glares down at me. "That's for the King of Cochas to decide."

They can't take me. What will they do to me?

Their cold resolve, guilt, and suspicion hits me as hard as a stone wall, but I push back at their emotions with the panic that swells in my stomach. I'll make them feel what they're doing to me.

"Yakua, stop struggling." My father's voice slices through me and I let the emotions flit out of my fingertips. "You make yourself look guilty."

The High Priest lifts my chin with a gloved index finger. "Some may presume your innocence, but I make no such allowance." He leans closer. "Thank you for that demonstration. If I felt your power, subtle as it may be, I'm certain my soldiers did too, and a bevy of witnesses is always appreciated, though no one recognizes Amoya Roca's power better than me."

I have to escape, but guards cover the exit from behind, so I wrench free of the guards who hold me and run forward. My muscles take over, but I have nowhere to go.

"Grab her!" the High Priest cries.

The guards lunge forward and force me still.

I twist toward my father as much as I can. "I'll fix it," I say. "I didn't do anything wrong. I swear."

Zarrill's gaze follows me as they drag me out the door. I want to hear her thoughts, to know if she believes them. Does she think I'm capable of treachery? Does my father?

The guards turn me and let me walk, though they tie my wrists with rope and surround me on all sides.

Dirty, tear-streaked heads turn as we cut through the village. I press my hands to my face, but they'll know me by my dress, by my straight hair. The giants caused this mess, not me, but they'll love another reason to hate me.

We ascend the mountain in silence, and I wince every time weight presses on the arches of my feet. We hike through the same jungle I passed through earlier in the evening when I fled down the mountainside, worrying that my whole family might be dead.

Though I know everyone is safe, my anxiety cripples me. What's going to happen to me? To my family?

I limp up the steep stone path as the sun rises again and rub the sleep from my eyes, a retinue of guards panting behind me. Servants have torn down the King of Cochas's tent by the temple, so it lays in a pile of multi-colored fabric on the ground. They fold it up, likely hurrying to escape in case the giants come this way.

Scattered deer still graze, but the place lacks the magical luster it had when the pipes played. The colors are bland, almost as if my dance with Sunqu hadn't happened, and we never spotted the Mungacu.

The king, Kunica of Cochas, perches on his golden palanquin, cape in place, feet crossed, ready to be picked up and carried to his fortress—a three-day hike from the coast along the Qori Mountains.

He wears all his finery, but up close, premature aging lines his face, though his hair is dark and thick, sweeping across his collarbone. Dark bags weigh his eyes as if he's spent many sleepless nights stressing over his future and the future of his kingdom.

While his priest appears angry, the king simply looks worn.

"Did you speak to Sunqu, the glass-maker?" the king asks in a tired voice, looking at his priest. "Did he agree to come?"

What could they want with Sunqu?

I search the priest's face for answers.

The High Priest nods quickly. "He did, yes."

"And is this her?" The king's gaze flicks toward me.

"Yes, I have no doubt."

The king's eyes rove my hair, down to my eyes, and finally to my feet. "She even looks like the princess, except for her hair." He rests his chin on his fist. "It's too straight. But we can make do. Even without her extraordinary charms, she's beautiful enough to tempt him."

"She's exactly what we need," the High Priest says. "If the emperor sees the value of glass like I do, he'll be loath to dispose of us. The two of them together will give our kingdom a fighting chance."

I'm not sure what the king means, and now I'm more confused

than before, because they dragged me here for criminal accusations, not to offer me a job. Though he speaks of two people, not one, and I don't see anyone else in the conversation except me, the king, and the High Priest.

Leaning back in his palanquin, the king sighs. "Let's get this over with."

Only a few hours ago, the High Priest accused me of being a traitor. Have they forgotten?

I twist my wrist to disentangle myself from the High Priest's grasp and step away from him. "Why have you brought me here?" My anger throbs with each syllable. "And why are you talking about me like I'm not standing right in front of you?"

King Kunica drags an idle finger down his golden armrest. "Yakua Lamar, we have watched you closely these last few days—"

"Yakua Roca."

The High Priest shoots me a glare, but the king ignores him.

"Yes, Roca," the Kking says slowly. "I knew Amoya Roca, your mother, well."

I suck in a breath. I knew she tried to steal the throne, but I've always wondered how close she got. Apparently, close enough to know the king on a personal level.

The High Priest steps forward. "She tried it on me, my king. I felt it."

King Kunica casts his brother a fleeting glance. "I never thought I would say this, but we are fortunate you walk in your mother's footsteps. Your talents are exactly what this kingdom needs. Yakua Roca, I'm in a grave situation and have chosen you to bear a heavy burden to preserve the future of our kingdom. The High Priest accused you of treason by consorting with the Emperor of Isul Urqu. I know this is not true, but it must become so. You must relinquish your family, your old identity, and become a princess of Cochas."

The ground seems to drop from beneath me, until I'm floating somewhere between Valhanen and Uru Hlocha, the upper and under worlds. Pressing my palms together, I help my feet find the grass again. "You want me to marry the prince?"

I came to the festival for Darhi, but I suppose a prince would make an agreeable alternative. Even if I have to relinquish my family, I can ensure they have everything they require.

The king raises an eyebrow. "No, you won't marry my son. You'll marry the conqueror of Isul Urqu. The prince of Cochas must not know what has happened here. He has spent the last several years traveling between kingdoms to learn their customs, and he can't know you aren't the young girl he left behind. No one must know, except the glassmaker I'm sending with you, not even your family. To them, you are dead. Executed here, tonight."

"Executed?" Like I feared when they arrested me, this will soil my family name. If they aren't ruined already, my sisters will have no hope of emerging from destitution. My father will curse me to his grave and the villagers will remember me as my mother is remembered. People will say my family is better off without me, that they knew I was rotten from the start.

The king leans forward. "Your mother convinced many people to do things they did not wish to do among the noble Huya clans in Cochas. One of my closest advisors died shortly after he invited her to his home. She came for my throne, and I cannot forgive her for that. But, if you save this kingdom, your mother's sins will be forgotten."

How dare he speak of my mother in such a way?

I bow my head so he can't see the anger brimming beneath my skin, though I force my voice to remain calm as I look up. "You have ruined what little reputation my family has left. You have destroyed my family. And you ask that I do this for you?"

The king straightens on his throne. "I have no intention of being cruel, I assure you. Being a princess of Cochas on enemy territory is no small request, I know that. But your family will be dead in a month if I don't send you. What is more important? Their lives or their reputations?"

I glare at him because I know he's right. Their lives are more important, but it hurts to know the only people in the world who cared for me might hate me too.

But how does me becoming a princess save their lives?

"I believe you understand my dilemma." The king fiddles with the golden threads weaved into his robe above the thick belt at his waist. "The Emperor of Isul Urqu fell upon our borders last year. Since then, he has amassed a grand empire and has gained control of many neighboring kingdoms with his unique ability to raise loyal giants from the stones of the earth. He wishes for Cochas to join his empire as well. His army, including his rock giants, is far greater than ours and would destroy Cochas in a matter of days. My choice is death at his hand or relinquishing my throne. If I step down, he'll allow me to continue governance as Chief Judge but, in return for his mercy, he has asked for my daughter, the princess, to wife, though he has never met her before."

I haven't seen the king's daughter in person but have heard much of her loveliness. She should be about my age. Perhaps the rumors are enough for the emperor to want her, despite not having seen or met her before.

"Why not send your daughter like you were asked?"

Why me?

Blood drains from the king's dark cheeks. His entire body sags, though his fingers tense over the arms of his throne. The High Priest glances at him with tight lips, but the king doesn't take his eyes off me.

"The princess of Cochas," he begins in a halting voice, "killed herself two full moons ago when I made the conqueror's request known to her. The attack your village received from the giants stemmed from her having not arrived at the capital already. In fact, the giants attacked all the northern seaside villages in a matter of hours. The emperor is an impatient man."

People would have spoken about the death of a princess, but I haven't heard a word.

"Why? Why would she do that?"

She has a kingdom that admires her and a father who does too.

King Kunica shuts his eyes, the veins in his forehead standing out against his skin as he takes a deep breath. "She struggled with the idea of leaving her home and beloved kingdom behind." His words sound empty, but he did just lose his daughter. "I need someone to take her place, ensure that this marriage happens, and convince the emperor that there's no reason to attack our kingdom. Turn his thoughts of warfare to thoughts of peace."

"I'm very sorry about the princess. Truly, I am, but is there no one else who can do what you want me to do?"

The king shakes his head and his throat bobs as he swallows. "No. After my daughter died, I threw the festival to find her replacement. I will admit I hoped to stumble on Amoya Roca's talents but did not dare to hope I'd stumble on Amoya's only daughter."

He needs me. So does my village—the entire kingdom even. And, of course, it's my fate to be chosen as a hero, and still be hated wherever I go.

"Then here's my price. I expect my family to be elevated to the level of Huya as soon as I'm gone. I want them compensated and I want my father to be in command of all shipments that come through our village."

The High Priest folds his arms over his robes. "Your family cannot be elevated after your arrest. The clans would want a reason."

His tone sends a flash of irritation through me, but my feet stay firm in the sodden grass. Raising my chin, I count on my ability to strike fear in people simply by looking at them. "My father is a hardworking man. I'm sure you can think of one."

The High Priest's voice rises. "If you refuse, if you fail or are discovered, you and the King of Cochas will be killed, and the entire kingdom, including your family, will be forced into slavery."

Digging my heels into the grass, every muscle tense, I hold my ground. "Make my father Master of the Docks and I'll be your princess."

The High Priest nods at a guard, who steps forward and draws his sword. "We don't make deals with commoners. You won't leave this mountainside as Yakua Roca. In fact, if you don't accept our deal, you won't leave this mountainside at all."

My heart leaps into my throat.

As I stare into the High Priest's black eyes, the truth in them glares back.

King Kunica raises his hand, his forehead wrinkled as he fixes his gaze on me. "We can make it work." The lines in his brow ease. "She's our best option, Gothlu."

Jerking his chin toward the king, The High Priest's eyes widen. "But my king—"

The king slices the air with his palm, as if his brother tore his refined exterior and let loose a flare of impatience. "Brother, I have stood by you in every mistake you've made, even when it almost cost me my throne. Our goal is to protect our families and this kingdom. The throne is lost, and it's not because of Amoya. Vengeance will do nothing for us. I know you're trying to make amends, but Yakua is not Amoya. She has no history of deceiving you. Give her what she asks. We need her."

I struggle to hide my astonishment.

My mother didn't mention the High Priest, Gothlu. Not once.

The High Priest opens and closes his mouth and then faces me, his hands clasped behind his back, his shoulders slumped. "As you wish, my king."

The king reclines in his throne, massaging his forehead. "I've been in turmoil these last few months. Your acceptance of my offer, Yakua, allays my concerns for now. I hope our kingdom is as important to you as it is to me. We have to fight for it—you and I."

Except the king doesn't plan to fight for our kingdom with me; he plans to send me to fight alone. If I fail, it doesn't matter what my father or the clans think of me. Everyone I love will be enslaved or dead.

"Unfortunately," the king continues, "you are supposed to be on your way to the emperor, so there's no time to train you. You'll have to figure out how to act like a princess as you go. Speak as little as possible and remember the gods in all things."

Impersonating royalty should be easy enough. I just have to act pompous and unfeeling, just as any highborn does.

The High Priest tugs at my arm as servants bring forward a much smaller throne and lower it to the grass.

"One more thing." The king holds up a finger and touches it to his chin. "The emperor is a distrustful man by nature. You must use your power to sway him to your side. Make him trust and love you and make certain your marriage is assured. Though he has promised peace if I send you to him, he isn't known for keeping his promises. He has been engaged to other princesses before that he didn't marry. Don't let him slip away, or the entire kingdom will pay the consequences."

I'll do what I must, but I promise him nothing.

"I am sending a glass-maker with you," he continues. "To gift his glass to the emperor in hopes that the emperor will see our nation as having worthwhile knowledge and commodities that he would lose if he demolished us."

Relief sweeps through me. At least Sunqu will keep me company.

"You have servants to escort you as well. I chose a few who didn't know the princess. Gothlu, please." He looks at the High Priest who gives a stiff bow, leaves, and returns a few moments later with a servant in simple clothing.

The servant steps between the king and me and bows. "Welcome back, Princess Nalia." His bare chest is well-muscled, just like the men who man the docks.

Princess Nalia.

I roll the name on my tongue as I step onto the throne and lower myself onto the thin cushion.

"Dress the princess for travel," says the king.

Their eyes bore into my shoulders as I settle, gold pressing against my arms, cool and solid, gleaming brighter than my glass slippers.

Two women step forward and sit on either side of me. They brush my hair, pulling the strands tight as they braid it with beads and set a feathered headdress on my head. As they work, a man paints my face and hangs emeralds around my neck. He slides gold rings and bangles over my fingers and arms, so I jingle as I shift. Then they retreat and a final servant offers a dress with extravagant blue designs. They set up curtains to shield me and I undress, stepping into it, before she ties the fabric at my back.

When the servants step back, the king surveys me with a critical eye.

"She's ready," he says.

My throne teeters as servants raise me onto their shoulders.

I didn't get a priest, high priest, or a prince, but an emperor. Still, I can't decide if this is a good play, or a terrible one. My apprehension makes me wonder if I'll regret this for the rest of my life.

Glancing over my shoulder, I catch one last look at my village, nestled against the trees on the water's edge. I might never hear the waves crash on the shore again, watch crabs crawl across the rocks, breathe the salty wind, or listen to Naya's laughter.

Unless I return one day as another person entirely, the people here won't recognize me until they spot my straight, black hair.

My throne rotates as the servants face the mountain trail, but the leader motions for the procession to stop. A figure approaches without a hint of surprise in his dark eyes, a pair of sparkling glass slippers hanging from his fingers. For once, he's not smiling, but smiling or not, I'd recognize Sunqu anywhere.

CHAPTER SEVEN

SWEAT DRIPS DOWN MY face and cloth sticks to my skin as the blue river line stretches for miles ahead and weaves through desert dunes—its cold, sweet water too far away to reach. We traverse the entire Isthmus of Chira within a week, and the sandy miles beyond it inch beneath the servants' feet. The river stretches wider as we near, while the sun sears my skin through the thin shade cloth overhead.

My throne dips to one side as the servants set me down, bow, and make for the water's edge.

Throat burning, I stumble after them and a servant intercepts me as I near the shallow waves of the riverbank. "Princess Nalia, please." He nods to a bowl of fruit placed on a low table at the top of the hill. "Help yourself. There's no need to drink straight from the river like we do."

Ravenous, I leap for the water, drain the bottle, and shove food into my mouth. My tongue laps up every bite and I could swallow the onions whole, but the servant's mouth hooks down in disapproval.

He offers a shallow bow. "As princess, I'm sure you always remember to give thanks and honor the gods."

I let the tiniest drop of water drip into the dirt until the beige sand swallows it. "To the gods. May they live on in the stones of our path," I mutter loud enough for him to hear. Then I force myself to chew more thoroughly as I search his face for any hint that he suspects who I am. He wouldn't chide the real Princess Nalia, would he?

I suppose I never saw the princess, nor did I get to see how servants interact with royals.

Water trickles over rocks black with moss, but the air is so dry it sucks the moisture from my skin. As I chew my food, I let my toes sink into the sand, where the heat of the sun doesn't permeate.

Sunqu relaxes on a rug with the King of Cochas's guards, away from the servants and me and closer to the distant mountains. Meanwhile, the servants create a circle on the riverbank, dividing themselves from me.

Among the servants of the king, I am no longer Yakua, so they can't hate me by my reputation. However, when I sit beside them, they don't acknowledge me like I suspect they should. Perhaps it's a difference of rank.

I should be grateful for this. It means fewer grave glances, solemn stares, and whispers that make me a ghost on a gilded throne, hoisted up on the shoulders of servants that don't belong to me. But I'm disappointed anyway.

All I have now is Sunqu, the only piece of home left.

When I stand and approach him, the guards watch, their eyes wary. Sunqu doesn't turn until I prod his shoulder. As he looks up, his quick and guarded glance fills me with uncertainty when I can't pinpoint the reason for it.

"Can I speak with you?" I ask.

"Now?"

The guards' faces don't change. They only stare into the crackling flames of the fire.

Should I be concerned?

I nudge him and drop my voice to a whisper. "Because I need to ask you a question."

He stands slowly and bows to the guards. "Excuse me."

His footsteps crunch in the sand as he follows me toward the river, where the water smooths and hardens the ground.

As we reach the riverbank, I pull up my dress to keep the hem dry and round on him. "What are you doing here? Why are you ignoring me?"

The last time he ignored me was when we were kids—after he said my mother was horrible and I should let my father move on. I told him he was a jerk, and he was so ashamed, he wouldn't look at me for months. When I beat his scores on our history test, he congratulated me anyway and looked so sad I couldn't help but forgive him. Back then, I was angry. This time, I'm everything but.

He shakes his head. "Yakua, I'm expected to teach you how to behave at the capital, and a teacher role is what the others expect from me. You need to treat me like your tutor, or they will question what our relationship is."

"What do you mean?"

Sunqu sighs. "You can't talk to me like a friend when the others are listening. When you need me, come when the servants and guards are not watching. We can do etiquette lessons at night when they're all asleep. You'll also need to pay attention and do some learning on your own. So much depends on us." He looks away.

He doesn't need to finish his thought. I'm very capable of grasping how dire my situation is.

If the princess doesn't show up when the emperor expects her to, both our families will be dead or worse.

"Did they threaten you too?" I ask.

Rather than answer, he stares off, like he's thinking, remembering, or trying to decide how to answer.

"Did they?" I demand.

"No." Sunqu straightens his back. "I came to teach you etiquette, but also to give the gift of glass to the emperor and prove our kingdom produces worthwhile commodities that he would lose if he destroyed us."

I recall the king mentioning this role for Sunqu, which means he understood that Sunqu is a good person and that Sunqu would come for the same reason I did—to save his father and our kingdom. Except doesn't Sunqu's father still need his protection at home? He has no one else.

Either way, I'm glad Sunqu's here, though I'm angry that the king bullied Sunqu into coming, especially when Sunqu was so excited at the festival for having someone recognize his work.

"Did you know they were sending me?" I ask. "In the tent at the festival, did they tell you they planned to arrest me?"

Sunqu's face darkens and this time, he meets my gaze. "I didn't know their full plan until the moment they arrested you. The king briefed me as they dragged you up the mountain." He couldn't have warned me.

"The King of Cochas asked if I wanted to start a business in the capital of the new empire alongside the princess of Cochas and I agreed," Sunqu continues. "That is all."

His tone is defensive, though I accused him of nothing.

"I understand," I say, to mollify him.

I thought, with the health issues his father had, that he wanted to stay with him in their shoe shop in Cochas. That's why he left his apprenticeship. When I spoke to him in the shop, I didn't expect him to listen. I didn't think him ambitious.

He nods, and with a half-hearted attempt at a smile, trudges across the sand to rejoin the circle of guards.

Tearing my eyes from him, I start to walk toward the group but hesitate. I have nowhere to go. Sunqu doesn't want me to interact with him, so I meander to my bags and pretend to rifle through them until the servants stand and pack up the food. One ushers me to my throne and the servants lift in unison as I sit down. Sweat pours over their foreheads and glistens on their backs. As their muscles ripple across their shoulders, a breeze carries the smell of their labor to my nose.

I turn away.

Weeks pass beneath our feet, the thrill of new lands hardly touching the ache of leaving home behind. Then the river splits in the distance. One side cuts to the sea, while the other veers to the right where the sand rises into hardened and jagged hills, streaked with multi-colored dirt as varied as a rainbow. Then the hills dip and the river curves into a row of gray squared rock walls with rectangular openings and tall doors. A stone image of a hawk perches at the top of the largest opening, its beak extended to the sky.

Wind sweeps the strands of hair that escape my braids into my face and eyes. I brush them away.

"What's that?" I ask a servant beneath me. "Is it the sacred sun city? Are we there already?" I heard the emperor's city is at the top of a mountain range, with waterfalls and buildings encased in gold. This city doesn't have the splendor I imagined, but is a practical, plain, and sturdy fortress, with the most exciting element being the sand it's built on.

While I want to be done traveling, I hope this isn't the golden destination I was promised.

One of the servants looks up and a bead of sweat slides into his eye. He blinks. "No, princess. This is Paria. We will stay here for one night only."

Paria, the city of priests, founded by the god of water and rainstorms, Parifalko, on whom we depend for livestock. Darhi, the priest I went to the festival to meet and marry, will make his annual pilgrimage here soon, just as every priest does. It's the landmark of the gods, a city of enlightenment, and a place where every kingdom preserves peace through shared philosophies. The Highest Priest of all the realms resides there.

Has Darhi, along with every villager in Cochas, heard of my death? Do they thank the gods that I'm gone? Do they believe the accusations?

Sunqu is the only one who knows the truth.

He walks behind me, his hair cropped from when he cut it just after we left Cochas several weeks ago. Carrying a massive backpack and several bags like a common servant, Sunqu stares off into the distance, as if the mountains fill his thoughts and not just his vision. He strides beyond the line of guards, far enough away I'd have to shout to get his attention—behavior no princess should undertake in any company, even one comprised entirely of servants.

The servants still seem to fear me, though they aren't from my village or from any of the local clans and shouldn't know my reputation. They don't fawn over me like I'm a princess either.

Back at home, I made my own food. No one carried me anywhere, and the only elaborate dresses I wore were the ones I made myself. After over a year of listening to parents complain that the daughter of a Heliray-worshipper is teaching their child, they'll have to find a new teacher who'll accept my meager wages. I don't want for anything, except better shade, the occasional opportunity to run to the ocean cliffs and swim in cool water again, and a friend.

Despite the relief these changes have brought, I can't forget what's waiting for me at the end of this journey. Who is the conqueror I'm expected to marry? Is he as terrible as they say?

The stone buildings draw closer as the sun sets. Stars wink in the sky, and I squint to see the proud hawk I noticed earlier as donkeys and cows graze within short fences. Then the wooden doors of Paria open and the wind stills.

Servants ferry me inside, where dozens of red-stained altars dot the ground of a massive courtyard. Clinging to the walls of thatched houses, a musty, sweet smell welcomes me, the houses forming a tidy line behind the altars and extending on for several rows.

My servants lower me to the ground at the threshold of the furthest house, where a priest wearing a feathered hat and cape opens the door. A row of women waits inside, also in priest's robes, with a washbasin, blankets, and deerskins. They help me undress in silence and then leave, save for one attendant, who folds her arms and stands in the corner of the room.

I wrap myself in my own arms, clutching my mother's necklace to my stomach so no one sees it. Anyone who does catch a glimpse of the necklace will wonder why a princess would wear jewelry with silver snakes. I miss my mother, but right now, I miss my sisters most, and it's like I'm carrying them all with me.

When I turn to the skins and blankets on the floor, silence greets me like an old friend, until I'm jolted awake the next morning with squeals and terrified brays, shaking me from a restless slumber.

Shooting upright, I snap to my feet, my own fear already making me stronger as I rifle through my clothes. Everything is dirty, so I throw on yesterday's dress, tearing the edge as I trip over it and stumble outside. Hordes of deer and donkeys gather in the plaza, all in line for the altar, with not a soldier in sight.

"Princess Nalia."

My eyes snap to the left, toward the source of the voice, where a young priestess wears a simple dress with a striped sash and a long, red cape. Her hair, speckled with red, spills down her back in a luminous sheen, but her eyes carry the grimness of a woman who will never experience the joy of an ocean sunset.

As I look at her, she cringes at my expression. "I'm sorry, princess. I didn't mean to frighten you." She faces the deer. "It's a sacrifice to the gods for the food shortage in Dokas."

"I'm not afraid."

She crosses her arms over her robes. "Then I'm sorry I misunderstood."

Turning from her, I watch the sacrifices too. My village relies on imports from Dokas to survive the winter. A shortage in Dokas means a shortage at home.

Filling my chest with air, I give my heart a chance to slow, hoping to avoid the energy crash that comes when I don't use my power. I have no reason to manipulate anyone now.

Arms still crossed, the priestess studies me out of the corner of her eye. "You dressed yourself?"

"Yes." I check my sash and the gems that glitter in the folds. They're all intact. I hide the rip. "Did I miss something?"

"You are wearing the same dress. Do you not have fresh clothes? I can get you a clean robe."

She suspects me.

"Thank you, but no." What would a princess say? "I panicked at the sounds and grabbed the first garment available. I'll change here shortly, but until then, I thank you for your offer, but cannot accept it. A robe would not be suitable."

The priestess gives me a concerned look. "A sacred robe would not be suitable?"

I spoke too quickly.

Searching her face for any indication her question was the test her tone suggests, I attempt to backpedal. I have no desire to offend her. "I have not earned the right to wear the robes of a priestess."

"I see." Her frown softens as she turns to the crowd of deer before the altar. "We sacrifice livestock to bring rain, princess. Without rain, the kingdoms have no crops. Without crops, the people die, including those in royal houses such as yours. In a sense, all the kingdoms of Hallja depend on those who wear these robes. You're from Cochas, yes?"

The deer knock into each other as they stumble across the stones. "I am."

"Have you been to Paria during a sacrifice?" she asks.

"I have not, but I'm curious."

Her fingernails dig into the splotched skin of her arm, where patches of pigment have flaked away. "Before the gods left Hallja, they asked us to remember them and make sacrifices in their names to bring blessings and, potentially, to bring the gods back themselves. Do you see those people sitting by the altar?" She points to a group of men and women sitting in a circle, their hands tied behind their backs and their eyes glazed, likely from sedatives. "They volunteer to be sacrificed to save the kingdoms from famine. There is no higher honor. Their lives are not cast off easily. We remember them for their selfless acts."

The local priest, Darhi, made similar sacrifices at home In Cochas. I'm familiar with the practice, especially since my mother was a priestess herself, in a way.

The priestess' gaze moves across the field to where Sunqu sits on a rug with the servants over the rainbow sand, watching the sacrifices and drinking wine with his back against a gray half-wall. The wavy curls in his hair flutter as his lips move, the servant beside him nodding in response.

They enjoy his company.

"I like your countrymen." She gestures to Sunqu, though I haven't given her a reply. "The servants attend to that man without being asked, though it's clear he's little more than a servant himself. They must be the best of servants."

She inclines her head with a benign smile and leaves before I can answer.

Is it true?

A servant refills Sunqu's drink and pours his own into the dirt for the gods, though they're supposed to be my servants and rarely do this for me.

Instead, everyone's eyes, even the priestess', are little knives on my skin.

It's a recognizable emotion, this petulant envy that perches on my shoulder, but it's strange to have it bite so hard. It won't help me though, so I use my power to pluck it from my threads of emotion and toss it aside.

When I felt disjointed at school as a child, I'd curl up on my mother's lap. She would hold me tight and comb my hair with her fingers. "I had so many plans for my future," she often said, "but I gave them up when I married your father. I became chained to family and expectations. They tried to put knots on me. But it doesn't have to be that way for you. I have so much hope for your future, Yakua. You have the same powers I have, but you still have your freedom. Don't let it go. You have the power to control your future."

I'm controlling it now, but I need clean dresses.

The King of Cochas sent me with so many and they all carry sweat and grime. Even my own clothes, buried at the bottom, stink. Do the gods send princesses clothes from Valhanen? If they do, I need to pray a little harder. I can't allow the servants to continue treating me like an outcast instead of the princess I need to be.

If anything is a measure of how well I manage my role as princess, it'll be how my servants treat me.

Crossing the stones of the plaza, I sink my feet into the warm sand as I stop before Sunqu and the servants, inches from Sunqu's tunic. As I level my gaze at him, he arches an eyebrow. "Yes?"

"I need my dresses cleaned."

He leans back on his palms and the rug rustles as the servants around him shift. "What about your maids?"

"I'm requesting you."

"Why?"

Because the servants would respect me if they saw him do the same. "Do not make a habit of questioning your princess."

I'd rather not talk to him this way, but the others need to see me princess-ing as a princess would, and he's the one who told me not to treat him like a friend. He'll understand.

His dark pupils consume the brown of his irises. I haven't seen him look at me that way before, with pointed disappointment.

"As you wish," he says.

Sunqu stands to extinguish a candle perched atop a stone-carved depiction of Ma Jocoya, the goddess of health and happiness. With the other servants in bed, the moon silhouettes Sunqu.

He pauses before the statue, bows his head, and jumps when he turns and nearly runs into me standing directly behind him.

"Yakua, what are you doing?" His voice chills. "Princess Nalia, I cleaned your dresses. They're drying."

I don't want to do this, but I also can't have this conversation with the servants around. As I reach for his hand, I check myself, since it's possible that we don't have the relationship we had a few weeks ago, and tuck my hair behind my ear instead. "Sunqu, I need your help. I need to earn my servants' respect. I need people to believe I'm a princess, but I'm failing."

He sighs, the divot on his chin more defined than usual. "You can start with ordering the right people to clean your dresses."

"I'm sorry, but I had to find a way to talk to you alone, and you haven't taught me nearly as much about etiquette as you're supposed to."

He rolls his eyes, but the corners of his mouth turn up.

"Please, Sunqu," I add. "I embarrassed myself with the priestess today. While I know traveling has been strenuous, there's so much I'm ignorant of, and I can't fail at this."

Sunqu glances around the courtyard. "Then remember, it's considered inappropriate for a princess to be out alone after dark with a man." He hesitates, meeting my gaze. "But I suppose it's too late for that. I'll come to your tent as often as I can, but we can't be seen alone together.

"You have to know the servants already suspect you're a stand-in princess. I've heard them talking about how cruel the emperor is, and how they wouldn't send their own daughter if they could help it either. They've watched you with your offerings. Princesses aren't so flippant when it comes to the gods. And you were overwhelmed with the finery when your handmaids dressed you. A born-and-bred princess would be used to fancy dresses."

His words stir my own misgivings, resurfacing them.

Sunqu continues without waiting for my response. "I recommend you thank the servants for their services and remember the gods. You are an example to everyone around you. They expect you to be pious."

I've already started the habit of sacrificial prayers, as my servant requested. As for thanking the servants, I haven't done a lot of that, but I can fix it. It's not that I wasn't grateful. I simply assumed they preferred my mouth shut, so I accepted their help in silence. "Anything else?" I ask, my mouth dry.

"That will be a good start." He points to the statue and then to the floor. "You're welcome to begin now." As he steps back, his mouth quirks, though he doesn't explain why. Then he makes for the thatched huts.

Lowering myself to the ground, I press my fist over my heart as we often do in prayer, bowing my head as Sunqu had, but no words come to mind.

Looking up again, Ma Jocoya's flat features and stone eyes don't carry any warmth as she glares down at me. Her mouth will never open. If the gods return, it won't be because I spent my night here.

The gods live on in the stones of our homes, our paths, our statues, but I can sense animation spirits and manipulate the emotion within them. Still, the only awareness I sense is my own.

CHAPTER EIGHT

SMOOTHING THE FOLDS of my freshly cleaned dress, I step into a reed boat that will soon carry me across the Cochmayu River. Water slaps against the sides, the boat sinking into the water with the addition of my weight. I won't miss Paria, especially not the priestess with the knowing gaze.

The servants disperse and Sunqu departs from them. There are several reed boats available, but he strides straight to mine, sits across from me, and turns his back to me.

I rotate so the gold in my headdress jingles, maybe to remind Sunqu I'm alive, maybe because I want to annoy him for ignoring me, but Sunqu doesn't move. He must have a reason to join me, even if he didn't want to speak.

The boat lurches as a servant pushes it into the water, the shore shrinking as rock and gray buildings meld into the rainbow sands. On the distant bank, tiny structures grow into bronze pyramids. The gentle twists of rocks carved by the river in Paria become hardened walls of copper. Silver gleams with harsh lines and deep grooves. A line of cattle grazes on a riverbank, carrying the stench of manure on the wind rather than the hint of salt that blows over the beaches of

Cochas.

As princess, I should know what this place is. It's highly likely that Princess Nalia has traveled here before. Instead of asking the servant closest to me where we are, I scoot closer to Sunqu. "What is this place?"

"This is the kingdom of Ragua, founded by Raguary." Sunqu says under his breath. Ragua is the god of metals and treasure.

My servant, the one who is a head shorter than me, has a friendly face with a wide nose, and carries more girth to him than the other servants, speaks with his usual slow cadence. "We have entered the new empire, princess, and now your home. Isul Urqu, the capital, is only a few days from here. Four or five, maybe."

The boat rocks as Sunqu shifts in his seat.

It doesn't feel like home, more like enemy territory, with sharp edges and hard places. I almost prefer Paria. However, if Isul Urqu is to be my home, I don't want it to feel like anything but an extension of Cochas.

"It's more extravagant than Paria," I say, letting the simple statement sit without communicating the rest of my thoughts.

Sunqu regards me for the first time since the prior evening. "Paria was simple and beautiful. I haven't seen sand like that anywhere else."

He thinks I had a problem with Paria, that my distaste for leaving the city of priests behind stems from a desire to abandon the simple for the city of gold. Has he forgotten who I am?

"You misunderstand me," I say, but I'm too angry with him to explain myself further. Instead, I ignore him and watch the water's edge draw closer.

Perhaps wealth is what I should strive for, and when I obtain it, Isul Urqu will redefine both our worlds. I've heard many stories about the gold that coats every rock and woman's dress. The city is said to shine as bright as the sun it represents and to stand so tall that the city touches the clouds.

The servants sit motionless in the boats as we reach the shore, but when the boats knock against the bank, they stand to tie them up, their faces grim. We march in silence through the kingdom of Ragua and choose a steep stone path on the outskirts where gnarled jungle trees hug the mountainside.

As we ascend, the servants' breaths shorten to ragged gasps, and their steps slow. Sunqu hovers close and moves rocks or carries bags whenever a servant asks. But as we hike further, we take shorter breaks. Almost like we're running from something, though no one mentions what.

My throat dries after hours of sitting on a hard seat that rocks back and forth. I claw at my throat and take off my headdress. "Can I get water? Food?"

Only the sounds of shifting rocks and footsteps greet me.

I lean back, my throne digging into my shoulder blades.

In Cochas, I would have helped, just as I bagged and carried fish for my father to prepare for the market, but I wasn't a princess then. Still, it's odd to be carried when I have two working feet.

They set me down for lunch and several of the servants disappear for a time. When they return, they bring potatoes they boil over a fire with herbs.

Massive spider webs hang from branches and stretch across the trail, far wider than any web I've seen in the Qori mountains by Cochas. Inside the long, white-webbed funnel, furry eight-legged creatures peer out with wide, round eyes.

As I watch, one of the servants ignores the spider webs, glancing into the trees with a shiver, though it isn't dark yet.

Rather than be alone, closer to the muted creaks of the jungle, I join the circle of servants, bunch up my dress, and sit without invitation. The guards do the same.

Mutual fear makes us equals.

As everyone hunches over their steaming soup, flinching at the slightest sound, I grow taller, more aware.

A servant dishes a plate of food and passes it to Sunqu, who then passes the plate to me.

"Thanks." I take the plate from Sunqu, and he hands me a stone.

"It's a dining stone for your offering," he says.

Smoothing the face so it doesn't show my annoyance, I douse the urge to tell him I already know and smash a morsel for the gods. "May the gods live on in the stones," I say, forcing as my piety into the statement as I can muster.

The servant starts passing Sunqu another bowl, pauses, and passes it directly to me, the muscles in his thin arm flexing as they tense. I freeze before taking it.

"Thank you," I say.

He smiles, showing me a row of yellowed teeth.

I turn away and chew my food, my chest filling with an overwhelming jumble of confusion that I prefer to hide until I can pluck it free.

But he has to be kind. I'm the princess they're escorting.

An owl screeches, causing a to servant jump. Sunqu's eyes narrow as he surveys the trees. Crickets cheep, and an animal screeches beyond the thick tangle of jungle plants. As the breeze shifts, a chill penetrates the wool around my shoulders.

"Are we not safe?" I ask.

The servant's throat bobs as he swallows. "We need to spend as few nights on this mountain as possible."

"Why?"

The trees sway and his eyes follow the pattern of leaves.

"I don't trust these trees," he says. "They don't drink from the ocean's water."

"You're worried about the trees?"

Trees don't have spears or spikes, or fine little poison teeth, just groaning trunks and branches that crack as you step on them.

He takes a deep breath. "I don't mean to scare you, princess, but travelers have gone missing while hiking this trail. This is the only passage to Isul Urqu from the eastern kingdoms, but there are rumors of a Dragunche."

"A Dragunche?"

I haven't heard of it. The tales can't be worse than the stories told of the Mungacu at home, and in all the years I've lived in Cochas, I only ever saw the creature at a distance. "I would think it's the Perja we should worry about." They stalk the highest mountain peaks and cast fear over the kingdoms with stories of their strength, claws, and almost-human abilities to communicate.

He licks his lips. "No, the Perja stick to the glaciers. I doubt we'll see one in these mountains. A Dragunche is a demon of Heliray. I'd rather see a Perja than a creature from Uru Hlocha. We'd have a better chance against it." He pauses and an eerie silence stretches between us.

"If you have to go to the bathroom, don't walk over that way" another servant warns. "There's a web there."

The servant brushes off his legs, as if sensing phantom webs, and shivers "Sorry, princess. Don't worry, we'll get as far as we can. If we spend the night on this mountain, we'll put extra guards around your tent. You have no reason to fear. We're close to the emperor. We'll be rid of these spiders soon enough."

In three days, I'll escape the dry heat of the desert and the wet, frigid hands of the mountain peaks. Whether he means to protect me or not, this servant's assurance is the kindest thing anyone has said since we started this journey.

"Thank you," I say.

Once we finish eating, the servants put the fires out. Sunqu sneaks into my tent, brushing aside the fabric flaps that tie to make a doorway. When he sees me, he smiles, as if coming to teach me etiquette is what he looks forward to most.

He sits cross-legged on the floor in front of me. When we've done these sessions in the past, he usually draws on blunders I've made to give me feedback for improvement.

Tonight, he stares at me, crinkling his forehead and squinting one eye. "I'm not sure what to go over this time," he admits.

If he's run out of topics, I can come up with my own, because the everyday life of the city I'm about to venture into never ceases to intrigue me.

"What can I expect from Isul Urqu?" I ask. "Do you know?"

He blows air out of his mouth in one quick gust. "I know some things. Most are rumors. Others are what the princess herself told me." He pauses. "It's all very grim."

It can't be more grim than what I've heard already.

"The King of Cochas told me the culture there is different than at home," Sunqu continues. "In Isul Urqu, you must speak only when you're asked a direct question and give as little information as possible. People in general like to be listened to, but in Isul Urqu especially.

"They have traditions around how you approach the emperor, and harsh punishments for petty crimes."

"Is that all?" I ask, barely keeping the sarcasm out of my voice.

"They have violent games too. And people are so afraid of the emperor, that no one confronts him. He hardly bothers with a guard."

I suppose I can respect that, but it doesn't make me feel better.

As Sunqu lets silence stumble forward, my anxiety grows to bridge the empty spaces, festering in the dark corners between words left unsaid.

I'm not sure I'll ever be ready.

With each sunset, the days before I meet the emperor narrow; I know that. But the further we leave Cochas behind, a heaviness settles on my heart. It's been weeks since I last saw Naya's smile and her uncontainable giddiness. I miss weaving blankets for her. I even miss Zarrill swimming beside me. She could cut through the ocean waves as easily as Mungacu, but she never left me behind. I miss my students and the pride I felt in their accomplishments, especially when Oci, my little protégé, recited the stories I loved as a child.

Yet now, the servants' collective fear and the way the guards raise their spears as we pass beneath arched trees and brambles make my stomach churn.

Decaying leaves melt into mud. Vines caress moss-coated stones and the scent of death and life saturates the thin mountain air.

My throne wavers as a servant slips, scraping his knee. Blood pours down his shin and I cling to my armrest as Sunqu reaches up to steady me.

"Please," Sunqu says. "Let me take a turn."

The servant clutches his leg, his lips pinched. "I can't—" But the other servants lower the palanquin and step back.

"You can and you will." Sunqu drags the man to his feet and binds his leg.

The servant's cheeks flush. "Thank you, Sunqu."

"Let it rest, Manco." Sunqu lifts him and sets him on the floor of my throne. Afterward, the servants raise the palanquin again and Sunqu takes Manco's place beneath me with the bags he carried still on his back. The other servants wince and shift their grasp on the handles.

Manco bows his head, his hair slick with sweat. He must be the same age as my father and might have a daughter, too.

I aim my gaze at the trees, tall with wide canopies, and let my chest rise and fall so I don't have to look at him and he won't feel compelled to speak to me. If someone talks to me, I'd rather it be because they want to, not because they have no choice.

"I'm sorry, princess." Manco hunches over his leg.

He does look sorry, with his eyes downcast, his shoulders slumped, but I can't think what he's sorry about. "What do you mean?" I ask.

He glances up. "I failed in my duty. I'm supposed to carry you, not be a burden."

For a minute, I thought he dreaded having to sit beside me. Instead, he's embarrassed that he must be carried when I've been sitting here for hours. Not only that, but I've ignored this man for weeks, not caring to learn his name because I assumed he didn't like me. Though he's shown nothing but kindness.

Rather than let the shame of this realization fester, I dip my head. "I hope your leg gets well soon," I say. "Though I'm sorry you're hurt, I'm glad for your company."

He gives me a shadow of a smile, his cheeks still pale. "Thank you, princess. I'm happy to offer conversation whenever you need it."

I wiggle on my throne, twisting around for a cozier position, though nothing helps. As uncomfortable as the hardwood with plated gold felt against my back, it was never so unbearable before.

If I don't allow these men to carry me like a princess, they won't have to guess I'm not who I claim to be. They'll know.

Another servant slips over a boulder and sweat stains his tunic from his neck down to his waist. He breathes in labored gasps.

I don't care.

"Stop." The throne lurches forward, despite my command, so I try again. "Stop!"

The throne shifts as the servants set it down again and Sunqu gives me a sharp look as he releases his handhold.

Stepping off the throne, I brush off my dress. "I will walk from here."

"You are a princess," Sunqu points out. "Or have you forgotten?"

I meet his gaze with what I hope is an equally fierce expression. "My back hurts and my legs need to stretch. I will walk."

The servants glance from me to Sunqu, their faces red with exertion and their mouths pressed shut.

Sunqu blinks. "As you wish."

Hiking up my dress, I press forward with the servants over the path of boulders. Their movements ease as we crest the point of the mountain, descending the other side before ascending again. Though my lungs struggle to expand, I push forward anyway.

I've hiked enough mountains in my life to be used to this.

The sun drops in the sky as we near another peak and the servants stop on a grassy outcropping to set up tents. They start a fire and prod logs with sticks as smoke settles over the camp.

I sit beside the fire, watching embers spark and fizzle into the dark earth. A servant stares into the depths, red light bathing his straight nose and deep-set eyes. Sunqu settles on the grass beside him, his hands on his knees.

Interrupting the silence, Sunqu asks, "Where are you from, Wykuru?"

The servant called Wykuru looks up from staring into the fire, the lines in his brow smoothing. "From the island of Holya. Have you been there?"

Sunqu shakes his head.

"It's on the southwest coast of Cochas, by Tarya. It's beautiful. There are plants in the jungles that are so lush and green you can't help but touch them. When you do, they shrink away and hide until they feel safe again, then reopen as green as ever. Have you heard the tales of Holya and Tarya?"

Sunqu warms his hands over the fire as shadows dance across his face and chest, though his expression is warm. I'm relieved to see this happy, contented side of Sunqu return after these weeks of traveling.

"I haven't," Sunqu says.

"There was once a daughter of Ma Cochira who conceived a child but didn't know who the father was. She turned to the gods for answers and learned that the father was Skapu, god of the mountains. Skapu demanded that both she and her child travel north to the frigid weather of the Skarag mountains to be closer to him and leave the sea forever. To escape this fate, Holya, daughter of Ma Cochira, threw herself and her child into the sea. Together they formed Holya and Tarya, mother and daughter islands. Tarya has more mountains and hills than Holya does, but I prefer the flat landscape."

I turn in the opposite direction of the fire and walk to the edge of an outlook where the face of the mountain plummets. Peaks rise on both sides and in the distance, another peak punctures the clouds with clusters of white glaciers. I try to fill my thoughts with images of these immense straight-up-and-down mountains, and not images of drowning babies, but it's hard to do.

If the gods were good, why would a mother throw herself into the sea with her child to avoid them?

We pray every day that they will return to us, reclaim their kingdoms, and bring back the age of creation and power when the gods made humans more than they were. When they mixed their blood with ours. The blood of the gods has all but died out in Hallja. Outside of the emperor, I am the only person I've heard of who has manifested their ancient abilities.

The servant, Manco, dumps my bags of clothes beside me and limps to toss my sleeping skins into a tent. "Here you go, princess." He smiles and I smile back.

"Thank you."

He hesitates. "I really appreciate you being willing to walk so far. I'm sure my leg will feel better by tomorrow, so you won't have to do it again."

I meet his gaze. "Take as much time as you need to rest."

He gives me a thankful nod and limps away as I turn to my tent with the same little tear by the door that I recognize each time we stop. I can't figure out how they keep track of which tent belongs to whom.

Another day gone and we're several miles closer to our final destination. I'll be married soon, but not to Darhi or a prince. To a conqueror.

Marriage to an emperor has more fanfare and bigger emeralds. I'll have fish in the storerooms that could feed thousands. I'll never wear another dirty dress, nor should I have to endure another sneer, but my stomach tightens as I think of the unknowns.

The clans whisper of his cruelty. He conquers nations, killing without remorse.

I hike through dangerous mountains to be his bride, but I can't imagine happiness at his side, no matter how big the throne. Will I ever find happiness again?

Manco's voice outside penetrates the thin fabric of my tent. "The guards are here for you, princess, if you need them. I will be back in the morning. Don't leave anything outside your tent, or you might find spiders making homes in the morning."

"I'll keep the tent shut, thank you."

Rocks poke through my deerskins that night, and the cold nips at my ears, despite the hat and thick blankets I hide beneath. My breath makes white snakes in the air, and I wish I could return to the heat of the Cochmayu River, a place I hadn't appreciated enough.

Still, unease curls inside me.

How will I fare once I get to Isul Urqu? And what will keeping an engagement intact entail?

CHAPTER NINE

W E ASCEND THE MOUNTAIN again the next day, the clouds settling around us in swirls of white. I pull every scrap of cloth over myself to keep my teeth from chattering. As we wade through bitter rain and mist, the servants' feet move surely across the wet boulders, but I cling to my throne, waiting for someone to slip.

For three days, we climb. I pass out every night, whether I walk on rocks or not, and dread getting up the next morning.

Until the fourth night.

The servants put out the fires and don thick shawls. Meanwhile, Sunqu packs what remains of our meager dinner. The familiar way he moves makes my queasiness settle. How his hair curls as the wind ruffles it.

I miss his smiles and gentle teasing at the base of the cliffs of Cochas, where we belong. The sound of waves crashing on the shore, of rocks tumbling off the cliffs and hitting the water, the drag of my father's catch across the stones outside and the sharpening of knives before he slices the fish open, Naya and Zarrill sleeping so close I can hear their steady breathing.

"Are you ready?"

Manco stands over me, both hands clasped behind his back.

Swallowing hard, I say, "Yes," before I add, "Do you miss your family, Manco?"

The corner of his mouth twitches into a pained smile. "Every day. I have a few teenagers as old as you are and one toddler. Their mother is the toughest woman in our village. She takes care of them all on her own and has for years. Every time I return, they're a little older and there are a few more experiences I've missed, but the pay I get as a servant is far more than what I'd receive working in my village. I understand if you're homesick. I'm no stranger to that feeling, but it'll pass. We're meant to survive."

He's been separated from them for years and I'm complaining about a few short weeks.

As I struggle to grasp the homesickness and remove it with my power, the way I would remove a sliver, it simply returns, stronger than before. At least Manco gives me hope I can move past it.

I follow him to the tent, erected at the foot of a massive tree, its trunk coated in moss. Hundreds of tree roots spring up from the dirt and create a patchwork of wood vines. He hands me clean towels and blankets and bows low, his hair hanging in his face. As he backs slowly away, still with a slight limp, I open the tent flap. He's ever kind, despite having carried me longer than I've stood on my own two feet.

"Thank you, Manco, for being a friend to me," I say.

I wish he might know how much I mean it.

His eyes shine with a warmth I've overlooked in the past.

"I'll see you in the morning, princess."

The tent flap shuts behind him and I cover myself in blankets, ready to close my eyes and forget how deep the bitter air reaches into my bones. But I can't keep my eyes shut. The peace I felt earlier vacates into something dark, quiet, and wrong. I try to fill it with images of Cochas and the beaches in all their golden warmth.

An ear-splitting scream quivers the walls of my tent. Another follows, with footsteps that dash through the grass outside. Weight moves and someone grunts. Then a body hits the side of my tent and sticky, dark liquid soaks through the thin fabric. A metallic scent wafts in the air.

What's going on?

I can't go outside, but I can't stay inside either.

Instead, I freeze in place as terror grips me, though the terror is soon replaced by a flowing power that radiates heat down to my fingertips. My thundering heartbeat slows as strength fills my core.

Footsteps race across the mud and my tent flap opens. A dark shape fills the doorway.

"Yakua!" Sunqu's urgent voice penetrates my soul, ripping me out of a strange, uncomprehending stupor. I've never felt so much fear, so much power in one place, not even when the giants came. They demolished homes, but most of the people got away.

People are dying all around me, people I know. Their lives leave this world, their emotions snuffed out like dying flames.

"Yakua."

My eyes snap to Sunqu standing at the opening in the tent.

He rushes toward me until he's standing over me, gripping my shoulders. The dark shapes of his lips move while screams drown out his voice. He shakes me again so my teeth chatter. "Yakua, you need to leave. Now!"

As I strip off my blankets and layer on coats, pinpricks of fear vanish as more lives are taken. Another one goes and I stumble, like I've been punched in the gut. I suck in a breath and turn to my pillow, snatching my mother's necklace from beneath it.

Red liquid coats the chain and pools on my tent floor. I wipe the necklace off and stuff it in my pocket.

A set of hands grabs my arms and flips me around. Sunqu's eyes are wild. "Yakua!"

The screams outside have quieted, the fear gone, except Sunqu's, though the wildness of their voices still echoes in my ears.

"Yakua, we need to run!"

He pulls at my arm, but I drag him behind me as I sense another presence. It's not the emotion of fear that alerts me, but the absence of it. The deep chasm suggests a presence with little emotional aptitude, as if it's a creature who can't feel emotion, or exists in another world, where I cannot access it.

It doesn't know where we are yet, but it'll find us soon.

I lift a hand as I inhale, pulling in the strength of my power, drawing on Sunqu's fear without his permission, because if there's ever an excuse for it, it's now. Though I have little experience exercising my power, I hope it's enough.

"There's something here." Sunqu chokes on his whispered words.

"I know."

"I don't know what it is," he says. "Everyone's dead."

"Manco?"

Manco carried me all the way here and answered any question I asked. He set up my tent every night. He became someone sturdy, sure, and familiar over the weeks of traveling, and I just got to know him these last few days.

I sense the creature approach as Sunqu nods.

Closing my eyes, I fight the grief that threatens to replace the fear I'm clinging to, but I can't let the fear go. It's what makes me strong.

Sunqu steps out from behind me, reaching for the flap again.

"Be still," I hiss.

But it's too late. The flap opens without him touching it.

The air inside the tent stirs and every muscle in my body freezes until a bone-chilling whistle splits the tent. At home, I jumped off cliffs, fought strong currents, breathed air into Naya's lungs when she nearly drowned, and watched my mother die. But the fear I felt then dims in comparison to the terror that stabs my heart as Sunqu staggers into me, though he covers me with his arm. While I manage to stay upright, my legs want me to cower beneath the deer skins.

As the fear sinks in, so does my power.

"What are you?" Sunqu's voice trembles.

Greasy strings of hair hang in the white face of something almost human, with broken bones for teeth. It wears a robe of decaying vines and beneath its slumped shoulders, a pungent smell brews of mildewed moss on river rocks. Two pinprick eyes on either side of a hooked nose illuminate the tent in a soft, blue, ethereal glow. "The queen of Uru Hlocha desires to grow her kingdom." Its whispering voice makes me shiver. "She calls you home."

Uru Hlocha is the underworld, and the queen has to be Heliray, the goddess of death.

Sunqu's back presses against me. "We can do whatever rituals and sacrifices Heliray requires. Just tell us what you want."

The creature's mouth opens in a laugh and the whistle returns, louder than ever, and reverberates in bursts. Sunqu clutches his ears, but I let mine ring even after the creature's mouth closes.

Its pale eyes flicker as it turns to me, and I return its ice gaze.

I drop my blankets as it considers my features, stepping around Sunqu, toward the drifting ghost until the smell makes my stomach roil and I can count the teeth behind its dried-up lips.

Pain shoots up my arm as Sunqu grips it, trying to pull me back.

"Death is rest." Its voice shrills from between its teeth. "It's rejuvenation and nothing to fear. Soon this will all go away. You'll never feel fear again."

I grip my mother's necklace in my pocket, letting the familiar warmth of the metal embrace me, giving me courage. Fear is my closest ally, and I can use the emotion to send the creature away.

The hairs floating around the creature's head settle. The vines that make up its robe meld and the flickering eyes glow brightly as if… as if it recognizes me.

I hear my mother's voice in my ears.

You're my daughter. And we don't let anyone tell us what to do.

Raising my mother's necklace so the giant emerald blazes, the creature hisses softly and bows.

"Ma Roca," it murmurs. The hairs on its head flutter again as if beneath water.

"Leave," I command, putting the full force of the power flowing around me into that word. "Now."

The creature's dark form shimmers and I glimpse the shape of a young woman, much like myself, in the red robes of royalty. Her eyes are wide and full of dread like they must have been when she was alive. Or perhaps because I make her feel that way. Then, like the light of a dimming candle, the creature vanishes.

Sunqu turns. "Where did it go?"

"I banished it."

Somehow, I harnessed its animation spirit and altered its emotions without touching it, though I haven't done that before. Either that or it simply obeyed me. I'm not sure. Either way, the thing is gone, and the fear fueling me makes me want to run the rest of the way to Isul Urqu and not pause for breath, though my brain reels with the horror of our encounter.

Sunqu's eyes go to my necklace, and he takes a half step back.

This time the fear comes from him, though not as strong. It billows inside me and pulses like the adrenaline I felt on the cliff's edge.

I clutch the necklace tighter in my fist. "It's gone," I say.

His mouth gapes. Then he opens the tent flap, peers outside, and checks inside the tent one more time. "You're sure?"

"It won't come back." My voice sounds odd even to me.

I can make Sunqu obey me too, and it wouldn't matter whether he's afraid of me or not. I can mold him into whatever I want.

Sunqu wipes his forehead with a shaking hand. "I–I don't know what to do. I woke up and everyone was running and now no one is." Crumpling to his knees, he clutches his hair with his hands.

I can't manipulate or control him.

So I reel back the emotions that fight to escape. As I contain them, my power snuffs out as fast as throwing dirt over an earthen oven. My vision careens, but I hold to the tent and manage to stay upright.

Everyone is dead, including Manco, the only servant who ever spoke to me. And I almost used my power on Sunqu.

The wind hisses, but nothing else stirs.

My father was always afraid I could inherit my mother's abilities and persuade someone to do what I wanted against their will. But no one has ever obeyed me like that demon did. It called me "Ma Roca."

"Ma?" Sunqu asks.

"My mother is dead, and I'm the last to carry her name."

It knew me and gave me a title of respect.

Sunqu drops his hands and looks up. "Are there more of them?"

I clear my throat. "I think we should leave." Blood covers my blankets, and I can't sleep with the fading bodies of my guards and servants.

"It'll be dangerous to hike the rest of this mountain in the dark." Sunqu rubs his eyes. "But I don't want to stay here either."

Fortunately, the stones on the path are laid out so it's difficult to miss. Without my servants, we have no guides to help us if we get lost.

"We'll have to abandon our supplies," he continues, "and hope we don't have far to go. We could follow the stone trail for days, hope for places to stay along the way, and pray we get to Isul Urqu before more demons and hosts of poisonous spiders find us.

Once we arrive at the sacred sun city, what then? I no longer have an escort. The small threads that make me royal have snapped in a single night, and if I can't pass as a princess, Naya, Zarrill, my father, and my stepmother are all slaves or dead. Though they didn't know it, they count on me.

"I'll pack my things," I say.

After packing the things I'm able to salvage, Sunqu and I leave stones over the hearts of the dead servants to honor their passing. We don't want to linger, so we don't have time to dig tunnels and bury them in the hills above a river, as is custom. As we finish, I hurry after Sunqu toward the mountain trail, hefting my backpack, and preparing for the long hike ahead.

Hours later, a bitter cold freezes the outer layer of my skin as the blood inside me burns. I stagger up another rock stair and press my palm against the slimy vines while rain trickles down my face, seeping into my clothes.

When I inhale, I breathe in mildewed air.

Everything I need weighs on my back in one giant bag. It doesn't help that funneling so much emotion into the demon at the campsite drained me physically too, but not as much as restraining myself from using my powers on Sunqu did. When I don't use the fear that feeds my power, it weakens me.

I can barely walk, much less climb boulders. The servants must have had legs given to them by the gods to carry me so far with all our supplies on their shoulders.

Except they're dead now. Manco too. Whatever they gifted Manco with, the gods didn't do much to protect him.

The shadows between stones meld together as darkness settles, and Sunqu pauses where the side of the mountain plateaus. "I think we should camp here for the night, before the temperature drops."

I halt behind him as he drops his bag and fishes out the fabric for the tent. "Can I help?"

"Sure," he says, though the end of his statement curls with a question.

His lack of confidence irritates me. Choosing not to explain all the times I went camping with my mother, I press my lips together, deciding to show him instead.

Taking the ropes out of his hands, I string the cords through the fabric. The sun sinks fast and a chill sets in. We work quickly as we right poles and tie them in place. Sunqu opens the door, tosses our belongings inside, pulls my backpack off my shoulders, and throws it in after.

I rush into the tent and shiver as he ties the tent flap shut behind us and yanks a large fur blanket out of his bag. I pin my arms to my sides to keep myself from snatching the blanket so I can wrap it around my shoulders. He lays a few thin deerskins on the ground, barely enough for one person, and drops the blanket on top.

With one hand over the fur, he pauses and doesn't meet my gaze. "We only brought one set. Yours had..."

His voice fades, so I finish for him.

"Blood all over it."

The blood of my servants.

A burning sensation tingles my nose, and I turn away, wanting to pluck the emotion from my thoughts, but resisting out of respect for my servants' memories.

I can curl up in a tight ball on the floor—but I won't survive the night without something to keep me warm.

"We'll have to share," I tell him.

He continues to avoid my eyes as he motions to the skins. "After you."

I lay down and pull the fur over my shoulder up to my chin. Warmth envelops me and the shivers racking my body dull. I turn on my side as Sunqu lies down on the bare tent floor.

"Don't be ridiculous," I say. I lift the blanket up so he can cover himself, but he stays as far from me as he can without losing heat. Tension radiates from the roundness of his shoulders as silence settles between us.

As I squeeze my eyes shut, images of blood oozing through the tent burns through my eyelids. I can still smell the metallic scent of death, still see the blue eyes of the Dragunche glowing in the night. My throat constricts as I gaze into the empty darkness, insects chirruping outside, followed by a low, throaty howl.

While I enjoy the fear that stirs my blood at the top of the cliffs, tonight I can barely breathe as a renewed sense of dread overtakes me. With it comes a flare of energy that usually accompanies fear, sensed by my power. It's not a fear I can claim as mine. Instead, it's an emotion I sense from Sunqu. Though we don't touch, the emotion envelopes me.

Twisting toward him, I reach out a hand and touch his arm, the muscles flexing beneath my fingers as his entire body tenses. He probably sees the same images I do, which means neither of us can escape what happened the night before.

I promised I wouldn't influence him, so rather than calm him with my emotions, I try to inject the feeling into my voice. "Sunqu?" I whisper.

His arm doesn't relax, and I can almost glimpse his profile staring at the ceiling of the tent, eyes wide open.

Edging closer, he doesn't move as I press against his side. He probably can't.

Perhaps my presence will be comforting. The gods know I can use the comfort, too. The fear that emanates from him shifts into a new fear—fear of loss, fear that something that was can never be again.

I run a finger down the curves of his arm, listening to the soft patter of dewy rain.

He turns his head and looks at me.

"Sunqu?" My voice is almost unrecognizable. It's not the host of emotions that my powers draw into me at his touch that makes me repeat his name, but the smoky glint in his eyes that torches the darkness.

I can't breathe with him looking at me like that.

He inhales sharply at the sound of his name and drags a finger down the edge of my jaw, winding a hand through my hair. His other hand pulls at my back and draws me across the velvet deerskins until I'm pressed against his chest, his warmth enshrouding me.

The night stills and all I can hear is the steady beat of my heart. I cling to his broad chest as if all that happened with the Dragunche can be forgotten for just one night.

Before I can kiss him, however, he pushes me away, shaking his head and curling up further away than he was before.

He doesn't need to explain why.

I know.

Tomorrow, we arrive in Isul Urqu.

Tomorrow, I meet the emperor.

CHAPTER TEN

A PERPETUAL MIST clings to the mountain's steep face, the path's stones and surrounding jungle covered in moss and webs. The moss might be beautiful if it didn't swallow my feet with every step.

I can't bend my knees one more time, but I have to. My whole body trembles as the air snatches warmth from my skin and replaces it with fog.

Ahead, Sunqu leans against a stone boulder and crosses his arms. He hasn't said a word about what happened in the tent, but waits quietly every time I fall behind. It makes me walk faster and push harder to thwart the gap between us.

His silence bothers me, but not as much as the images that stick to my eyelids whenever I close them. I can still taste the saltiness of his lips and feel the heat of his breath.

"Are you all right?" His voice carries through the thin air. We've climbed several peaks, and likely have a few more ahead. I don't know if I can make it over another.

"Fine," I say evenly.

I've agreed to marry an emperor I don't know, one who has destroyed my village and threatened my entire kingdom. Why wouldn't I be fine?

Sunqu scales several more boulders and pauses at the top, a smile dawning. "We've arrived." He points into the mist. "It clears up ahead."

My desire to see the city where I am tasked to live, a capital that must be a reflection of the man who rules it, propels me upward until adrenaline sweeps through my muscles, drowning out the whining of my knees on each stair.

My breath catches as I join Sunqu.

Just as a wave dissolves over the seashore, a collection of clouds part over the mountains and little black dots dive in and out of the wisps. Threads of light illuminate a vast city, perched on a massive, circular mesa with carved stone giants evenly spaced apart, their backs pressed against the steep cliff face. Each giant has a crude face with greenery that grows from the cracks. Their gold embellishments reflect the sun as waterfalls on either side of them sparkle.

They can't be the real giants the emperor created. They stand too still. When the emperor's giants attacked my village, it was dark, and I'd looked out from the top of the mountain. The giants were gone by the time I arrived, so I didn't see them in detail, but they were very much alive and moving.

Rumors circulated in my village that the emperor was descended from Mirchira, the god of creation. During the early age when the gods walked among us, Mirchira emerged from the sea and created giants to keep him company. However, the god of creation wasn't satisfied with their simpleminded nature, so he destroyed them and created humans in their stead. No one had seen giants in many lifetimes before the emperor came. No one could stop the giants, not even our armies in Cochas. But here, wedged against the cliffs at the edge of the raised city, these giants are artwork.

In the city itself, thatched homes huddle against garden terraces, and a massive fortress of a castle is built against a pointed mountain in the middle of the mesa. The castle has square rock walls that tier up to the top, painted with gold to match the giants that guard it.

Heat thaws the ice in my bones and my fingers tingle, as if the city itself is a source of heat and I've finally breached the perimeter, but the warmth doesn't reach my heart.

"They say the emperor created those giants himself." Sunqu's voice takes on a note of wonder. Of course, he, more than anyone, would appreciate the artistry of the giants.

Rather than remind him that giants like those demolished villages, including our own homes, I look around for a place to bathe. I'll need to change and wear fresh clothes. They expect a princess, not a pauper, and I have lost both my escort and the throne they carried me on. I can't fail my family the moment we arrive.

Sunqu shakes himself. Then, as if guessing my thoughts, adds, "You can bathe at the river. I'll be your escort, introduce you, and explain your lack of servants. You don't need to say a word."

Opening my bag, I check that the finest princess gown I brought remains in one piece. The fancy headdress and emeralds sparkle without defect. The box with my shoes in it lies at the bottom, alongside my mother's necklace. I clutch the bag, so the contents chink together. "I have everything I need, then."

My knees creak as we descend the mountain to the river below. We'll have to ascend once more, but it won't be so hard with such a fascinating view around us, especially knowing we're safe, with a limit to the number of stairs left to climb.

On the riverbank, Sunqu turns his back, his hands clasped behind him. "You go first."

"Thanks." I double-check that he faces away before I drop my bag on the riverbank, undress, and jump in. The icy water strips away the grime from the last few days, but my teeth chatter. I crawl back out and, without looking, Sunqu hands me the cleanest blanket he has in his bag. Then he strips off his shirt and slips into the river as I change.

I turn my back, but it's hard not to look at him when he steps past me, putting his shirt back on so the thin fabric sticks to his skin. He runs a hand through his wet hair. It's grown longer in the last few weeks.

Clearing my throat, I say, "What do you plan to do once we get there?" Though I leave out the part where I remind him I'm getting married.

I know part of his answer already, but I need something to think about other than how good he looks and how very unappealing getting married to a man I've never met sounds.

"I told you already. I came to pitch a new commodity and prove Cochas is capable of producing more than just fish."

A commodity like my slippers. I slide them out of my bag and put them on last.

"But where will you live?"

His voice turns brusque. "I'll figure that out when we get there. Are you finished dressing?"

"Yes."

Sunqu turns, a strange look in his eyes. His hand twitches as he takes a hesitant step forward, then closes the gap between us.

He reaches for my face and tucks loose strands of hair behind my ear, taking care not to touch my skin. I should say something, but I stand still, the words trapped in my lungs. As he retracts his hand, he clenches his fist, and his face becomes a tortured mask.

"Why didn't you tell me?" I ask.

He gives me a sharp look. "What do you mean?"

His feelings are spilling out, flooding the air, even if I can't sense them. They're in his gestures, in the anger he displayed when I accepted this marriage. In every glance.

"How long have you loved me?"

He studies me. "You're marrying the emperor. Both our families depend on you. Our entire kingdom relies on you."

And I feel all the weight of it. "How long?" I repeat.

Water drips from his hair. He meets my gaze and doesn't flinch. "All my life," he says.

How did I not see this before?

I suppose I didn't think it possible.

My throat knots. I want to tell him I care about him, whatever happens, and I do care. But we can't be together, so it doesn't matter whether I love him or not. Shouldn't matter…but does.

"Do you…" His entire face scrunches with sudden anger. "Do you feel nothing for me?"

My hands shake and I ball them into fists.

Emotions are messy things. I'm not sure what I feel for him, but I know what I can't feel. We came too far to forget our duties.

He slings his bag over his shoulder and stacks mine on top of his. "I get it." Both bags together tower over his head. "If we're going to finish this, you need to be careful, Yakua. I told you the servants suspected you weren't the real princess. They feared the emperor would see through you. The King of Cochas is playing a dangerous game. Are you ready?"

What am I giving up by walking up those stone stairs?

Despite feeling rested, climbing the stairs seems more daunting than ever.

Whatever happens, I must secure the throne.

Am I ready?

"I am."

But as I stoop at the riverside for a handful of water, it doesn't soothe my throat.

"What does a princess do that I don't?" I ask.

If I still come short, I need to know. This is my last chance to improve.

"Smile more." His eyes crinkle at the sides. "Stop looking at people like you're contemplating how to swallow them whole."

Funny how difficult it is not to glare at him.

He ignores me and continues. "You've made a lot of improvements over our travels. I think you're as ready as you can be. Just remember that Princess Nalia grew up being respected and wasn't cast down by anyone, especially not her clan." His expression turned thoughtful. "A princess has faith in herself. And if she doesn't, she pretends to."

I'm not sure what he means. Does he think I don't have faith in myself? Rather than ask, because I'd rather not confirm it, I change the subject.

"You respected Princess Nalia then? You knew her well?"

His eyes take on a faraway look. "She reminded me of you sometimes. I was sad to hear of her passing." He presses his lips together. "One last bit of advice—"

He raises his hands to show me a few paper-thin scars on his palms and fingers. "The glass I work with is a tricky material. It can be hard as the granite that forms our ocean cliffs, or it can break into thousands of shards that slice your skin and burrow deep. Walk like you're treading glass, Yakua. Talk like anything you say might cause those shoes to shatter."

"Will the shoes shatter?"

"Not those." His eyes gleam. "I promise."

I reach for his calloused hands but let them drop almost as soon as I touch them. We can't repeat the night before. I'm at Isul Urqu now. My kingdom needs me to marry a different man.

"It'll be fine, Yakua," he says, as if realizing how grim his words sound.

"No, it won't."

It's a statement of fact, one I've accepted, and I don't care to examine the emotions I have around that statement. Rather than pause to think on it, I motion for him to follow. "Let's go, we're already long expected."

Stairs that cut into the sheer cliff lead directly upward, with the occasional tree branch protruding from the rock.

My thighs burn and my legs weigh more with each step. I straighten my spine, like a princess would, and push my hair from my face. Past the giants, up the garden tiers.

We pass a small outpost of guards, their spears leaning up against the rock walls of a small hut, sheltering them from the oppressive heat of the high-altitude sun. Their eyes slide past us, busy with their drinks and clearly expecting no foreign threats, and wave us by without speaking to us. A man and a woman traveling alone cause little concern for kingdoms like this one.

Continuing down the streets of the village, we pass carved stone statues of the gods lining the road on either side. The black dots I noticed earlier circle high above me—the Folqus of Isul Urqu. They're giant birds that feed on dead flesh and carry the weight of dying souls into the afterlife, to Heliray if she still reigns over Uru Hlocha, the underworld. I didn't expect to see a Folqu myself, even at a distance.

Then the fortress I'd seen from the neighboring mountain casts me into shadow. The great doors bear depictions of the sun and the Perja—a sign of life and dominance over it. Another set of stairs rise to a wall, and beyond that, the hand-carved palace doors. Only the wealthiest merchants in Cochas have wood in their homes. My father would have loved the geometric designs and friezes of gods on the surface. Perhaps I will learn to love the richness of this city too, if I live long enough.

Perhaps not.

A soft breeze stirs the hair on my arms.

Clink, clink, clink.

My shoes hit the stones. My dress drags and my neck strains against the weight of my headdress.

Behind that wall, the emperor waits. He could kill me, sell my family into slavery, trample my kingdom, or toss me aside like a common beggar. Or I could convince him to love me.

A line of guards on either side of the door survey me. They wear pointed gold hats and matching waistcoats.

"Princess Nalia of Cochas, to see the emperor," says Sunqu in a grand voice.

He lays his fingers over my hand, squeezes, and lets go.

A guard raises a golden spear. "We are expecting her. But where are her servants?" He scans the stone road behind me, like he's expecting a procession to show. "And her escort?"

"We were waylaid on the trail. All were slaughtered except the princess and myself. Please inform the emperor that the princess of Cochas has arrived at last."

The guard beckons to the other, younger guard, and mutters in his ear. As the second guard inclines his head and disappears inside the doors, the first waves at a line of sentries standing at the bottom of the stairs. The sentries disperse.

I don't have bath salts to wash with. The emperor might smell me from across the room. If I throw up, that will only make it worse.

Sweat prickles my skin.

"Now is the time for your glare," Sunqu whispers with a small smile. "Be fierce."

It's too late to turn back. In this moment, I can become someone great. I can protect my kingdom, my family, but I must keep this marriage intact.

I straighten my shoulders, my fingers tingling as my power detects the fear beating through my blood. They lead me through the double doors of the wall, into the grounds where another path leads to the palace entrance.

"Take your shoes off," the guard says as we reach the palace doors.

I always imagined wearing my glass slippers when I first saw the emperor, but I stoop, taking them off, and hold them by my fingertips.

A man slings the straps of another bag over my shoulders, weighted by something that clanks like rocks. My insides pitch and I wobble on my aching heels. "What's this?"

"You must bear a token burden to meet the emperor."

They want to make this as hard and as humiliating as possible. I might remind him I walked three days in the freezing cold with a massive bag that was burden enough. However, my tongue doesn't work properly.

Sunqu takes my shoes from my hands and his lips twitch as he shoulders his token burden, or bag of rocks, in addition to both our travel bags.

"The emperor has been informed. You may proceed," the guard says.

The doors creak open and light falls on a quilt of interlocked stones.

"Princess Nalia of Cochas," a voice echoes.

The name is still strange when applied to me, like they've inserted a jagged rock in the prongs of a golden necklace meant for sapphires and opals. The reality of my dishonesty strikes harder in this formal setting.

I want to correct them, but I don't.

Just beyond those doors, the emperor will see me. What will he think of me? And what will I think of him? Will the people here fear me too?

Sunqu lets go of my hand. His emotions must have melded with mine because I didn't realize he held it, but I'm vacant without his touch. I walk ahead, as they'll expect me to do, dragging the weight of the rocks with me, and rely on the security of Sunqu's eyes wherever he stands. The room goes on forever until the floor bends into a raised platform.

You are my daughter, Yakua, the memory of my mother's voice whispers.

I look up.

When I dreamed of the emperor's face, he often looked angry and cruel, dressed in blood red. Other times I imagined a loving and kind face. Instead, the golden feet of a throne stick out beneath a woven screen that obscures the emperor from view. Uniformed servants in white and red stand in ranks on either side.

"Where is her escort?" the servant on the right asks. Gold and red lines his simple loincloth and he wears a chain around his neck with a single shell. The two servants beside him keep their heads bowed and have matching seashell tattoos on their wrists—the ownership markings of slaves.

Sunqu steps forward and bows beside me, only a few steps away, and the bags he carries teeter. He manages to keep himself upright and straight. In his arm, he holds my shoes and a box I haven't seen before. "They were killed on the trails by a demon called the Dragunche. We barely escaped with our lives. I have escorted the princess for two nights since we lost our servants and guard."

The servant grimaces. "We have heard rumors of dark spirits on the trails. This is concerning news we will have to investigate further. But how are we to believe this is the princess? Do you have proof of her heritage?"

Sunqu opens the box and brings forward knotted threads with shells and cut stones hanging from the strands. The positions of the shells and stones record our history. This one likely chronicles the Cochan monarchy, including Princess Nalia. Sunqu never mentioned the King of Cochas giving him anything for the emperor. "I recovered this from the possessions of the king's guards after they were killed. I have a gift as well from the people of Cochas." He produces a dazzling seashell from his pocket. "It's made of a new material called glass, encrusted with gems, to remind the emperor of our shared history and heritage."

"Glass?" A new voice cuts in from behind the screen, layered with subtle confidence. "I haven't heard of it."

Sunqu inclines his head, still holding the shell aloft. "Not many have, my emperor."

I can't tell if the emperor observed me through the screen. I can only see the faintest outline of him. But he must care more about his future wife than a glass gift from a foreigner.

"Who are you, to be sent by the dethroned King of Cochas?" the emperor asks through his screen. "Are you High Priest? Or a clan leader?"

"Neither, my emperor. I came to bring the gift of glass to the new empire, as an offering of peace and celebration for the emperor's upcoming wedding. I'm the man who first created this material, and I hope to start my trade here at the capital."

"Your name?"

"Sunqu Sua of the Phaqcha clan, my emperor."

"You are welcome here, Sunqu. I accept your gift and I'd like to see it closer. Lift the screen."

Servants pull on ropes and the screen rises to reveal a man on a golden throne, his hand in a fist, inches from his chin. He has thick, unruly curls, a sharp jawline, and dark eyes that look out beneath thick brows. He glows in his white robes, stark against his dark skin, darker even than Sunqu's. The shining patterns that adorn the floors, the elaborate gold sun, and the gold-leaf pillars dull against the powerful arch of his eyebrow and shape of his lips.

He's beautiful.

Like a perfectly poised, venerated human that embodies everything I wish I could be. This is a man no one dares to mock or scorn.

The emperor gestures to a man in priest's robes. "Ranu, come see this. Does this not look like the ice that the Perjas carve?"

I learned a long time ago in school that the gods created the Perjas to carve memorials in the ice of the mountain peaks to commemorate and remember the gods after they disappeared from the mortal world.

The priest called Ranu strides forward and bows. Turning to Sunqu, he squints at the curves in the glass as Sunqu holds the shell beneath his careful gaze.

The emperor leans forward on his elbows, lifting his chin to see better. "It doesn't melt, see?" the emperor says with barely suppressed excitement. "It's a purified, exalted stone. We can replace our stone statues with it in Mirchira's honor."

"Yes." The priest's eyes glitter as the emperor motions for a servant to take the piece from Sunqu and then watches the servant whisk it away. "I'm pleased to meet the inventor of this fine new material. Please return tomorrow. I would like to discuss the potential I see in you."

The emperor's gaze strays from Sunqu and travels from my legs up to my headdress without reaching my eyes. As if he doesn't expect to see an expression there. Or doesn't want to look at me—really look—any more than the clans of my homeland do.

"As for the princess—take her to her rooms."

My wrath at his offhanded dismissal boils over as a servant with a necklace of shells appears at my side and nudges me in a new direction.

Letting my token burden fall from my shoulder, I don't bother to pick it up. If he doesn't care about me, I don't care about his ridiculous tokens, and I can't leave until I've spoken to the emperor and established some basis for a relationship.

How dare he dismiss me?

But the servant pushes harder. "This way," he says.

As I stumble toward the door, the emperor's cool voice speaks from behind me, but I can't catch the words, though I'm loathe to leave Sunqu, my only source of comfort, behind.

The servant leads me down an empty, gray hallway and all sounds of the emperor die. We leave the palace and cross green grass to a line of small huts against the city's only mountain, still within the wall that protects the grounds of the emperor. He takes me to a hut nestled against a line of trees and stands aside as I push through the drapes covering the door.

The hut is simple, a place of bed skins, stone walls, and basic necessity, with a handful of tapestries to warm the stone walls. It's a place to live in uncomfortable solitude until called upon.

It doesn't matter that I don't get to stay in the palace, not if I can't talk to the emperor even when I'm in the same room with him.

Anger won't help me right now. There's nothing I can do but wait until the next time I see him, but after several attempts of trying to pluck out my anger with my power, the anger returns just as strong, so I pace the length of my hut, ignoring the comforting bed skins and hearth as if they're nothing but dirty rugs.

CHAPTER ELEVEN

DAYS AFTER I MEET THE emperor for the first time, I drag a deerskin pouf toward me and use it to support my foot as I strap on sandals. In addition to the bed skins and hearth, the servants furnished my hut before I arrived with extravagant rugs and tapestries, ceramic vases, sculptural wall reliefs, and the softest blankets.

Servants bring baskets of gowns, headdresses, beads, and precious stones into the sunlit room.

I fidget with my dress, paint my face, put my headdress on, and then take it off again. As I set it on the pouf, light bounces off the metallic sides. If only I could bottle that light and surround myself in it, so I'm a little less me.

That's what they want, right?

Why hasn't the emperor called on me?

If he had any suspicions of being tricked, I'd be dead already. But that doesn't change that I arrived without a retinue of servants and without a clean dress. The emperor won't forget this, and it can't happen again. No one can suspect I'm anyone but who I claim to be.

A servant lays a hairbrush on my table and backs slowly away. She looks a few years younger than me, with an honest, open face, like many of my students in Cochas. By now, they'll have a new teacher. The news about me will have traveled. My students will call me a traitor, too.

"What's your name?" I ask.

The young woman's eyes flit up. "Irenti."

I spent weeks with Manco, my old servant, and only took an interest in him as a person days before he died. I can do better than that. I will do better.

"Thank you, Irenti. You've done well."

She blinks. "You look lovely, princess." Then she bows, a fist over her heart with a thick, likely gold-plated, bangle that covers her wrist.

An obsidian mirror hangs from my wall, my reflection staring back on its surface. Birds chirp outside, and the fresh fragrance of honey and flowers waft through the open door—evidence of a brighter world.

I reach beneath my pillow and run a finger over the gems on my mother's necklace.

When Irenti leaves, I bring out my necklace, but holding it doesn't offer even a taste of the boldness that burned in my mother's eyes, in her raised chin, or in her swift stride that lives on in my memories.

Irenti said I was beautiful, but I've been told that my whole life and people still distrust me, still jeer at me. The emperor hardly looked at me. So what's the value in it?

Since I don't have shells for offerings, I kiss the emerald instead.

"Please, make the emperor like me," I whisper to my mother, hoping she heard.

I have to make him like me.

Because I don't want to think about what could happen if he doesn't.

After days of sitting around, I'm about the abandon my hut and search for something to do, perhaps woods to explore, when a servant knocks on the wood paneling of my door. "The emperor is waiting for you," he says. "Follow me."

I stand so fast I surprise myself and almost topple over. Then I follow him to the palace, past the guards, through the front doors, and into a banquet hall decorated in stone carvings of giants and gods.

The emperor doesn't look up as I cross the floor, the heels of my slippers clattering against the stone as I move to sit at the far end of a patterned tablecloth stitched with gold.

This time, dozens of people occupy the space between us, but there are no screens to obscure his lips as they curve. He raises a golden glass to pour an offering to the gods. His coarse, knotted curls gather above his forehead and tumble over the close shave on either side of his head.

He wears a simple tunic rather than his robes, with sleeves that hug his arms. As he sets his glass down, he rests his chin on his fist. His cheek dimples, but he doesn't smile. He doesn't eat either.

The woman across from him gestures with her hand, subtle hints of gray in her black hair. He nods several times, but then his eyes travel down the table to me.

I avert my eyes, but when I look again, he still watches with his chin tilted up and his brow furrowed. His lips pucker.

Should I be flattered?

Instead, the world is in shadow while the sun glares in my face.

I sacrifice my food offering for the gods and then spoon the rest of my food into my mouth, eating with as much delicacy as I can. Pinching the golden chalice between my fingertips, I tip it, ever aware of the emperor's eyes on me, and let water slide down my throat. My stomach growls, but I eat slowly.

Finally, he looks away, and I'm able to breathe again.

His mouth moves as he speaks to someone else.

The woman he's talking to turns to her food, looking down at the vegetables on her plate. As she faces away, the emperor scowls and glances at me again. I meet his gaze, remembering Sunqu's words about smiling, but the emperor doesn't act fazed by my eye contact. Instead, he takes a swift swig out of his goblet and rises to his feet. The men around the table stand as if waiting for this precise moment.

"It's time," the emperor says.

What does he mean?

Sitting beside me, a man rubs his hands together, bustling toward the door where the other men collect. None of the women move, as if this is a normal thing I should expect, like the sun rising or the grass turning green.

A servant positions himself behind me and beckons with two fingers.

"Me?" I point to myself.

He nods.

The emperor wants me to join? Or watch from a close range?

Perhaps he wants to get to know me after all.

But headdresses, gold medallions, and capes rustle as the rest of the women rise and follow me out of the palace to a set of stone benches beneath shade tents. The servant pushes aside a curtain to reveal a large playing field with lush grass, walls of stacked stones, and two enormous posts with hoops. Far below, the emperor stalks across the field with a rounded stone tucked under one arm.

"The men play Fidichi," a soft voice says at my side, "the day after the star, Kurku, shows itself. We watch from up here." A woman settles on the furs next to mine and spreads a golden cape around her, though her outfit exposes her legs and stomach. She wears a gold-plated skirt and a headdress with turquoise feathers, with her long hair pulled behind her neck. She sat at the breakfast table earlier, only a few chairs away from the emperor.

"We don't play Fidichi in Cochas." If we played any games, we raced with rowing boats or swam the length of the beaches. "What are the rules?"

"Cochas? That's a long way. What brought you to the sun city?"

Perhaps the emperor didn't make everyone aware of the identity of their future empress, but he should have. The announcement must be forthcoming. "I'm Princess Nalia." My title should explain enough.

She clicks her tongue. "And you didn't learn the rules? But I suppose it was your brother who visited a few years ago, not you. I thought every royal had at least heard of it." Pointing to the gold hoops on either end of the court, she says, "It's simple. They pick up that stone ball and try to get it to the other side of the court without dropping it. They usually play ten-on-ten. The other team tries to intercept their passes or get them to drop it before they reach the other side. If the other team intercepts it, they can carry it back with an advantage. I'm Cuxy Pa, by the way."

I nod my acknowledgement, fighting a surge of embarrassment that threatens to color my cheeks at my clear ignorance of upper-class ways. "Thank you for the explanation."

As I turn from Cuxy, the men below spread out across the stone court, the emperor crouching into position, his hair hanging in his face.

Cuxy leans on the overlook. "Emperor Huamar might be strong—"

I silently test his name on my tongue. I have yet to hear someone refer to him by his actual name and I like the sound of it.

"But," she continues, "I wish he played with a heavier stone. The bigger the stone, the harder the game. He's too reserved. Now, who is that other man? I haven't seen him before."

She points to a shirtless Sunqu, with his hair cut so it waves over his forehead. I force my gaze away from him, but despite my best efforts, my traitorous eyes drift back.

Another woman kneels beside Cuxy on the beach, leaning against her shoulder. "The man with the wavy hair? He's gorgeous as the ocean at sunset." Despite her colorful language, she manages to sound bored, as if ocean sunsets are a regular thing and she's seen enough to throw them away.

Though he does look gorgeous—like all my best memories of home. "He's lovely," I say, but my voice is stiff, bordering on sarcastic.

While I have nothing but good things to say about Sunqu, I don't want her looking at him.

The woman beside Cuxy studies me, but I keep my focus on the game.

"Do you know him?" the woman asks.

"He's my servant," I say, perhaps too quickly.

The emperor won't invite someone below nobility to his table and this woman wears emerald beads around her neck. She won't stoop to a servant, especially not my servant. Even if he isn't, exactly, my servant. Or a servant at all.

As a glassmaker, he shouldn't have any reason to cross paths with her, unless she wants their paths to cross.

She smooths her cape. Disbelief adds a hint of character to the boredom in her voice. "Is he really? Odd. The emperor doesn't play ball with servants."

If Sunqu never speaks to this woman, he won't know I claimed him. If he finds out, this conversation will certainly bite me, but it's too late to resorb my words. "I can't control what the emperor does with my servants. He is the emperor."

Cuxy chuckles as the woman's eyes narrow.

"Pacay," Cuxy says, "this is the princess of Cochas. Princess Nalia, this is my cousin."

"Are you really?" The woman called Pacay lengthens her mouth into a lazy smile, the narrowed incredulity gone. "I saw you at breakfast and figured you'd just arrived. I promise I've no intention of stealing your servants, even if they are handsome. Though you do a fantastic job making this particular servant sound interesting. Entertaining, even. But all the princesses who come here are our best form of entertainment, you especially."

All the princesses? Surely, I'm the only one. Unless the emperor has a sister I've never heard of, but I must have misheard.

"Welcome to Isul Urqu, Princess," Pacay says. "We wish you an abundance of good food and fortune."

I need to be more tactful. I don't need negative opinions from the nobility of Isul Urqu the moment I arrive. While I can tell her about my engagement, the emperor might want to make the announcement himself. At the end of the day, I need to let Sunqu go. He deserves happiness too, even if it's with someone else.

"Thank you," I say, "but I would happily recommend you to Sunqu if you'd like."

Disinterested and remote as she might seem to me now, she could grow on him the longer they know each other. Perhaps I shouldn't cling to him so tightly.

Patting the stone bench with both hands, Pacay says, "I do love a man with intrigue, but we will speak of him no more."

Cuxy gestures toward the men as the stone moves between players. Below us, Sunqu grunts as he swings the stone toward another, taller man. "That's my husband, Opo-Mayta. He is the emperor's general."

Tearing my eyes from Sunqu, I fix my gaze on the man Cuxy points out.

Opo-Mayta still has the unwrinkled and unfettered signs of youth. His dark hair doesn't contain a single strand of gray, nor is his smile touched by years of death and warfare, and yet he holds kingdoms at bay.

Cuxy wears her role well—wife of an emperor's general in a gold and red tasseled ensemble with finely woven patterns.

I was right not to anger her.

"He is young, isn't he? He must be a natural tactician for the empire to have grown so much with him at the emperor's side," I say.

Though her smiles were warm before, Cuxy's smile broadens. "He is." She peers at another woman, seated on the other side of the shade tents, and purses her lips. "The Huya didn't always support him, but they embrace him now. The emperor has full confidence in his abilities."

In Cochas, the Huya were the noble clans unrelated by blood to the emperor. The class structure between Isul Urqu and Cochas must be similar.

The woman Cuxy glared at sits with a straight back as she looks out at the players. It's the woman with the hint of gray in her hair who spoke to the emperor at breakfast. She has a flat, severe mouth and wrinkles around her eyes that don't come from laughter.

The older woman must notice my stare because she lifts her chin to meet my gaze, her lips pulled down at the corners. "Pacay Viri-mac." She nods with forced civil deference. "Cuxy Pa." Her eyes find me again. "And who are you, child?"

"Princess Nalia of Cochas."

The older woman's upright posture stiffens. "Welcome to Isul Urqu, princess. I'm Lina Illapu, of the Isul Huya clan. I came to watch my sons play." She jerks her sharp chin to the court. "Ichu and CoccoInta. I'm sure you'll get to know all the Huya before long." She clasps her hands on her lap and returns to motionless watching.

Cuxy leans toward me and whispers, "She's one of the original Huya of Isul Urqu. They think they're better than the rest of us."

Pacay rolls her eyes in a slow, careless way, smiling as she does it. "The emperor doesn't trust them, so he brought the families he could count on from Chira. We help him keep control of the city." Unlike Cuxy, Pacay doesn't bother to whisper.

Lina's eyes fix on us again. Her left eye twitches before all three women return to watching the game as if nothing has been said.

In Cochas, my father bowed when the Huya passed, but never spoke to them. He said they counseled the King of Cochas in heavy government decisions. Lina must claim a high position in the city's politics, or the emperor wouldn't have brought her to his table and invited her sons to this game.

I can say something kind to Lina and earn her trust and respect, but if I did, I would alienate Cuxy, whom I have befriended in a small way. I can't afford to offend the general's wife.

Instead, I will stay neutral by saying nothing.

Lina stands and approaches in a royal purple dress with woven square patterns at the hem. As she stops in front of me, she looks down her nose at me. Her light amber eyes, a unique color I haven't seen before, flash. "Princess Nalia, Chira is a kingdom that hasn't known prosperity since the days of Mirchira. Isul Urqu has always been prosperous because of the Huya clans. If you marry the emperor, I urge you to repair the rift between us and appease the original god of Isul Urqu, which is Isul, not Mirchira. If you don't become empress, I pray Heliray is kind to your soul." She bows her head, turns, and leaves the benched seating area.

My blood chills. She must be aware of the impending marriage, yet she still questions it.

Pacay and Cuxy watch my expression, as if they're curious to see how I receive Lina's words. Cuxy, at least, has the decency to pretend to study the artwork on the decorative pottery to my left. Pacay has no staring inhibitions.

While I'm no stranger to being stared at, it increases my discomfort.

I came all this way to marry the emperor. I've only been here a few days, and he hasn't tried to get to know me. If he changed his mind, it will explain why he never spoke to me. If he chooses not to marry me, what then? I can't go home. Nothing good awaits the traitor of a kingdom on the brink of war.

The king wants me to use my powers, and I have to do it without Emperor Huamar noticing, but how do I do that without getting close to him?

If the emperor changed his mind, why hasn't he sent me home by now? The King of Cochas warned the emperor was fickle, but he did say the emperor intended to marry Princess Nalia. The king wouldn't have lied.

Would he?

Confusion and despair spin in my head, but they aren't fear, and they don't make me stronger. I'm too faint to use my powers to pluck them out.

The men hoot below and Sunqu grins widely as the emperor slaps him on the back. If I were down there with them, I could toss the stone through all the hoops and not sweat half so much. With one touch, I could tweak the emperor's emotions, convince him not to fear me, but to care about me, and we could get this over with. Provided I'm as good at convincing someone to love me as I hope I am.

"Princess." Someone taps my arm. The cushions beside me lay bare, empty of both Cuxy, Pacay, and Lina. The stone arena is quiet and still, devoid of the emperor and his retinue. Somehow, I've lost track of passing time, as well as the people around me.

"It's time to go," the servant says. "They expect you in the weaving room."

They expect me…in the weaving room.

They also expect a smile and a warm speech, no matter what concerns rumble in my head. "Yes, of course. Thank you."

The smile doesn't come., though I follow the servant inside the doors, down the hallway, and into a small room tucked away to the right, filled with tapestries, rugs, and weaving tables. Under better circumstances, I might have loved the coziness of this room, with scented candles that hint of fresh jungle air and fragrant flowers.

Mountains, snakes, giants, and Folqus cover the walls in brilliant arrays of colors with such incredible craft that I might have stumbled on Ma Frigello's personal weaving room—the goddess who first taught the clans the art of spinning.

Pacay takes one look at the weaving tables and crinkles her nose. "They couldn't think of anything less boring for us to do?" She heaves a dramatic sigh and slouches to the corner, where she sits in a pile of skirts and fiddles with the strings in the fabric, refusing to touch the weaving instruments.

Pulling a weaving table closer, a servant spreads cloth at my feet, and I reach for the brightest strands of deer wool. They slide between my fingers, smooth as mountain grass. I haven't made anything for sheer enjoyment before. Everything I've made in Cochas was for necessity, though I enjoyed adding patterns of my own. My father hung the rugs I made on the walls to keep the rooms warm in the winter. They also kept the dust and dirt out.

What would the emperor like most to see on a tapestry or rug?

Lina Illapu sits at the loom by an empty hearth and eyes me. "You look comfortable. You've done this before?"

"I have."

At home, Naya would have asked me to make her something. She would have brought a bucket of seashells to sew in and would have sat up all night watching until I finished, her legs crossed and her hair wild in the dark. I always envied her curls.

Lina bends over her loom, cutting off any further conversation.

When she spoke to Cuxy, she mentioned Lina was part of the original Huya of Isul Urqu. The empire hasn't been around long, which means Lina either came from another kingdom, followed the emperor from his home, or was a survivor from the early wars when the emperor first appeared on the battlefields.

Rude or not, I have to ask. If my days are already numbered, it doesn't matter what I do. If not, understanding the political landscape of the city matters.

"Are you—" I search for the best way to phrase my question, "from the old city? The original Isul Urqu?"

Lina doesn't look up. "I am."

Her homeland now belongs to the emperor, and she serves him as an advisor. She might like this setup, but she might also hate it. Her feelings likely depend on how she feels about the emperor, and how close her family was to the throne.

I entwine my strings and pull the stick, so it slaps against the wooden edge. Cuxy mirrors me from across the room, using cream strands that gleam with hints of gold.

As empress, I can make a difference to the people of the empire. I can stop wars. I could rid the mountains of the Dragunche. What kind of impact would I have had as a fisherman's daughter in Cochas? Very little.

The threads of my rug knot. I untie them and keep going, my fingers moving faster as I go, until Lina pauses to watch.

Cuxy ties the ends of her rug and folds it. But I'm still going, my pattern detailed with glowing red embers, black mountain peaks, gray smoke.

"What is it?" Cuxy asks in a hushed voice, her mouth round.

"The giants," I say.

I don't have to say anything more. In fact, I don't say more on purpose. To Cuxy, the giants are a symbol of her husband's strength and prowess, of her family achievements and pride. To Pacay, they are what they are to Cuxy. To the emperor, they are his own instruments, his creations, and even an extension of himself. To all of them, the giants are wondrous and praiseworthy.

But Lina is more complex.

She might see the giants as Cuxy did, but I suspect that she'll notice the town depicted in the corner that the giants destroyed, and the trail of blood in the giants' footprints. Perhaps she will wonder if I understand her perspective.

With this tapestry, I can touch them in different ways.

"It's wonderful," Lina says in a dry voice.

Lina's tone and expression must speak leagues because Pacay stands from her corner to join us and admires the giants too, though her gaze lingers on the village in the corner as well, as if she picks up on the subtleties too, though I hope I'm wrong.

Cuxy unrolls an exquisite rendition of a Perja. Perja are predators that roam the mountain glaciers. The paws of the creature nearly spring from the cloth and the eyes glow with rubies. "It's a gift for the emperor. Perhaps I can repay my family's debt to him for our good fortune in a small way."

"He'll love it," I say.

Cuxy's cheeks glow.

Lina ties hers off, which has illustrations of the sun over the mountainous cliffs at the edge of the city, with glimmering threads of gold.

As Cuxy gathers her tapestry, she leans toward me. "If you don't give your tapestry to the emperor, I'd love to have it." She squeezes my arm before following Pacay out. The last thing I hear from either of them is Pacay telling Cuxy I might be far more entertaining than she hoped.

After brushing loose fabric off her lap, Lina smooths her dress and leaves her loom. She stops before passing me by. "Princess, I'm sorry about what must have happened to your kingdom, what's happening there now, and what's about to happen. But if I were you, I'd keep the tapestry and not bother with the emperor. Keep your dignity if you can. You have no power to change what's coming." As she leaves, a couple more women I don't know trail behind her.

But Lina Illapu doesn't understand.

I was sent here because I'm the only one with power. I just hardly know how to use it.

CHAPTER TWELVE

STARS FLICKER OVERHEAD in a stretched, black tapestry as I climb a grassy hill with garden tiers cut into the sides. A servant with a shell necklace dangling on his chest walks a few steps ahead and glances over his shoulder as he crests the top. Hitching up the front of my gown, I follow him, a warm breeze brushing my ankles.

The dark outline of the emperor's palace pierces the midnight sky on my right. All around us, the city swells with rivers, waterfalls, and cliffs. Though I can't see them, I know the giants stand below us, still as a woven tapestry, but big enough to crush the world beneath their feet.

"This way," the servant says, motioning me down the path toward a rounded stone structure built on the edge of the hill with one giant window facing west for the setting sun, though it set some time ago. The roof is open to the stars.

As I enter, shallow stairs lead to an altar, encircled by a group of men with their faces tilted upward toward the bright full moon that flings light into the constellations. One man glances my way for a moment before returning to his stargazing.

They are likely making recommendations for planting at specific altitudes or pondering the well-being of our flocks based on the light and dark spiritual energies that surrounded the river in the sky. With everything my stepmother taught me about her garden and with what I have learned in school about the stars, I can contribute to this conversation, if they'll let me, though the climate here differs somewhat from Cochas'.

Would that be wise?

From what I've observed, the women here don't speak with the men unless there isn't a man to be a spokesperson for their family. Has this always been the culture, or has this been a recent practice? In Cochas, it depends on the family, but the mother's family holds the family name. My mother was the dominant personality, though she had no family. When my father remarried, my stepmother was timid, so my father assumed the role of spokesperson.

I cannot pretend my upbringing is the norm in any culture, and I'm uncertain how to act in this scenario. In the end, the person I need to like me is the emperor.

Even as I think this, the servant veers toward a woven blanket on the lower level, leading me to where several women sit and watch. I pick out the regal chin of Lina, Cuxy's kind smile, and Pacay's disinterested smirk.

Lina meets my eyes and there's a knowing expression in her eyes that I don't like.

The servant wants me to sit away from the emperor again, and Lina expects it. Lina knows he intends to cast me off like a star that winked and fell from the sky. She, like the others, is waiting for it to happen, but my family and kingdom count on my success. Not to mention I don't know what the emperor will do with me if this doesn't work. If the emperor decides without telling me that he wants to break our engagement, I have nowhere to go except back to the

Dragunche.

So I turn on my heel and stride toward the men.

I can't sit idly by and wait for my kingdom to fall.

The servant looks back, but I don't wait to see his expression. I won't be cast off. If I have any value to the emperor, he needs to be aware of it, and I'll never have a chance to succeed or fail with my power if I'm not able to try.

Two men stumble aside as I slip between them, though I don't bother apologizing. Sunqu talks with Emperor Huamar near a pile of large stones, his mouth set in a false smile, the bright Sunqu I know buried somewhere deep within him. We're all wearing invisible masks, hoping to enchant.

When Sunqu spots me, his eyes widen, and his lips stop moving.

I hope I'm not making a huge mistake.

Sinking to my knees in front of the emperor, I dip my head. "My emperor, I've spent time studying the stars in Cochas." It isn't a lie. "I know the constellations are different here, but I know I can help with your predictions if you'll allow it."

Emperor Huamar's dark eyes fix on me with the same intensity as when I entered his throne room, his expression both guarded and attentive. He's taller than I expected, and his bulky shoulders loom, wearing blood-red robes with a gold belt and a simple headdress.

He's silent as he regards my appearance, but then his mouth twitches.

"What do you predict?" he asks.

Crickets chirrup as I scan the stars, and everyone's eyes are a weight on my chest, but I pick the thread of unease from my emotional strings and use my power to toss it aside. I can embellish the truth a little if it pleases him, and perhaps he'll appreciate praise.

"The stars tell me we'll have another illustrious season under your rule, my emperor."

"Will we?" This time he does smile, just as he did when he played ball with the others. I surprised him—in a good way. His teeth are even, with a thin mustache on his upper lip that accentuates the lighter skin of his bottom lip.

"Yes, there are no famines and no early frost. The thaw will come on time, so we need not fear early planting. The fish will be plentiful and even the kingdom of Hlos will dig up hordes of gold. The gods have blessed your rule."

With the eternal summer that graces Isul Urqu, a lot of this is true without me needing any star-reading talent. Though I did see the plentiful fish in the stars, I embellished the rest.

"And what makes you say that?"

I point to the dark spots, devoid of stars that form distinguishable animal shapes. "The constellations Hanup and Luthuya are connected, the celestial flames vivid, meaning the blood of the gods is strong in our leaders."

My mother hammered the basics into me as a child. But when I read the stars or recited poetry, I've never said anything so false. I've also never been so desperate.

Sunqu raises an eyebrow, but Emperor Huamar continues to grin.

"You're a brave one, Princess Nalia," he says. "I like that." Putting his hands on his hips, he rocks on his heels in the grass. "Tell me more. I'm eager to hear what else will go well during my reign." His tone is sardonic.

I can't tell whether he likes my ploy, or if he's laughing at me and I don't appreciate the latter.

At least he knows my name.

I bow, stiff with unease. "Of course."

He steps closer. "And perhaps," he pauses, "you and I can spend some time together afterward."

If he doesn't like me or care about me, at least he's intrigued by me, and I can get close enough to fix the rest, though I dislike the close proximity.

"You're from Cochas, correct?" he asks. "Does that mean you like to swim? Or am I overgeneralizing?"

I search his face for answers, my confusion impeding my tongue. He shouldn't have to confirm I came from Cochas. He attacked my village and demanded to marry the princess. What trickery is this?

How does he not know what kingdom I came from?

Something is wrong, and it takes all the strength of my powers to wipe my horror from my expression, replace my emotion with cool tranquility and respond to his question.

"I love swimming," I say. My voice sounds mechanical, even to me.

What am I missing?

"Then I will send a servant tonight to bring you to me as soon as the sun sets. I have somewhere I'd like to take you. Every princess should experience this beautiful city, especially one as stunning as you are."

I snap my attention back to him. For now, I'll have to focus on his words and consider the meaning behind them later. Otherwise, he may catch on that something's wrong, and I can't have that.

"Just come yourself," I say in my smoothest voice, "my emperor." In Cochas, I never had suiters, but if I did, they would come to my doorstep and I would bridge the formality that existed between titles, if I could.

The emperor's expression doesn't change, though he might not have liked the suggestion. A bead of sweat tickles my cheek as the emperor blinks.

Both Sunqu's eyebrows rise and I'm sorry he must witness this, but he has to know this must be done. His family depends on me as much as mine.

At last, a smile tugs at the emperor's mouth. "I can do that."

While I managed to snag the emperor's attention, it doesn't solve the problem that the emperor seems to have no idea that we're engaged.

I don't care to celebrate.

Above me, black spaces shift in the cosmological river and new animal shapes appear, but they don't give me answers.

General Opo-Mayta Pa approaches the emperor and nudges him. As the emperor turns to face the general, the servant who brought me prods my elbow and bows. I turn to the servant, unwilling to ignore him but unhappy about leaving my conversation with the emperor. Still, I watch the emperor out of the corner of my eye as he walks with the general to the other end of the room, speaking to him in low, hushed tones.

The servant clears his throat. "You have been requested to join the women." He points to Lina, seated with her legs folded and her back straight.

Cuxy smiles at me.

"Please," the servant says.

If I want to speak to Emperor Huamar again, I'll have to shove a few people. To be honest, I need some time to myself to think, and I'm almost grateful to go to the blankets. Besides, I already have a night planned with the emperor and, out of respect to Manco's memory, I shouldn't be rude to the emperor's servant.

"Thank you," I say.

Pacay makes room for me as I join them, between herself and

Cuxy. She leans toward me and whispers in my ear. "He's not your servant, is he?" She nods at Sunqu who is still speaking to the emperor in the corner. Sunqu's tunic glitters with gold threads against his dark skin and simple headdress. The servants in the room wear plain loincloths, except for the emperor's personal servants, whose loincloths bear the patterns of Mirchira and have seashells around their necks. None of the servants wear headdresses.

A slight miscalculation. I never expected the emperor to dress a common man like a prince. Is this a standard custom here?

Rather than ask Pacay, I press my lips shut.

"You know," Pacay says, leaning back on the blankets with her fingers splayed out, "you might be one of my favorite people here. You're all kinds of fun. You haven't been here very long, princess, so I'll let you in on a secret. There are only five Huya families from Chira. The Isul Huya families won't have anything to do with us. I haven't seen a wealthy, handsome Huya I didn't know in a long time. I'm grateful to you for bringing him here and I promise I won't tell him you claimed him as your servant. You probably won't stay long, and I doubt Sunqu will leave when you're gone."

I meet her gaze, and she flinches the way people usually do when I stare them down. While I don't usually find any enjoyment from people's reactions to me, I like watching her squirm.

Sunqu will see through her, but what bothers me is everyone's expectation that I will be gone soon. Like this city is one giant stone and I'm an oyster, knocking pathetically against the side, trying to leave a mark.

What scares me is that I'm starting to wonder if it's true.

CHAPTER THIRTEEN

THE STONES ON THE FOOTPATH shine with moonlight as I step outside my hut and let the curtains flutter shut. I miss the warmth of my fire and the elaborate rugs on the walls inside, but tonight the emperor has asked me to wait for him, so I inhale fresh air and let it fill my lungs, hoping it will calm my thoughts, which jump between wondering what my future here will hold and what the emperor thinks of me.

He hardly cares enough to remember what kingdom I traveled from.

My origins say so much about me. My family customs, my skin tone, the straightness of my hair. I can't keep thinking about this. It's not helping.

Any sense of achievement I once felt fades to dull embers as the sky darkens to black. He should have come by now.

Pebbles crunch down the footpath as dark hair takes shape, revealing the emperor's head as he rises over the slope. Then comes the robe with the red sash, the sandaled feet, and the broad shoulders.

Hiding my annoyance before it can betray me, I bow, my fist on my heart.

He stops in front of me, sturdy and proud. "Princess Nalia, I'm late. My attendant informed me of the arrival of a few long-awaited guests I had to attend to before I came." His robe cuts into a wide V down to a sash that wraps his waist, pinned to the robe with a brooch of Mirchira's staff insignia. Between the fabric, his smooth skin stretches over defined muscle, highlighted by moonlight.

My annoyance ebbs, but only a little. He could have sent a servant to let me know. Would that have been so hard?

Still, I push this aside. The emperor's busy and, at the end of the day, my feelings don't matter. I suppose he knows this as well as I do.

As I straighten, I glance over his shoulder, and am grateful to see that no one accompanied him. "You didn't bring attendants?"

He heeded me when I asked him to come alone.

"I wasn't raised with attendants." He takes a step back, his smile becoming sly as he twists his body and raises his hand, palm up. It's as if he takes immense pride in his statement. "I have no more need for them tonight than I did as a youth. I suppose it explains why your challenge interests me so much. I have missed walking alone." He offers me his other hand. Calluses cover the thick skin across his knuckles and the top of his palm, still visible in the dark.

Taking his hand, his fingers close around mine.

At his touch, two sets of invisible threads tug at me as my magic senses the emperor's emotions. Apprehension and something akin to disgust crowd my head. Is he disgusted with me? It might be residual from the meeting he came from. Still, I use my power to push his emotions aside and replace them with wonder and fascination. His emotional pipes bloat, as if there isn't enough space for those emotions to push through, so I let the emotions go.

Rather than call me out for my meddling, he pulls me down the footpath with a gentle touch and leads me to the tiered gardens that overlook the city beneath the palace.

The moon brightens the hillside enough that the petals give off a dull shimmer.

"I charged my servants to plant every kind of flower they could find here." He touches a petal. "Aren't they extraordinary? This is the true power of my empire. It brings together all varieties of people and unifies them. This garden wouldn't be nearly so beautiful with only yellow blooms. Our unique challenges and backgrounds beautify the world around us. Wouldn't you agree?"

"I do."

It's a beautiful statement, but would he consider a solemn daughter of a Heliray worshiper someone who would beatify his garden? Probably not.

If all the kingdoms join, it eliminates the need for war, though the last squabble between kingdoms hasn't been for some time, not since our priests began their journeys to Paria.

The flowers thicken as we walk further down the tiers. My stepmother often brought new buds inside to brighten the windows, but her flowers don't have nearly the variety these do. Her flowers are more distinctive though. They carry the personality of Ma Cochira and her ocean in their sharp teeth and vivid colors. They are beauty with a bite.

He turns to me. "Do you like flowers, Princess Nalia?"

Flowers shrivel when they're cut. My father ruined all the times he brought my mother flowers when he brought them to my stepmother instead, though my stepmother lined the house with them for all to see.

I love my stepmother, but she can't replace my mother.

"I adore them." The word "adore" stales on my tongue.

He clasps his hands behind his back, rocking on his heels with misplaced pride. "I thought you might."

Thinking of flowers and my step-mother brings me full-circle to my family and the goals I had coming here. I want them to know I didn't soil the family name, but am making it greater.

For this to work, the emperor must connect with me. How do I make a stranger connect with me when I've only been able to make Sunqu, who is kind to everyone, like me?

The emperor turns a corner and vanishes behind taller plants. Attempting to keep pace, I speed up, but when I reach the spot, there are only more flowers that lift their petals to the clouds. "Emperor?"

"Right here, princess."

I flip around and he stands behind me, the barest hint of a smile on his lips.

Did he do that on purpose? He might be toying with me, but to what end? I'm not sure. Perhaps he simply means to flirt, and I'm over-analyzing the situation.

Touching his arm, I say, "I thought I scared you away." The emotions from his animation spirit flood back into me, this time with the curiosity I hoped to find in him.

The emperor slows his steps but continues through the flowers, pushing them out of our way. "I hear you wove a tapestry of my giants. I'd like to see it."

If he has heard things and bothered to listen, he must have a healthy amount of curiosity for me then.

Good.

We pass a prickly yellow flower, with spikes that end in a soft pink. I eye the thing as we leave it behind. Perhaps it isn't so ugly after all. I can learn to like flowers, if I focus on the aspects of them I can relate to.

Like the flower, the emperor is handsome. Would marriage to

him be so bad?

I tighten my grip on his arm, but he doesn't seem to notice.

"I'm told it's clear from your tapestry you weren't brought up for weaving." He chuckles.

I continue walking, but my hands turn to ice.

What does he mean I wasn't brought up for weaving? I was one of the best weavers in my village. My rendition of the emperor's giants was so stunning that everyone in the room came to see it. Or am I remembering wrong?

He gives me a quick, sidelong smile. "I was glad to hear it. Weaving is a brainless exercise, something only a princess has time to master. It's a sign of a pampered, shallow, worthless woman. I haven't met a princess who didn't stoop to that level."

All my years of practice and all the rugs hung on the walls of my childhood home are stamped with shame in a single word. I pride myself on those achievements, as little as they are, as brainless and shallow as they seem to him.

But what makes him say they're incompetent works of art? That's incorrect, and it bothers me that he should think less of my abilities.

Who told him this?

My brain goes to Pacay. It must have been her. Who else would have said that about me?

I can drag him to my hut and show him the tapestry hung on my wall, but instinct tells me this will have the opposite effect of what I hope and come off as petty.

Instead, I fall into the opening he has given me, allowing the lie to slide easily through my lips, through gritted teeth. "I hate weaving, too," I say.

We pass more flowers, and the rooftops of the village below looks like part of another world, like the little houses are water and I'm oil poured over the top. "In Cochas, we do less frivolous things with our time." I hope he doesn't ask me what because I can't tell him I spent my free princess time teaching poor children. Princesses have more ostentatious jobs, whatever those are.

His sandals pick up dust as we walk, the flowers turning to crops, tomatoes and carrots and fruits that grow in the high mountains.

"What was Cochas like? Is there anything of value there?" he asks.

It must have been worth something for him to send an army to conquer it.

At this point in our conversation, I'm not inclined to like him, though I hope he can recover, or my future here looks grim indeed.

"Cochas is beautiful," I say. "It was warm all year round, not unlike here, with salty air and humid breezes. I used to jump off the cliffs that overlooked the ocean." My heart skips a beat. I shouldn't have said that. I imagine princesses don't jump off cliffs. "I'd love to take you there someday," I say quickly. "There's a temple in the mountain that's beautiful at sunrise. My father," I swallow, "used to hold festivals and sacrifices there. He would love for you to see it. It's our most sacred spot."

I need to speak smoother, not so fast and jumbled, or he'll tell something is amiss.

The emperor intertwines his fingers in mine and my power senses a subtle yearning that floods in from his touch. I push on the emotion as gently as I can, until I've awakened it, and the emotion sprouts tiny buds, growing fast.

A rare sense of pride radiates within me at this small sense of accomplishment.

He pulls me closer. "I wonder, would you prefer a different place to this? One even more sacred? I have a place I'd like to take you to.

I haven't taken anyone there before, so you must keep its location a secret." His golden headdress gleams.

This is a milestone I didn't expect—for him to take me to a secluded place that holds such significance. Does this mean I'm doing well?

Pressing into him, I lean into my success. "I would be flattered."

He squeezes my fingers. "Follow me then."

Retracing his steps to the palace, he crosses the grass to the jungle trees and motions me toward a path that ascends straight up the mountain. We hike with our hands inches apart. When I slip once in the mud, he doesn't catch me, but he tries. I recover on my own, clinging to the vines that sweep across my path.

My breath comes in ragged bursts as we turn a corner and cross a rope bridge further up the trail. A waterfall on one side rumbles into a stunning lake where the reflection of the moon glitters on the crimped surface. Sharp, rich red petals flower from their stems and deep purple bells arc to form soft shapes, the colors barely distinguishable in the magic of the darkness.

"This place is especially sacred to me, which is why I protect it from the rest of the city. I renamed it Mira-Tamya when I conquered the old Isul kingdom."

"What was it before?"

"Isul-Fuyu, but now that the god of this city is Mirchira, not Isul, I think the new name is appropriate."

The emperor is a demi-god of Mirchira, so, of course, he wishes to rename the locations, especially this one. He can rename whatever he pleases. What it must be like to act as you please without fear of everyone's opinions!

He tugs my hand, and the bridge sways as we cross. Birds chirp as they flit through the trees and the emperor slows near the middle.

"You said you like cliff jumping. The spring at the bottom of the waterfall is deep enough you could jump, if you wanted." His deep voice saturates the thick mist that swirls around us, and the moon reveals yellows and greens in the dark brown of his eyes.

I peer over the side of the bridge. "Is it?"

The lines on his chest deepen as he laughs. "Yes, but you're not actually going to jump."

"Am I not?"

The noise of the waterfall drowns my heartbeat as he rested his hands on my hips, leaning close. The scent of salty ocean spray fills my lungs as his lips part and he pauses, inches away, but then draws back. "Of course not." He clears his throat. "It's far too high."

He doesn't know me.

Shall I introduce him?

Excitement and hunger emanate from his hands, which still wrap mine. He wants me even if he doesn't act on it. His emotional energy crashes all around me.

"If I jumped, would you follow?"

His smile fades to pursed lips and the excitement I sensed in him earlier flips to an equally strong anger and fear. I did something wrong.

"I'll jump first, of course," I rush to say, though I'm surprised he's not more bold, like the man I envisioned him being when I first saw him in the throne room.

His smile returns, fainter this time. "Of course."

I peer over the rope that lines the edge of the bridge, and my lips dry despite the damp air. This isn't my usual space for jumping and while I love dangerous activities, I'm not stupid.

A mist clings to the rocks against the mountain and obscures the faint outline of the spring below. I can make out a few rocks, but the water's surface is dark and murky, though the rocks seem far enough out of the way.

I twist my torso to face the emperor again. "You're sure it's deep enough?"

He cocks his head. "Yes."

Do I have a choice?

I'm not sure.

Looking down again will only make me second-guess myself, so I toss my sandals and leap into the abyss. A thrill electrifies my spine and shoots down to my toes, charging me with energy as my power absorbs my fear.

If I excel anywhere, it's here in the air, above the water, seconds between life and death.

The water stings my feet and arms, and my lungs compress as I sink too deep, but I push upward, and my head breaks the surface. Swimming for shore, I heave for air, gasping in mouthfuls of it as I hike through the jungle up to the bridge. My dress clings to my thighs as I drag the water-bloated weight of it.

He waits where we stood before, so I cross the bridge and grip his hands. The mist from the spring sparkles as it billows around us, smelling of rain.

I pull at the threads of his emotions, this time for faith and bravery. Out of practice as I am, the exercise comes naturally to me, my mother's teachings from childhood coming to the forefront of my mind.

I'm prodding the animation spirit, bending it to my will.

My energy ebbs, but not much. I only dry out my reserves when I refrain from using my magic. It won't hurt to prod Emperor Huamar to jump, and it will build a false sense of camaraderie. This time, the emotive air flows without inhibition, as if his mind grows receptive to the change.

"Will you try it with me this time?" I ask him.

He considers me, his eyes a little wider than usual, though his confidence and determination return as he squares his shoulders. "I will."

At least the emperor is braver than Sunqu, in some ways. Sunqu would never consider jumping, not even for me, but he also never allowed me to touch him because he knew what I could do.

He knew I could influence him to do what I wanted.

The emperor's hold on my hand tightens as he peers over the edge. Again, I'm surprised at his willingness to show this weaker side of himself. It doesn't make me think less of him, but it does alter the image that I maintain in my head.

As I send calming emotions through to him, he looks at me, gives me a half smile, and steps off the bridge, exactly as I hope.

It's almost enough to make me smile as I fall beside him.

He lets go somewhere in the air. A loud splash announces his landing and my own feet hit a split second later. My arm stings more than before as water soaks my dress and tows me down, heavier this time than when I jumped last. My mouth and nose fill as the faint light of the moon above darkens.

My brain struggles to comprehend what went wrong and what I did differently. Am I dying? Did I come all this way for this?

A strong hand grasps my wrist and yanks me upward until pebbles scour my chest.

"You're crazy." The emperor drags me across the shore, panting, until we both collapse on the rocks.

I cough and water streams down my cheeks. My chest expands and I inhale without issue, but when I sit up, my arm lances with pain. Little rivulets of deep red swirl down my arm as I clutch it to my chest, cascading down to my elbow until the wetness drips onto the pebbles, where water absorbs and scatters the color.

The emperor wraps an arm around me while my arm throbs, but it looks worse than it feels. I must have smacked it on the rock, hard enough for the rough edges to scrape off layers of skin.

He studies me with his head tilted to the side. "I don't know anyone else who jumps off cliffs like you do. I wish we could come here every day." Pebbles shift as he moves to his knees, lifts a finger, and drags it down my uninjured arm, leaving a trail of gooseflesh.

If we married, we could come here as often as we liked. Why does that not seem like an easy solution to him? He's the emperor.

He hoists me up, so I sit on his knees, my wet dress splayed across the stones. As he tilts my chin, droplets rain from the curls of his hair onto my face.

His lips hover inches away, his eyes locked on mine, unflinching under my stare, which has frightened so many.

Do I want this? I never thought I would, and I'm still not sure.

He presses into me, his skin warm and wet. As we kiss, he tastes of river.

I clutch his robe in my fist.

"You're beautiful when you fall," he says.

"I have to be good at something, emperor," I say, trying not to sound sarcastic, "if not weaving." I investigate the hard contours of his back with my good hand, but he pulls away.

I'm sorry the moment must end, but I remind myself it isn't real, not when I spent most the night fiddling with his emotions to get him this far.

"You can call me Huamar, if you wish," he says.

"Huamar," I repeat.

He touches my cheek with a light finger, and I turn my face away before remembering this might offend him. It's not that I don't want to use his name, or that I don't like him touching me. Instead, a distaste for what I must do, and the situation I'm in, settles inside me.

No amount of kissing changes the fact that my kingdom is on the brink of war, that his giants demolished hundreds of my people's homes in a single night, that I came all this way to marry him, only to have him ignore me and not remember why I'm here. He hasn't brought up the engagement once.

Have I established enough of a relationship that I can bring this up?

Something tells me no, I haven't, and it frustrates me more.

"You should wrap that arm," says a withered voice. Smoke fills my nostrils as the figure of an older woman crouches over us. I scramble away from the emperor, the taste of his lips still on my tongue, though it has gone acrid.

"If she had landed a stone's width to the right, she might've died." The woman glares at the emperor. "But perhaps you didn't notice the buckets of blood she's losing, though it seems pretty obvious to me with the way she clutches her arm." She studies my face, as if trying to make out the color. "Are you all right, child?" Her suntanned nose has a ball at the end, giving her a unique witchy look, though her eyes peer out with kindness.

How long has she been watching?

"I'm fine." I hide my bleeding arm behind my back and wring out my dress so I don't have to meet her eyes.

I don't like showing weakness, especially not in front of the emperor.

She crouches beside me. "Please, let me help." Tearing off bits of her sash, she binds my arm so the blood soaks the cloth, but no longer drips over the stones. A wide circle surrounds me in the dark, black with a reddish tint.

She doesn't look like a healer but wears a colorful robe, long as her ankles with diamond designs while thick, braids of gray hair pour down her back.

"Who are you?" I ask.

The emperor never told me he has people that live around his sacred places.

"She's one of my mystics," the emperor says in a tight voice, "dedicated to Mirchira." He opens and closes the hand that touched my face, as if uncertain what to do with himself.

While the emperor didn't mention that anyone would be around Mira-Tamya, he did talk about mystics. She must do her ceremonies in the spring.

The mystic dips her head to the emperor. "This girl will need her arm washed and rebound. I suggest you take her to a healer. I will go now." She stands and backs slowly away, respectful despite her chastising tone.

The emperor exhales as I wring water from my hair and clothes. "I guess this night is over," he says in a low voice.

I force what I hope is a smile. Our moment before can't be recovered, but I don't mind. The memory has been made. He knows me better than before, and hopefully will want to do this again. If he does, I'll have more opportunities to prod him to care for me the way I need him to. By then, I might have the answers I need to explain his behavior since I arrived.

"My arm will heal beautifully," I say as my head starts to spin. "I'm sure."

It doesn't make him smile, though. Instead, he loops an arm behind my knees.

"What are you doing?" I demand, though I appreciate that he's considerate, and not at all like how I imagined he would be after all I heard about him.

He grunts as he lifts my feet and the rest of my body off of the ground.

As he carries me, I clutch my arm, disinterested in the idea of not using my own feet, though the loss of blood drains my energy as much as not using my power does. "I'm fine. I don't need to be carried."

His breath rustles my hair. "I can't have it be said I left you to die at the foot of my most sacred mountain."

Because he doesn't want me to die, right? I wait for him to add something more, but only snapping twigs and the emperor's steady breaths follow.

I don't like the doubt that creeps in as my vision hazes at the edges.

As I settle into the warmth of his arms, he carries me to the palace, passing the elaborate guarded doors on his way to my hut. My dress drips on the threshold as he sets me down on the doorstep and crouches to look me in the eye.

"I'll send a servant to attend to you," he says.

He kisses my fingers, steps back, and lets my hand go.

I watch his form walk down the path to the palace, wondering if leaving an injured girl on her front porch is a normal thing in Isul Urqu, or if the emperor is unvaryingly thoughtless.

Pressing my back against the wall of my hut, I muster the energy to stand and haul myself inside. When I do, Irenti rushes toward me and helps me to my deerskins.

"What happened?" she demands.

I sigh. "I did a dumb thing."

But my brain returns to the emperor, analyzing his actions on repeat, until I my brain is more broken than the torn skin on my arm.

CHAPTER FOURTEEN

GLIMMERING GLASS and obsidian slippers. Colorful hems on multi-layered dresses with flowers and tiny animal tributes to Ma Hlocha. White beads and gems that dangle from headdresses of the finest gold. The chink of corn falling on brittle pottery. The slap of feet from dancing couples. The steady beat of drums that continue on into Uru Hlocha, the underworld.

Then a ceremony and a speech. Emperor Huamar in white and gold robes standing before me, both my hands clasped in his.

What will his face look like if we married? Will he be smiling? Frowning?

Does he hate me too?

I straighten the headdress on my head as my servant, Irenti, smooths my hair, ensuring I look my best in case I see the emperor today.

Irenti brushes my hair's straight ends for the final time. "Your hair shines like spring water," she says. "Straight and long as I've never seen."

She has a pretty face of her own, with a small chin and nose, and amber eyes. Her hair is mostly straight, like mine, but with a subtle wave, though not as long or as black.

Squeezing Irenti's arm, I say, "thank you." Her comment is kind, but she has to be, and sometimes I wonder if every word she utters is calculated, as mine are. She may be paid to say what she says. "Can I ask you a personal question?"

"Of course. Anything," she says, her face smooth.

Turning on my chair, I face her. "Did you come from Chira? Or have you lived in Isul Urqu all your life?"

She looks different from the emperor and the families he brought from Chira. They have more curl to their hair, like my family in Cochas. Irenti doesn't. Irenti also has amber eyes, which many who originated in Isul Urqu have, including Lina, though I never saw amber eyes in Cochas.

She bites her lip. "I'm from Isul Urqu, yes. From the mountains outside it, actually."

Then she would have been here during the war, when the emperor came with his giants to take over the old kingdom.

"Are you happy to be part of the new empire?"

I can picture him striding before his army, spear in hand, a legion of warriors behind him, the giants in the distance. Every story ever told is influenced by perspective and remembered best by the victors. Even stories of the emperor.

I know how we view him in Cochas, but how is he seen in Isul Urqu?

"Yes." She runs the brush through my hair again, catching my bandages from my cut last night. I flinch and she pulls away, quickly changing direction until her brush snags at my dress, popping loose one of the gems so it rolls down my sleeve to the floor.

"So sorry." She stoops to pick it up.

I only have one other dress this fine. As I check the sleeve, I'm relieved that the dress has so many gems I can't tell where it unfastened. Taking the gem from her palm, I set it on the table. "It's fine."

She faces away. When she turns back to pin my hair, her nimble fingers fumble and my hair falls out into black, straight strands.

Clearly, she doesn't feel like she can talk to me because she's not telling me the full truth. Is she afraid?

I could reach out, touch her, and read her emotions, but they're clear on her face.

"Irenti, are you feeling well?"

She squeezes her eyes shut and nods.

"It really doesn't matter," I say. "The dress is fine. You can't tell anything is amiss."

She bites her lip.

"Or…" I pause, wondering how much to prod. "Is there something else?"

I grasp her hands, and she lets me, though a deep sadness emanates from her touch.

"Are you unhappy here?" I pipe my memories of the ocean waves crashing against the cliffs to calm her, the seagulls and pelicans that sweep through the air instead of the dark shapes of the Folqu birds on the Isul Urqu horizon.

She wraps her arms around my shoulders. "You'll be a wonderful empress, princess. I know you will be."

I will be if I'm allowed the opportunity. "You won't tell me what's wrong?"

She wipes her eyes. "Not right now."

As much as I wish to use my powers to force her to tell me, I don't know if it's possible. Even if I knew how, she should have the right to refuse.

The formal voice of another servant penetrates the curtain of my tent. "Princess Nalia has been invited to the palace to join Emperor Huamar for breakfast. Please be ready to leave as soon as possible." The shape of his shadow bows and the servant's heel grinds the dirt as he departs.

The Huya, including Lina, Cuxy, and Pacay, will be shocked to see me with the emperor after noticing how coldly he treated me before.

Irenti gives me a tight smile. "Are you ready?"

"Yes." I stand and Irenti attends me as I leave my hut. The servants at the door of the palace stand aside as I enter a bare hall with a single stone table. But I'm not the only woman in the room. At least six women sit on the rugs, none of them bothering to look at me. While Pacay and Cuxy aren't present, Lina stands in the doorway with her arms folded, a contemplative expression governing the wizened lines of her features.

Bowing, Irenti joins the line of servants as I walk slowly toward the table. No one moves, and the emperor doesn't look up. All the women wear headdresses much finer than mine, each bearing symbols of the different patron gods: grain for Ma Dokara, the tea leaf for Ma Jocoya, lightning for Ma Thala, the figure of a woman holding a golden rod for Ma Jaspu. They must come from different kingdoms.

More importantly, why are they here?

I lower myself down to the rugs at the end of the table, but my stomach must have shrunk to half its size because I can't bring myself to pick up my sacrificial stone to make an offering, nor take a single bite.

These women came for a reason—but not for me. I search each of their faces for answers, but they watch the emperor with blank, solemn expressions.

A lineup of eligible princesses to compete for empress.

I suppose it doesn't make sense for the conqueror to marry the princess of Cochas over any other kingdom. Cochas isn't the biggest or the wealthiest, but this means the King of Cochas outright lied to me. And I believed him. He didn't just want me to use my powers to keep the emperor, he wanted me to use them to secure him.

Anger swells, but with the king absent, the emotion won't help me. There's nothing to do except go along with the plan. Betrayed, I squeeze my eyes shut and pluck the bitterness from my emotional threads, letting it go, though the bad thoughts knock at the edge of my consciousness.

I'll deal with them later.

A woman with hair longer than mine leans toward the emperor, her hands upturned on the table. She has a sharp chin with a light freckle on the edge of her lip. "Emperors and kings are supposed to be ugly. When they sent me here, I thought you would be."

Emperor Huamar's cheek twitches. "Who says I'm not?"

"No one of importance." She fingers the edge of her bowl, tossing a strand of light brown wavy hair. Her gaze shifts from him to me and our eyes lock.

The emperor follows her gaze and I look quickly down at my broth, taking two deep breaths before peering up again. But they've returned to their conversation.

The princess on my right squishes a potato beneath a stone by her plate. "To the gods. May they live on in the stones of our walls," she says.

The food on the table disappears as everyone eats, but I can't join them.

I can't think of a single princess-like way to shout across the table at the emperor, or an excuse to stand beside him so I can use my power to force him to remember me.

Baring my teeth instead of smiling, my potato in my hands, I watch him as he continues his conversation with the other princess as if I don't exist. While I never cared for the emperor in any real way, I'm humiliated that he dared to kiss me yesterday, only to ignore me today.

I'm not someone to be ignored.

His lips compress as his square chin rotates to look up at me, noticing my heated gaze that could roast the sea serpent, Mungacu, on a pike.

"I'm better now," I say in a loud voice, nearly shouting across the table. I show him my bandaged arm so the other princesses can see, too. "I thought you'd like to know. You forgot to send your servant."

His mouth turns down. "I'm glad you're better."

I shouldn't have spoken. Instead of accomplishing anything with the emperor, I've angered him and embarrassed myself. It was rash, but he struck my pride, and my pride is all I have.

Forming a pond of fabric with my dress, I sink into it, ready to flop into the cold stones on the floor.

When the emperor left the night before, he kissed my fingers. While he forgot to send his servant, he was neglectful, not rude, though I clearly misinterpreted his actions.

A curtain rustles as an elderly woman enters the room and bows low to the ground. She wears a poncho over a long, colorful skirt, and layers of necklaces are draped around her neck. Conversation dies as the emperor stands with a swish of his robes. "I'm ready," he says.

The elderly woman pushes herself upright as he passed her and walks out the curtained door. Then she stops, the air thickening in the emperor's absence.

All of us at the table form a group. A guest party of eligible women, likely all princesses, except for one Huya woman, Lina, who still stands by the door.

The spokeswoman comes into focus and my brain locks on her words.

"Hello, guests," the woman begins. "I'm Drea Chiki of the Chiki Huya clan. As many of you have seen, we have brought princesses from each of the new empire's conquered kingdoms. The emperor will set up times to get to know each of you and I will assist where needed.

"When the emperor feels he has spent adequate time with each princess, he will select an undesirable princess to be sacrificed to Mirchira to celebrate his dominion, and a new selection round will begin. By the end, the emperor hopes to find an empress to rule at his side, but she must be trustworthy and deserving of her new role. He will give you tests to prove that you are capable. The first round will be to determine if he feels a connection to you. The second round will be a test of heritage. The rest will be announced when they come."

My mouth becomes a cave, dry and festering with anxiety. I have no royal heritage so a test of heritage can only end badly.

"For those of you not chosen to become empress," Drea continues, "your kingdoms will serve the empire in such a way as the emperor sees fit. Typically, this means your kingdom will be divided into slaves to build temples and stone statues for the gods and the new elite, those whom the emperor feels are worthy of the title. If you are sacrificed, you have bestowed the highest honor you can give the new empire—to be of service both in life and in death. The gods will bless our kingdoms for your selflessness and perhaps, one day, we will witness the gods' return."

Perhaps I have eccentric views, but I don't consider being sacrificed in a princess contest honorable.

Again, Drea goes on with her speech. "I wish you luck in the next few weeks. I will arrange meetings between you and the emperor to get to know one another. During that time, you'll have opportunities to charm him. The emperor has promised the Huya an heir to stabilize the empire and guarantee its future. You are all instrumental in accomplishing this."

She backs out the curtained door, her colorful clothes hanging from bony shoulders.

The real princess of Cochas must've killed herself for this reason; she knew she would die here in Isul Urqu. If she, a born and bred princess, didn't have a chance, what does that mean for me? I have to win the emperor over or I'll die in these mountains, kingdoms away from the sea where not even the stones I tread on will remember me. With a knife to the neck and one final gasp of air, I might as well not exist.

But I can't let it happen. The other princesses can't do what I can with emotions. But how far can I push before he notices what I'm doing? How easily will he bend to my will? I don't have my mother here to teach me and all I have to depend on are her lessons from my childhood, which I haven't practiced in years.

As the message sinks in, the fear that accompanies it gives me strength, but the strength leaves just as quickly when I don't use it, leaving me exhausted, with a renewed sense of dread.

Powers or not, the emperor said I was different, that he liked our adventures and my inability to weave. He must like me a little.

I'm already on my way to winning him over.

Except my confidence wavers as I consider how he left me bleeding on the doorstep, and how he ignored me at breakfast when he had other women to talk to.

Can a man like the emperor be won?

Even if he can be won, it means the other princesses failed, and if they don't succeed, they'll die instead. The horror of knowing I'm responsible for their deaths can only be eclipsed by the awful reality of my kingdom's collapse if I lose.

I'm drowning in a maelstrom of inescapable miseries.

"Princess Nalia?" A servant hovers at my side. "We need to clean up."

The other princesses have left, their bowls half-eaten on the table. Plates of pig and decorative fruit lay untouched, arranged to spoil. I pick myself up off the rug and stand.

"Thank you." My voice sounds faraway, but I force myself to stand straight even as my headdress weighs me down. Then I do as the servant desires, and I flee.

Everything spins as I lurch out the doors.

I need to be alone. I need time to think, to calculate, to plan.

An older woman with long, graying braids interlaced with beads drags along a cane decorated with flowers that she smacks the ground every few steps. It's the woman from the waterfall, the one who told him I needed to be bandaged.

I turn my face as she passes so she can't see the confusion, the horror that shreds my insides, but she pauses and folds her hands over the top of her staff. "Can I help you?" she asks.

"No." I speed up, rather than be seen in such a state.

I need to go where no one can find me.

"You're in more danger than you know," the elderly lady calls from behind.

Spinning around, I look back at her, unable to help it.

Her cheeks wrinkle with a sad smile. Then she dips her head, ambling off with her rose-carved cane in hand.

The sickness in the pit of my stomach strengthens. The danger

I'm in can't be worse than what I already know. When I accepted this task from the king, I never imagined a princess competition against princesses who have been born and bred to simper and woo.

I'm the most hated person in my entire village. I frighten people. Maybe he didn't realize this?

I need Sunqu, but as I search for him, scouring the grounds, the different rooms, the hallways, I don't find him, and the guards bar my passing into the village beyond the wall surrounding the palace, saying only, "you cannot leave the palace grounds tonight, for your own benefit," which only makes me angry in addition to tired and scared.

Stumbling into my hut, I curl up on my bed skins, covering my eyes with my hands.

At home, Naya would sit at my side when I was upset and rub my back. She would promise I'd find another way to teach the children in class who refused to listen. Or that I'd show the others someday how I could rise. She thought I could do anything. I need someone like her with me now.

If I fail, I won't see her again, nor anyone else in my family, not even my stepmother.

I face the fabric that covers the walls, the embroidery depicting giants on the ocean's shore and Perjas stalking the mountain peaks. But the Perjas' eyes lack the gleam I expect in a piece so fine, while the tapestry in front illustrates dozens of snakes, like the creatures my mother loved. I rip the loathsome thing off the wall and try to tear it in half. When that doesn't work, I let it hang there, crumpled and decrepit.

Standing over the shredded fabric, I dig my nails into my palms. Despite the emperor's actions today, I forged a connection that night at Mira-Tamya. He enjoyed the time we spent together. I can't let a bunch of powerless princesses discourage me, not when I can use my magic to make things right again.

I slide the finest gown I own over my head, the one with gold intertwined in each thread and wide sleeves that billow at my elbows with emerald beads.

I'll take him back. And on the day we marry, I'll make him regret ignoring me.

CHAPTER FIFTEEN

PUTTING ON MY HEADDRESS, I stalk down the hill to the palace and leave the row of huts behind, the mountain shading the path. Sunqu told me princesses are pious and showed it. If the emperor sees my love for the gods, it will elevate his opinion of me.

But more than anything, I need to find Sunqu. I need someone to talk to. After failing to find him yesterday, Irenti recommended I look for him by the statues of the gods in the palace.

The guards in front of the palace doors stand rigid, their spears in hand, their eyes on me as I approach. But the doors are open, and they step back as I stride past them into the empty throne room. I slip by the dining hall where the emperor eats at the head of the table with a dozen other men and women, including Pacay and Cuxy. None of them wear the elaborate gowns of the princesses he invited from the other kingdoms.

If he's hosting an event without inviting the princesses, he probably doesn't want me here, though the guards let me in. I tiptoe past the open door and stop on the other side. No one calls my name. No one notices me and I'm not sure whether to be disappointed or not.

So I continue on. I haven't been this far into the palace before, but Irenti said to go down the arched hall, so I follow her instructions.

A sharp pealing sound makes me freeze as it rings against the walls, pure and melodic, but unlike any bell that chimes on the docks of Cochas or any leather hammer Sunqu uses in his father's tent.

The laughter in the dining hall continues undisturbed, and I press forward. The ringing sound was strange, but not frightening. I'm curious to see the source.

As I creep down the hallway, the ringing increases in volume. Covered in carvings of the city's founding, the walls depict the clans as they stumble on the vast mesa amidst the mountains, beneath the bright sun, with springs and rivers. The people grin, their arms lifted toward the skies, likely praising the sun god, Isul.

Little rainbows light up the rest of the carvings in the hallway as it opens into a massive room with a tall ceiling. Over a dozen statues line the stone walls, many of them made of white glass, like the glass Sunqu made my slippers with. Others glitter, clear as ice, making my breath catch in my throat at their size and beauty.

Nothing like this exists in any of the kingdoms.

The sharp ring comes again, this time from the foot of a statue of a goddess where Sunqu swings a tiny mallet and chips away shards of glass, his shirt discarded on the ground. I pause as he chisels more glass to reveal smooth folds in the goddess's gown. The goddess has a petite face with seashells around her neck, a netted dress, and hair that coils down to her waist. Her eyes gleam—Ma Cochira, the patron goddess of Cochas.

She looks so real, like she might step out of the glass and reach out, her hair darkening and her eyes gaining the green of the sea. I could tell her all my problems and she would offer solutions. She might even tell me she loved the Mungacu too.

Sunqu exhales, steps back, and bows his head, his fist over his heart.

I can't stay quiet any longer. He needs to know how amazing the goddess looks.

Folding my arms over my chest, I say, "You're very talented."

He jerks and spins around, stooping for his tunic and slipping it over his head in one smooth motion. "I didn't see you there."

"I know. I haven't been in this room before. Sunqu, this is beyond anything I've seen from you. These are well done."

His cheeks color as he tucks his mallet into his pocket. "Thank you. The emperor agrees."

At least the emperor recognizes Sunqu's talents.

Again, my eyes are drawn to the differences in the statue's colors. "Are they all glass?"

"No." Sunqu stares up at them too, scanning the others behind Ma Cochira. "I stumbled on a clear stone when we hiked through the mountains and picked it up. While I started with glass, I tried polishing the stone I found and tried that too. The emperor has been mining for more of them. I call it 'diamond.'"

"What are they for? Is the emperor building another temple?"

Sunqu chews his lip, gazing up at the glass face of his creation. "He plans to build temples in each of the kingdoms to commemorate both himself and the gods. The slaves he takes from each of the kingdoms will build the glass monoliths, and I'm expected to teach them. He wants statues that rival the ice sculptures the Perjas create."

I don't need to ask the reason why. It's every priest's goal in the civilized kingdoms. "To bring back the gods." The Perjas were created by Mirchira and Skapu long ago, to ensure the gods were remembered after they disappeared. Those cat-like creatures used their claws to carve statues out of the glaciers in the mountains as tribute. They were also dangerous to approach and as cunning as any human. We didn't see them in Cochas, but heard tales of mountaineers finding them on the trails and having their limbs sliced off.

"No." Sunqu lowers his voice. "I don't think the emperor intends to bring back the gods. He'd prefer they stay gone forever. He just wants to show his dedication to their memories." He clasps his hands behind his back, over the folds of his tunic. "Because he's a demi-god. Honoring the gods is honoring him, in a way."

For being a demi-god descended from the gods, it's strange that the emperor doesn't want the gods to return. Everyone else seems to. Whether or not the emperor cares to commemorate the gods, the emperor's odd priorities don't diminish the statues' magnificence.

Stepping closer to the statue of Ma Cochira, I whisper, "She's beautiful."

Sunqu wipes his forehead with his wrist, shifting from one foot to the other. "Are you afraid, Yakua? Is there anything I can do to help you?"

I came to talk to him, but as I stare at the immobile statue, ready to spill my anxieties and nightmares right there on the floor, I take a steadying breath instead. I want him to see me as someone confident and capable, and I want the usual brightness to return to his features. "I'll be fine. The emperor won't allow me to be sacrificed or harmed." Though I know my words ring as hollow as the arched room.

"How can you be so certain?" he demands.

He's too smart to believe me.

"I spent a day with the emperor right before they made the announcement. We had… fun." The emperor trusted me enough to jump off the bridge at my side, didn't he? He seemed to enjoy himself, so it's not a total lie. I turn to Sunqu as his mouth twists into something far closer to a scowl than a smile. He needs a better explanation. "I just need more time with him."

Sunqu's expression doesn't change.

I turn back to the statue, so I don't have to face the doubt in his eyes. "I'll do what I have to do to save our kingdom."

Sunqu dips his head. "I'm glad to hear it. Excuse me." He strides down the hallway I came from and disappears into the other room.

I came for comfort and tried to comfort Sunqu instead. Neither worked.

As I look at the statue, my heart fills with a mixture of pain and longing for home, as well as pride for my friend's achievements. Her eyes sparkle like the sea beneath the sky. Like she wants me to know the waves haven't left my life entirely. Like she sees me.

I bow my head and touch my fist to my heart, doing it for the first time because I want to. "May the stones beneath your feet bring you life and comfort," I say.

Reaching out, I touch her glass dress, letting the cool, smooth texture pass beneath my fingertips. A torrent of anguish sweeps through me, followed by an anger that nearly stops my heart. I leap away, clutching my hand to my chest.

The gods are dead. This statue is glass, nothing more. But my heart hammers on.

The emotion of an animation spirit touched me beneath that transparent shell. I sensed life where there should only be cold, purified stone, like the statues I prayed to in Paria.

Hurrying away, I glance over my shoulder before I enter the hallway. The statue doesn't move. Ma Cochira stares ahead at the wall, her eyes flat, the sparkle gone.

As I pass the emperor's dining hall, he sits at the head of the table, laughing with his guests and picking at grapes. I hurry through the throne room and out the palace doors. The guards' eyes follow me as

I turn down the path toward my hut, their gazes still weighing on my shoulders as I close the curtain and press my back to the closest wall.

Ma Cochira simply looked so real that she felt real, too.

I was startled, that's all, with a fear that took root far before I saw the statues.

I squash a grape with my sacrificial stone, turn a few over, and squash it a few more times until seeds smear the table. The princess across from me watches with interest, but I ignore her. I have no interest in eating again, not with the emperor absent from the table again. I haven't seen him in days.

This is a bad sign.

The older Isul Huya woman, Drea, who announced the princess rivalry, enters the room and conversations sputter to a still hush. She stops at the head of the table. "I am to announce that the star, Kurku, is expected to shine tonight and that tomorrow we will have another game of Fidichi, which you are all required to attend. You should have spent time with the emperor since our last meeting. After the Fidichi game is over, the first sacrificial princess will be chosen, and the celebration ceremony will begin soon afterward. Don't be afraid, but praise the gods for your role in the success of the new empire."

Pausing mid-grape-smash, I look up.

I haven't spent any time with the emperor since the announcement Drea made, and now I can't help but wonder why. Does this mean he doesn't want to spend time with me? Doesn't feel the need to?

I could become the first sacrifice without ever having a real shot at influencing him. Before, I was too soft, too hesitant. I won't make that mistake again.

The last grape I clutch between my fingers drops to the table and rolls as despairing hopelessness carves a hole within me. I have no control over what happens after the Fidichi game. If I'm chosen and dragged away, my powers can only do so much. I may be able to persuade one guard to let me go, but what if there are more than one? There likely will be, and I've never tested my abilities at that scale.

It's terrifying in a way jumping off a cliff never was.

Drea lifts the hem of her dress and departs, but I need her to turn around and explain what she means. Did the emperor take the other princesses somewhere? Did he forget about me?

A princess with a small nose and too-sweet smile leans across the table. "I'm guessing the emperor took you to the waterfall as well?" she says to another princess.

"Yes, he called it Mira-Tamya," the other princess whispers, her arms folded on the table.

My stomach curdles. He told me the waterfall was sacred, that he never took anyone else there, that it was a secret between us alone.

Yes, my plan was to manipulate him, but he manipulated me first, and my blood burns thinking of it.

He used me.

My anger is worse than the fear, because it gives me no power, just a mess of emotions that confound me, and prompt me to do things I'll come to regret. I can't make mistakes, not here in Isul Urqu.

Within hours, I'm stepping down a set of rock stairs that double as seating for the sports field, the fabric of my dress pulling at my shoulders as my train trails in the grass. Across the stone field, the

Huya of Chira observe the game from where I sat previously when I watched the emperor play Fidichi before the rest of the princesses arrived. Fiery rays of sunlight glare on my shoulders as the princesses file down and sit in a line on either side of me.

Pebbles scatter down the stairs as another group descends to the seating a few rows above. They remain separate from us, their ages varied. One of the women has a rounded, pregnant belly, her cheeks blushing from the heat as she fans herself with her hand. Lina sits among them, two younger men on either side. It's hard to tell from where I'm sitting if they all share Lina's strange eye color.

These people must be the original Huya, or noble clan, of Isul Urqu.

Facing the field, I try not to look at the other princesses or even breathe deep enough to inhale the dozens of fragrances made to entice the emperor. They wear pale expressions, their lips pressed shut. There are four of them, besides me. Four princesses must die for my family and kingdom to remain intact. One of their deaths will be announced at the end of this game, and it could be mine.

One princess wears a necklace of blue rain droplet stones, with a long nose and small eyes. Her hair curls in tight ringlets around her fair complexion. Another princess has light brown hair—a rarity in the other kingdoms. The princess with the coca leaf engraved into her belt has all the right shapes while the princess the emperor prefers wears a dress made from the finest weaving I've ever seen, each thread stitched with gold. How will I compare to them?

Her hair is rich and shinier than mine, with a slight wave, and she has a small nose and big lips. Her olive skin sparkles in the sunlight as if she slathered her skin with oils before coming. I should have thought of that.

Thinking this way makes me squirm, but do I have a choice?

I can't handle this.

Men enter the field, more than in the previous game, with their faces painted like skeletons. Sunqu walks behind, his hair wind tossed. While I don't enjoy being here, Sunqu seems to, and I hope, for his sake, that he's happy.

Then the emperor strolls onto the field, bare-chested and in a loincloth, his hair braided to the side.

The other princesses lock their eyes on the emperor and clap on que, as the Isul Huya tap the tips of their fingers into their palms. The Chira Huya, or the Huya that came with the emperor from his own kingdom, spring to their feet on the other side of the field amidst roars of excitement, though I missed whatever they cheer about.

My hands won't stop shaking.

Rather than sit here and feel sorry for myself, I stand and approach the closest servant, standing by the overlook, holding a flag.

"Can I join the game?"

If I can surprise the emperor, perhaps I can curry favor, even if I've never played a game like this before.

The servant's eyes widen, and he glances between me and the emperor on the field, as if uncertain whether to repeat my words. "No?" he says.

Ignoring him, I lean on the stone wall overlooking the tournament, letting my dress splay behind me. "Can I join?" I shout, loud enough for the emperor to hear.

The emperor glances up, Sunqu too, but rather than the intrigued expression I hope for, his eyes flash, and I back away.

"Take her back to her seat," the emperor calls.

The servant bows his head, as if apologizing, and leads me to the benches where the rest of the princesses sit in despair, and I sink into my hatred for this man who once thought me intriguing and now thinks of me only as a princess who gets in his way.

Down on the court, the teams split again, and a player chucks the massive stone—twice the size of the stones they played with before—across the court. The emperor dives and catches it, his shoulder slamming into the rock floor. He didn't play so roughly in the previous game, but there weren't as many people watching then.

The steps quiver as cheers erupt, though the square boulders of the palace remain unmoving. Behind the palace, rise the distant pointed peaks of the mountains. Folqu birds circle above, casting shadows over the court.

I don't bother clapping. I couldn't act excited if I tried.

Sunqu catches the stone, and a man kicks him in the face, causing blood to gush over his lips and chin. The game wasn't so intense last time.

Somehow still laughing, Sunqu drops the ball and clutches his nose with both hands as the emperor lunges to pick it up. He waits while Sunqu stuffs a wad of fabric up one nostril and offers the stone back to him. Bowing, Sunqu accepts it. A kick to the face must have broken a rule because the other team stands back as Sunqu carries the stone across the court and swings it through the towering hoop.

A man raises his fist. Every player faces the emperor and bows in unison.

With the game ended, the emperor wraps an arm around Sunqu's sweat and blood-coated neck and limps up the stone stairs that surround the court, as if they're friends. As he nears, he lets go of Sunqu, straightens, and ambles forward with only a slight limp, though he winces with each step. He favors his ankle as if he twisted it. Ankle sprains should heal. Sunqu's nose, however, will need straightening.

But none of that matters. The game's over, which means the announcement has come.

The dresses of the princesses rustle, but more from the wind than because anyone actually moved. As the emperor grips his belt with both hands, his eyes sweep down the line, landing on me, and pausing.

Panic jolts my heart.

Does he plan to sacrifice me?

"I wish you could have joined us," the emperor says.

He speaks to me, not to the others, but maintains a cold reserve.

I don't believe him. If he wanted me to join, he would have invited me down, rather than turn me away.

"I've enjoyed my time with all of you these last few days," he continues. "But I've chosen today to declare who is to join Heliray in the life after this one."

He didn't have to take me to the waterfall, but chose to. I didn't tell him I don't like flowers, and he loves that I can't weave. I wrack my brain for when I mis-stepped. He's hardly seen me since that night, except for my outburst at the table.

Perhaps he intends to kill me for speaking out at the table, for accusing him of leaving me on the doorstep of my hut in need of medical attention and forgetting about me.

Oh gods, I could die today.

The emperor gestures to the group of Isul Huya and Drea, the announcer, stands from among them, bows, smooths her dress, and approaches with stiff steps. Then she bows again, her shoulders slumped. "The Emperor Huamar—"

The emperor raises a hand. "Please, Ma Drea, I would prefer not to be here. Take care of them for me." Again, his eyes find me and linger, though he continues talking and doesn't address me. "Sunqu, will you come?"

Sunqu exposes more bruises as he folds his arms, muscles flexed.

"I will stay."

The emperor's expression darkens, but he nods to the line of princesses and heads for the palace.

Drea clears her throat. "Emperor Huamar did not feel a connection to Princess Tullu of Dokas—"

The princess with the grain necklace stares at Ma Drea's back, her eyes wide. After a long, awful moment, she gasps, and her hands fly to cover her face as her sobs escalate in both volume and hysteria.

Ma Drea continues, speaking louder to be heard, "and has determined she is not a candidate to rule at his side. She'll be sacrificed at the altar tonight, overseen by the High Priest and the emperor himself. Every princess is required to attend." She offers a shallow bow, but not as low with the emperor gone. "A selection of people, including the nobles of the Kingdom of Dokas, will be tasked with building the first glass monument for Mirchira. Dokas is now absorbed into the new empire." She closes her eyes, as if her words pain her too. "Consider your time at the temple a chance for rejuvenation and respite from the cares of the world." She rejoins the Huya with one last incline of her head.

While relief cleanses me of the stress I agonized over all night and day, my stomach knots with guilt. And even the relief is fleeting because my safety is temporary.

Shadows from the Folqus circling above traverse Princess Tullu's exposed shoulders, like permanent storm clouds, growing darker and larger as she rocks back and forth.

I've never heard anyone cry like that, not even the families of Cochas, when they discovered their loved ones were lost at sea. It's the cry of ultimate failure. Of losing every man, woman, and child the princess has ever known. If I can't convince the emperor to love me back, it will be my cry, too. Cochas, as I know it, will be reduced to free clans and slaves, forced to build statues to reinforce their fear of his power.

Sunqu steps forward and drapes his arms around the frenzied princess, picks her up, and carries her off. The Chira Huya have already vacated their side of the court. The Isul Huya leave one by one, their expressions solemn, but unsurprised, as if they've witnessed an event like this before. But the princesses sit still, and I remain with them, my legs as stiff as my heart.

As grand as the palace is on the hilltop of Isul Urqu, it shivers beneath the weight of a thousand crumbling stones.

I want to be happy and free, like the days I spent with Sunqu and my sisters back in Cochas, but I can't be.

Forcing in a breath, I push out the guilt that stiffens my limbs, as cruel and heartless as it feels. I can't allow such emotions to cripple me and prevent me from strategizing my next move. While I pity the princess of Dokas, I can't allow her fate to be mine.

From here, I move forward, or die.

As I stand, the eyes of the guards and servants follow me.

My feet carry me down the roads, past terraces and houses, and into a market lined with tents. Dolls in one booth. Corn in another. I thumb through stacks of rugs, each holding a unique pattern with the emperor's likeness, or tributes to power.

Wherever I look, I see the creases on the emperor's hands, the curls of his hair, or his slackened jaw when I returned from jumping off the bridge, and I shiver with disgust.

There are too many faces to hide from, so I rush to my hut and snap the curtain shut behind me. Irenti, my servant, steps forward, but I shoo her away.

She doesn't go as I command, but rushes to fill a basin with water. My hands tremble as I splash it over my face, on my cheeks, chin, and eyes. I bury myself in a towel and focus on breathing.

I won't die here.

A voice calls from outside my hut. "The princess's presence has been requested."

Turning my palms up, I let the cool water snake between the crevices of my skin and pour into the basin. If the emperor wants me at the ceremony, I can't avoid it.

Irenti passes me a cloth as I straighten.

"Are you well, princess?" she asks, "How can I help?"

She can't.

I take a deep breath, pat her shoulder, and step around her. The hinges in my mouth don't work well enough to say a word.

Following the servant to the palace, I walk down a trail that leads into the town. The three remaining princesses join me, all except Princess Tullu, the one scheduled for the sacrifice. They hold their hands in front of them like I do, to keep their fingers from quivering. A man with skin wrinkled from too much sun waves us onto a boat far grander than any I've seen. The boats at home are simple reed boats. This boat is narrow, with ends that curve upward into a giant Folqu head and a small cabin in the middle.

He dips his paddle into the water. "This is a beautiful mountain," he says, as if this were a perfectly normal joy ride. "The rivers lead right to the temples at the edges of the kingdom." The boat picks up speed as he sits down, scanning each of our faces as he clears his throat. "The mesa of Isul Urqu is a circle. Did you know?" He waits before continuing. "With outcroppings where the giants stand, forming points around it. The temples are on sun rays, with windows facing west and east. We have been blessed by the gods for remembering them and for incorporating them into every aspect of our infrastructure," he pauses, "and so will you be."

I turn away, not because I'm frightened, but because his callous words make me want to push him overboard.

The sacrifices are sacred. I sacrifice food myself every day with my dining stone. I've sliced fish on the altar of the temple in Cochas to remember the gods. The priests sacrificed the selfless in Paria.

I can be selfless, too. I can be pious and play my part in bringing the return of the gods.

But I don't want to.

While these princesses agreed to come, knowing this would happen, watching them die brings me no comfort. And I have no desire to die. Not here, not in this way. And not by the whim of the emperor, who has turned the teaching of the gods to his own purposes.

Surely, the king of Cochas knew this, and I want to hate him for it, though he didn't have options either.

The river becomes a waterfall that splits at the cliff's edge, the top of a giant's head showing as a small island in the middle. The boatman paddles to shore and docks. He offers me a hand, but I ignore him and step off onto the smooth stones of the bank.

He bows as the last princess vacates the boat, then ties it up and gestures to a set of stairs that lead up a pyramid to a small temple on top. "The altar is inside."

I take the stairs one by one. Gold lines everything—the steps, the tiers, the walls, the windows. Friezes of the gods glare down at me as I sit on the ground, hunched as small as I can make myself in a gold headdress and black patterned gown. The other princesses settle behind me—more visible than I—as more people file in.

Lina Illapu settles at the front of the room with two younger men about the age of my father on either side of her. One of the men scowls with a scar mottling his upper lip. The other man scans the room with narrowed eyes as a woman sits beside him, touching his hand lightly with the tips of her fingers. His shoulders relax a little as more bodies fill the room. Cuxy and Pacay find seats beside Opo-Mayta Pa, the General of the emperor's army. A woman almost as striking as the General sits beside him, with features so similar to his, they must be related. Perhaps siblings.

A line forms between the two opposing sides of the Huya as the emperor enters. He hesitates only for a moment in the doorway before coming forward with a hand raised. "Stay where you are."

The High Priest follows, balding, with one eye a lighter shade than the other.

As the procession of guests ends, the priest sacrifices a lineup of deer, before cleaning his knife and the altar. Then a guard drags forward the chained princess, her eyes wide and her face as pale and gray as the most desperate storm clouds, her hands tied behind her back. She wears no headdress, and her hair is wild without it. Behind her, several more people follow, their hands tied behind them.

The emperor stands before the altar with his arms folded over his chest. His mouth twitches into a scowl. Rather than say a word, he jerks his chin toward the priest.

The High Priest gestures to the princess and the guard turns her so her back faces the emperor. She locks her gaze on mine and a single tear slides down her cheek.

I breathe in pity, as much for her as for myself, and let it spread to my fingertips, but there's nothing I can do for her.

"May the gods live on in the stones of our altars by the blood of our people." The High Priest slides a long, shining knife from the pocket of his robes.

The princess whimpers as they force her neck down over the altar. Her legs thrash. The shadows lengthen in the room as the knife rises and the setting sun baths the walls in pinks and reds.

The blade glints and I look up at the emperor as he turns his face away. Not unlike when he leaves before his announcements, he doesn't watch his own sacrifices. It's disrespectful to her memory and shows that he can't stomach his own actions.

With a slice, the thrashing stops.

"It is done," the priest says.

The emperor bows his head, keeping his eyes averted. "To Mirchira."

The Huya mirror him with murmuring assent.

Pointing out the temple window, the emperor makes eye contact with the guard, who picks up the girl up so her hair dangles like a cast-off rug. Blood trickles down the altar and trails out the door as he drags her outside. While the emperor speaks to Sunqu, I can't tear my gaze away from the bodies of the other sacrificed men and women as they're carried out too.

With each smearing of blood that is wiped off the floor, my compassion for the emperor chills a little more.

The ground trembles as if the gods give thanks for their meal, and the people in the temple vacate, including the other princesses. I stay because I want him to see me standing here, the only one in the room. I want him to remember me, though I'm not sure yet how I want to be remembered.

The emperor meets my stare, his mouth a tight line. "The gods will honor her for her sacrifice."

This is our custom, our religion. She served the empire by allowing her blood to go up as a plea to the gods. A plea for prosperity. A plea that the era of the gods will return. But the executioners didn't drug the princess like they usually do.

He did it all wrong, but I'm not in a position to tell him that.

I dip my head and turn to leave.

The emperor doesn't call me back.

As I follow the line of blood down the stairs to the bottom of the temple, the path cuts to the cliffs, looking out over the guardian giant pressed against the cliff's face below. I turn and speed up. I must know. I have to see for myself.

The land drops off into nothing but air and waterfalls, the face of a giant embedded into the rock beneath my feet, and the distant peaks of the Kichka mountains that lead into the nameless barbarian clans of the north.

I have always loved cliffs but have never felt so unstable standing this close to the edge where the trail of blood ends.

Down into darkness.

With one misstep, I could join the dead princess' glorious fall.

CHAPTER SIXTEEN

THE KNIFE PRESSES TO my neck in my nightmares, the trail of blood to the cliff's edge, and the bodies of my servant outside my tent cutting their likenesses into my brain.

A day passes. Two. I go to breakfast and try not to stare at the empty seat where the emperor usually sits. He hasn't been to breakfast in several days, which likely means he escapes with a different princess every night. It could also mean my turn will come soon, though the emperor hasn't approached me with an invitation. I'm not sure whether to yearn for my time with the emperor or to dread it, and I hate that I should have to do either.

Drea, the Huya woman who led the contest, stands at the head of the table and licks her lips. "I have been asked to announce the second round, which will test the strength of your connection to the gods and enable the emperor to determine whether you can withstand the storms that come from the throne. He will choose if this test requires a meeting in person or not. May the kindness of the gods live on in the stones of your huts."

I need to think of something else while I'm sitting around, waiting, otherwise, I'll go mad.

Plan for a way to avoid death when the time comes for the test of heritage, and I have no royal heritage. It would help to know what that test will be, but I have no way of guessing. Do I need to memorize the names of the kings? My mother taught me a few if I can remember them.

To convince the emperor I'm pious, I can continue making visits to sacred places.

What else?

I can attempt to smile more.

What else?

Drea leaves and the princesses file out, some of them without eating.

What else?

Returning to the silence of my hut with an empty head, I sit on the floor by my bed skins, trying to breathe and recall the sound of crashing waves, the salt water against my skin and tongue. But it was too long ago, and I can't bring back the excitement I inhaled on the edge of the cliff or the thrill of the plunge as I hit the water. All I can see is red and a drop off with bodies piled at the bottom. No ocean in sight.

My chest rises and falls, faster and faster, but the tension doesn't fade.

Remembering the solid walls of my schoolhouse pummels me with homesickness as the bright expressions of my students fill my mind, listening to stories of our ancestors as they sailed the sea. I'll take their parents criticizing me from the open doorway. I want Naya to sit on my lap with her filthy feet up on my dress, even if it means watching my stepmother arrange flowers.

Pattering footsteps approach and I squint through one eye as Irenti opens the curtained door. She bows as she tiptoes toward me.

"Princess?" she whispers. "Are you feeling well?"

"I'm fine." I squeeze my eyes shut to block out the memories of home.

The princess who died gave her life for the future of the empire. The people call her heroic. The emperor praises her name, though he didn't choose her to be his empress. She did her part in glorifying the gods.

"Can I ask you a question, then?" Irenti asks.

"Please."

"Do you love the emperor?"

I open my eyes. I didn't expect anyone to ask me that question, least of all Irenti. I picture the perfection of his face, alongside the lurking anger.

Why does he do what he does?

Whenever I asked Irenti questions, she gave me half-truths, or pretty lies. She's in his employ and not my friend. If I told her what I truly thought of him, she might go straight to him or one of his servants and repeat my words. I can't have him sacrificing me for not liking him.

"Yes," I say with my brightest Sunqu inflection. "I do."

Though I could try to leave, his servants and guards watch me wherever I go, including Irenti. Once I made it to the mountains, what then? I wouldn't make it past the peaks. I'd freeze to death. Nor do I want to hike for weeks through the jungles alone.

She bows her head again. "I want to help if I can, but I'm not sure how. If there's anything I can do for you, please tell me."

If she wants to help, she can answer one question.

"Do you know how many of the princesses he's spent time with this round?" I ask.

"I don't. I haven't seen him go off with anyone like he did in the last round." She fiddles with a strand of her hair. "But I know something that may comfort you. I heard a rumor that the emperor prefers you over anyone else, that the Huya are hopeful he might make a choice at last. There are rumors he kissed you." She searches my eyes.

She hopes I'll confirm those rumors, but until I know if the kiss matters, I'll keep that information to myself. He might have kissed the other princesses too and I don't want him coming after me for bragging about negligent milestones.

"The Huya are hopeful?" I ask, hoping she'll elaborate.

The only Huya nobles who ever paid me any attention were Pacay and Cuxy, and only Cuxy likes me. She hardly represents the entire Huya clan. Why do they care?

Irenti clasps and unclasps her hands, her agitation increasing my own because I want her to spill the reason now, rather than continue withholding it, but I can't make this easy and do what my mother would do and threaten her.

"Yes," she says, "They worried he would never marry. The Huya are divided between those of the old kingdom and the favored families that the emperor brought with him from Chira. If he dies with no heir, the empire would collapse. There would be war between the families and our people," she takes a deep breath, "might not survive."

He needs a queen. So why not take one? He has a literal lineup, but he'd rather sacrifice them one by one, using our religious traditions to disguise what would otherwise be murder, since I doubt the princesses would volunteer to be sacrificed if they had the choice.

A female voice wafts through the curtains outside my hut. "Excuse me," the voice calls, sounding older and wavering, not unlike the announcer the emperor uses at the palace, though she doesn't come in.

I can't forget her voice if I tried.

As I push the curtains aside, Ma Drea bows, though not very deep. "The emperor wishes to see you tomorrow for lunch."

My chest eases and I breathe deeper than I have in hours. At least he won't ignore me again. "Tomorrow?"

Her mouth stretches into a tight smile before she walks away, her hair shining with a few more streaks of gray than I remember her having before, but she looks all the more beautiful because of it.

That night, I sleep easier, but the next day dawns with new stresses because I worry about every wrong word I might say, any flinch I might give away if he touches me and I forget to act like I don't despise him.

The sun rises high in the sky and my stomach growls for food as a kingly figure strides down the path toward me wearing a multicolored robe with a feathered imperial crown. His formidable hair is braided in tight rows, rather than hanging in his face.

He gives me a crooked smile as he reaches for my hands. "Are we going to jump off cliffs again?"

"I'll jump anywhere you want. Just name the location."

He tugs me forward. "I have a few places in mind. Do you like to cook, princess?"

Cooking means spending time in the house with my stepmother and father together, their happiness a disease I can't escape from. The Yakua of months ago would have avoided the kitchen. The Yakua of today misses it more than anything.

"I could learn to like it if you want me to," I say.

"I would like that." Towing me toward the village, he takes me down the same stone stairs I descend so frequently. "I know you don't know poverty, but in Chira, cooking was always a challenge to concoct the best food with the sparsest ingredients. Would you like to make breakfast with me? We could do it in the imperial kitchens, with no servants or slaves to disturb us."

I recoil at his casual use of the word "slave." Perhaps he forgot he threatened to turn all the free clans of my kingdom into slaves. As I study his face, his features remain smooth. Clearly, I'm right. He has either forgotten, or he doesn't care.

"What would we make?" I ask, keeping my voice even.

His eyes gleam as we round the palace walls to the other side. "You mean what will I make?" He clicks his tongue. "I cook alone, but you can watch."

Still holding my hand, the emperor walks beside me down a short hill to the servants' entrance, entering a tunnel that swallows the sun in square stones, but I don't need light. The darkness wraps around me like a blanket.

"This way." He tugs me forward, my sandals slapping against the smooth flooring. We turn left and then right. A biting breeze tickles my skin, until a sweltering heat mixed with the scent of spices sweeps the chill away.

We enter a vast room of gray stone with deep pits, many of them filled with firewood and rocks. One burns brightly, but no one tends the flames. The emperor lets me go, marches up to the pit, and knocks over some logs with a pike. Bending over bits of meat, he lays them over a rock.

"What is it?" I ask.

"Mountain deer." He fills an earthenware bowl with water and pours quinoa inside, before setting the bowl over the fire and stirring it with a wooden spoon. "I'm making quinoa soup."

As I sit beside him, I stay far enough from the pit that I won't roast, and near enough that he feels like I'm not trying to avoid him. "I love soup." I've always enjoyed warm soup on cold, windy days, so it's the most truthful statement I expect to say all night.

"I thought you might," he says.

Eyeing him as he stirs, the flames brighten his cheeks, his dark eyes. He looks happy, in a way I didn't expect him capable, as if cooking brings back a boy who dipped beneath the water and never resurfaced.

The quinoa softens, and the emperor removes it, pouring in herbs. "Sometimes I go on hikes alone just to find these. I picked them fresh yesterday." He cuts up the deer meat, pours them into a bowl, and lets a small amount trickle onto the stones. "May Mirchira live on in the stones of this palace." He spoons a hot mouthful through my lips, and it burns my throat as I swallow. "And?"

"It's fantastic." Pressing my lips together, I savor the symphony on my tongue. It tastes salty and fresh and better than any soup I've tried.

"I can even work magic with potatoes, as difficult as that may be."

"I believe it." While my tone is falsely sweet, I can't help staring at him, seeing him in this strange new light. I don't know how to perceive him. If I consider food art, he is like Sunqu, enjoying strange forms of creating new combinations, new styles, new tastes. Unlike Sunqu, there is little warmth left in him, though embers burn through his eyes now.

"I grew up cooking with my grandmother," he continues. "She used to love soups with spice."

I didn't imagine this man who hides behind a screen to enjoy cooking. Stirring soups with his grandmother seems so ordinary that I question if he's being truthful.

My father liked cooking well enough if it involved fish. My stepmother loathed it and did it out of necessity. Her passion was gardening. Sunqu likes everything, even me.

I wonder if Sunqu likes it in Isul Urqu. Hopefully, Sunqu can find success here. Perhaps I can steer the emperor to consider making that success assured.

"You make cooking a work of art," I say. "Clearly, you have expensive taste, and the highest appreciation of fine crafts." Outside of weaving, of course.

"I do," he says.

"With Sunqu Sua being an artist, you must have lofty plans for him? That will pay well?"

The emperor's mouth quirks into a smile. "Across all the kingdoms, yes. He will be busy for many years to come, and even the gods will be envious of what I intend for him to accomplish."

I exhale with momentary relief, grateful Sunqu will continue being safe and useful doing what he loves.

"That sounds grand indeed."

Gathering additional questions, I choose a few that I hope will sound entirely innocent. "Can I ask you something else?"

The emperor lowers his soup. "Of course."

"Do you like being the emperor? Is it validating after being poor for so long?"

The emperor came from a poor country, and it's said he wasn't a king or wealthy at all. Little does he know, we are alike.

Perhaps he will appreciate my interest in himself.

A crease forms on his forehead. "I love being the emperor. I love raising up those who were once like myself. One day, I'll cast out the undeserving royalty in the kingdom for people who work hard and deserve the life the elite lead. I'll break those social structures down. I've already started to build a loyal following. Although it's wise to remember that man is really only loyal to himself."

Once again, he forgets I'm supposedly one of those royals. Or he doesn't care.

If he prizes the lower class so much, then he can accept a peasant princess over a real one. I could tell him the truth and become part of his loyal group, but I don't trust him. "If you hate royalty so much, why do you want to marry a princess?" I ask.

The corner of his lip turns up. "Because I can."

His words, so filled with bitterness, make my stomach turn with apprehension. He's so open about his answer, as if he doesn't care that I know he toys with me because he has the power to do so.

I swallow my unease, because revealing it will result in my neck on an altar.

"So if I were a fisherman's daughter," I continue, my throat dry, "would you not want me?"

He laughs, but the hand that grips his soup bowl clenches so tight that veins protrude around his knuckles. "Why would you ask such a question?"

The King of Cochas's deception might anger him. I shouldn't mention it. "It was theoretical." The lie stumbles across my tongue.

I need to be more careful.

The emperor picks up his soup and takes a long sip, the polish of the ceramic bowl gleaming from the heat of the glowing embers. As he sets it down, he studies me, and then he continues speaking in a softened voice, as if nothing upset him. "I like cooking. But what do you enjoy doing?"

It takes me longer to recover my wits and move on than the emperor. Shaking my head to clear it, I strain to think of hobbies. I can't tell him about weaving. He knows I like to cliff jump. I can't discuss my family—he might ask too many questions. "I love hiking," I say in a halting voice. I just don't consider it one of my pastimes. I do too much out of necessity.

"I see. Perhaps we can do that next time we're together." He finishes his soup, stands, and helps me to my feet so the warm broth in my full stomach sloshes.

When he faces me, his eyes glint.

"I'll do whatever you want to do," I say.

Except go to the temple and get sacrificed to the gods, of course.

I show my teeth in what I hope is a smile, not a grimace.

With a grin, he nods, and tows me out of the tunnel and down the stairs, away from the palace, into the village and along a burbling river, with rocks coated in moss. "Today, I want to show you the majesty of my city. It won't take us far from here."

Leading me to a large rock outcropping that overlooks passing boats, he motions for me to sit. Water meanders through the trees in a soft blue line, stretching between houses. With a touch of salt, it might be home.

I find a smooth spot and tuck my dress beneath me as I take my shoes off and dangle my feet over the side.

He gazes out over the water, already sitting. "You like it?"

"I do."

The corner of his mouth curves upward. "We have many rivers that sculpt the city. They weave through the hills and drop off the cliffs. I doubt you've been to the cliffs before? We could do that next time we're together too—perhaps visit some festivals."

He wants to see me again, so my company can't be too terrible, though I'm not sure how many of these outings I can take.

"I've seen the waterfalls," I say. My first sight of them was from the mountain peak, before I descended to the base of Isul Urqu's vast mesa. "I hiked up the side of the city to get here."

I push back the memories of my servants. Now's not the time to think of them, though I still mourn their loss.

The emperor must not notice the subtle change in my tone because he continues looking out at the city without glancing at me. "The eternal stairs? You came from the south then. Of course you did. It took some time for my army to climb those stairs. I remember them well."

I hadn't thought of that. With the steep cliffs and altitude, Isul Urqu would be nearly impossible to conquer, except for someone like him.

A reed boat drifts past. Most are built with the heads of Perjas or various gods, but this one has the head of a snake.

The emperor leans so close his chest brushes my arm.

As he runs his fingers through my hair, I sit frozen, berating myself for not being better at pretending to like it. Instead of pushing away from him like I want to do, I angle toward him as another boat cuts through the river.

He lifts my chin with one hand, and I stare back. His eyes search mine with an intensity in them that lures my heart into my mouth, despite myself. He rubs my bottom lip with his thumb and drags the small of my back toward him, his lips parting around mine.

I kiss him back, and don't cringe.

When he pulls away, he says, "You taste like the Cayuhu spice I put in my soup."

I assume Cayuhu spice tastes good, or he wouldn't put it in his soup. "I suppose if I had to taste like something, I'd prefer it was spicy. Did your grandmother use Cayuhu in her cooking?"

"No." He runs a finger down my side, and I force myself not to watch. "It's an ancient spice, not typically used in cooking. I've found it doesn't have a strong flavor, except to those who know how to look for it."

Perhaps, if I taste like Cayuhu, and Cayuhu doesn't have a strong flavor, he meant to insult me. I can't tell.

Resting my palms against his chest, I say, "What about your parents? You haven't talked about them much."

He tenses beneath my fingers, fear emanating from him. I sit back to read his expression, but he avoids my eyes. Once again, I broached a subject I shouldn't have.

A muscle throbs in his jawline. "What have you heard?"

I haven't heard anything, but he continues before I can say so.

"My father and mother didn't raise me. My grandmother and I used to hike for hours to find herbs along the trails, and we made the most amazing food together. Better than the finest cook here in Isul Urqu. I knew her better than I ever knew my parents, who rarely came to visit." His tone carries as much hostility as his touch.

Everyone in our clan speaks of the new emperor of Isul Urqu and how he took out the ruler of Isul, the most powerful kingdom in all of Hallja, which is the land that encapsulates all the kingdoms in the known country, but I haven't heard a whisper of his upbringing. "But your parents brought you here?" I've heard that much.

"They did, yes. My brother was the first in our kingdom to show potential power in generations. He could create things out of rock."

He picks up a few loose stones and squeezes them between his fingers so the rocks meld together. As he opens his hand, a small, rudimentary man stands, marches across his palm, and careens over the side. The man tumbles apart into several stone chunks as he hits the rock we sit on, the pieces lying still.

I stare at the chunks, awed by the fabled power that bought him his throne, so different from mine.

"Just small things," the emperor whispers. A vein stands out on his forehead from overexertion. "But my parents were so excited, they took him to the mystics to train. They wanted so much to improve the hopelessness in Chira that they left me with my grandmother. I didn't hear from them for years. They hated being poor, and they hated the nobles who took advantage of them."

At least my father didn't leave me. My mother wouldn't have left this world if she had the choice. I even have sisters and cousins who offer company whenever I need them, even if my cousins don't like me, and I have Sunqu.

Emperor Huamar looks up at the sky. "I sat in the fields as a boy and wished for a family who was present. And then the giants formed and stood up, almost like the stones heard me." His voice trails off. "The energy it took nearly killed me, though. I couldn't stand for almost three days. But I've grown a lot stronger since then."

"What happened to your parents?" I ask.

"They decided they would make better rulers than I would." He meets my gaze. "One thing the crown has taught me is that everyone wants power, and they all have reasons for deserving it."

His family must have been cruel to give him this outlook.

"You can trust me."

It's a lie, but I think he's been honest with me and for the first time, I wish I could return the favor.

The vein in his forehead throbs. "Sure I can," he says in a tone that suggests otherwise.

At least he's not stupid.

I touch his arm and use my power to send him the emotions I want him to feel—love, trust, belonging. But they bounce back, as if his anger is too strong to allow for anything else. I push harder.

"What are you doing?" His eyes narrow and he snatches his arm away. "What was that?"

My mouth gapes open, the explanation stuck on my tongue.

I pushed too hard.

He stands. "We're done here." Maintaining several feet of separation between us, he walks me back to my hut. I watch him go as the sun sets, but he doesn't invite me for anything else. He just goes, leaving me with the awful knowledge that I made a grave mistake.

I stand outside the door of my hut, the sun high in the sky the following day, as the emperor leads another princess toward the kitchens of the palace. He probably plans to make her soup with Cayuhu spices too before kissing them off her lips. She likely doesn't have magical powers to manipulate him with, but he might suspect me of having power.

Would the thought of me having power frighten him?

If he's frightened, how will he respond?

Probably by throwing me off a cliff.

Though the emperor says he doesn't trust anyone, not even his family, he keeps Sunqu close—always at his side and on his team when they play Fidichi. Everyone loves and trusts Sunqu, including me. Perhaps Sunqu can convince the emperor not to question my authenticity, or to think me capable of anything more than princessing.

Sunqu will fix it.

Rushing into my hut, I find Irenti sitting by the empty fireplace and kneel before her. "Do you know if Sunqu is working on his sculptures again? I need to find him."

"He might be. Or he could be home if you can find out where

he lives." She eyes me with a touch of wariness. "But if you go to his home, you might want to be aware—" she pauses, "there are rumors that he enjoys a visitor from time to time."

A visitor?

People don't "enjoy" visitors unless they're courting them, and I'd rather not think of Sunqu courting anyone. The very notion strikes me with ire.

"I'll try the palace first." I say. "That's where I found him last time."

Hurrying out the front door, I follow the path up to the doors with the guards in front, their spears pointed upward. When I stop in front of them, they don't move aside or open the doors.

"I need to see Sunqu," I demand.

They train their eyes forward.

I try again, tapping my sandal in the dirt. "Sunqu Sua?"

The guard on the right raises his spear. "He's not here, and you're not allowed inside at this time."

"Do you know where he lives?"

"He does not live at the palace." His voice is cold and final.

The man's tone worries me, and concern for Sunqu overtakes any other thought, especially that anything between the emperor and I might endanger him.

I'll try the village. Servants go to the market all the time and Sunqu himself might sell glass shoes there, or other wares. I suppose I never thought to ask him how he made his money, or if the emperor commissioned him for the statutes and paid him enough to give up his shoemaking business. Either way, someone must know where he lives. Darting down the stairs that cut into the hillside, I head toward the village.

The road leads me to the square with dozens of tents side by side, filled with flowers, meat, artwork, and whiffs of seasonings.

A woman shuffles flowers in a stand beside the hunched form of what looks like a beggar. She looks up and the wizened features of the emperor's mystic from Mira-Tamya scrunches as she meets my gaze. Then she nudges the man next to her and he stares, too.

She must have talked to him about me, though I can't imagine why with so many princesses to interest her. But she spends a lot of time around the palace, which means she might know Sunqu as well.

I approach them steadily. "You sell flowers?" I point to one of the less wilted ones. "I thought you were a mystic."

A touch of white fogs the middle of her dark eyes. "I am. But I sell flowers as well. I go to Mira-Tamya to reconnect to the creation and animation spirit of our patron god." She plucks a small bouquet. "Would you like to buy flowers?"

"No."

If she knew me, she'd know I'd only ever buy flowers to step on them. "Has something happened to Sunqu Sua?" I ask, holding my breath rather than allow myself to consider what could happen to him in this city. "He makes glass for the emperor."

Her expression softens. "He's safe."

I want to close my eyes, take a deep, shaking breath, and cry, but I'm my mother's daughter, and I never do that. Instead, I pick up a stem, and twirl it between my fingertips, though my hands aren't as nimble as usual and I fumble to hold it.

"Why did you help me at the waterfall?" I ask. "And speak to me outside the palace?"

She runs her frail fingers over the petals, and plucks one with a brown petal from a bouquet, tossing it in the dirt. "You have more friends than you expect, but not in the places you look."

That doesn't tell me anything.

"Do you know where Sunqu lives?" I asked instead.

The woman's eyes crinkle at the sides. "Not far from here."

Stepping forward in my eagerness, I knock a pot to the dirt so it crashes at my feet.

"I'm sorry." My neck warms as I stoop to pick up the shards, brushing my hands off on my dress.

She grimaces at the pot, but when she speaks, she doesn't sound angry. "I'll take you to him, if you'd like." As she picks up her staff, she circumnavigates the dirt, and steps over a few broken stems and limp petals. "But you must pay for the flowers."

I tug a gem off my dress in an obscure location and hand it to her. The dress will be fine. No one will miss a few gems here and there. "Thank you."

She waves me forward and surges into stride with so much speed I have to pump my arms to keep up.

Sunqu probably lives in a little shack on the edge of town. He won't have time to build or buy anything, especially with the small earnings of his father's tiny shoe shop.

We pass a group of men and women in a circle, all dressed in ragged clothes. Some of them hold pipes to their lips and puffs of smoke circle upward. As we near, the details of the pipes sharpen into the smooth, white contours of polished bone.

A man twists toward me, smoke billowing as he watches us pass.

I avert my gaze, though I watch him out of the corner of my eye.

The mystic woman slows and points to the circle of beggars with her staff. "Those are the mystics from the mines of Hlos. They escaped the war and are refugees here, but they have connections and ways of communicating to the gods that the mystics of Mirchira don't understand." She picks up her pace again. "Don't let them bother you."

Rather than respond, I hurry after her.

The houses we pass all have the same stacked stones and pointed, thatched roofs. We climb a steep hill as the bottoms of my feet ache. Back at the flower tent, the mystic woman told me Sunqu lived close, but we traveled as far as it took to hike to the cliffs from my home in Cochas.

The houses grow and the roads widen as a little girl hurtles into our path and stumbles to a stop, her curls bouncing around pink cheeks. She grins at me, still breathing hard, until my gaze connects with hers. Within seconds, her eyes widen, and she runs away, frightened.

It doesn't take much.

Picking up my skirts, I chase after the older woman. "How much further is he?" I ask, trying to force patience into my voice.

The mystic slows to a hobble in front of a well surrounded by grass and a little stone walkway. Garden boxes squat before a stone house. The house has a slanted roof and an arch with vines growing around it. She gestures to a richly carved wood door that no shoe or glassmaker can afford.

"We're here," she says.

She led me to the wrong place.

"This isn't it," I say. "Are you sure you know where he lives?"

Sunqu wouldn't live in a place with a view of the mountains and garden boxes in front. He doesn't care for gardening, not that I can remember.

"I assure you; this is his hut." She stabs her staff into the grass. "I'll leave you here. I must return to the market." Bowing, she scurries down the hill we climbed to get here.

As I face the hut again, the jagged mountains beyond it pierce misty clouds.

Rather than curtains, like most huts, the door is formed from wood, with carvings of the gods, colored stones to represent the four worlds, and the symmetrical patterns and waves associated with Mirchira to symbolize mankind's beginnings.

The four worlds include Uru Hlocha, the underworld, Valhanen, the upper world, Hallja, the world we know, and the world that was once the moon, though its name has been forgotten.

None of the carvings depict Sunqu's actual heritage.

Has Sunqu forgotten that Ma Cochira is his patron goddess?

I rap on the wood, and it swings open without a sound, except for a low murmur behind it.

"Sunqu?" The murmuring fades as I step into a massive, circular room with a low table, a fireplace, rugs, tapestries, and baskets of food. But no Sunqu.

Curtains sway across the room. There must be another room beyond it. "Sunqu?" I push the curtains aside.

Sunqu is seated on a stone bench, with none other than Pacay, the young woman I thought Sunqu would never stoop for, on his other side, wearing a dress that shimmers. Her hands rake his hair, while his fingers hold her chin. Fidichi paint smears his nose and exposed chest.

The two of them together whirl me to my earlier years, when I stood by the river where the clan buried my mother. My father took me by the hand. "Come, Yakua, I have someone you need to meet." He led me home, where the curtains my mother wove to warm the house at night had been thrown away. Instead, a younger woman waited inside, her hands clasped in front of her and her beautiful face smiling with careful hesitation.

"Who is she?" I demanded to my father.

My father stepped around me and clasped both her hands in his. "Yakua, this is your soon-to-be mother. In a few days, you'll be Yakua

Lamar."

My father hated my mother so much that on the day of her funeral, he had already replaced her. And now Sunqu has done the same to me, though I have done nothing to deserve it.

The same anger and hurt burns through the hole my father dug out all those years ago as Sunqu pulls away and looks up, horror dawning on his face as he notices me.

I refuse to be a child again, so I dam up those feelings, use all my strength and power to pluck them out of my emotional threads and toss them aside, leaving me cold and hollow, but in control of myself.

"Good evening, Pacay," I say.

They only look at me, and I enjoy their faces more than I enjoyed the emperor's soup. A part of me wants to sit on the bench beside them, but there isn't room. Instead, I sit on Sunqu's bedskins, leaning back on my palms to observe with my usual stare.

"Continue," I say. "There's no need to stop on my account." While my words are friendly, my tone is not. "But once you've finished, I have something to discuss with Sunqu."

Pacay gapes at me before her mouth relaxes into her usual bored expression.

Sunqu nods to her. "Give me a minute," he says, gesturing toward me. "We need to have a few words."

She gives him a disappointed look. "Are you two about to have a row? Because if you are, I'd like to watch."

Shaking his head, Sunqu points to the door and she strolls out with one last simpering look over her shoulder. As she leaves, he rounds on me. "Yakua, you can't kick my guests out of my house. What are you doing here?"

"I didn't kick her out. I asked her kindly if I could speak to you."

Honestly, I've forgotten what I came to talk to him about.

He stands in front of me, inches away, his lips creased, his eyes narrowed to points. The work of Pacay's hands has left his hair wild.

The King of Cochas can take everything from me. The emperor can bend me around his fingers, but they can't take Sunqu.

Wringing his hands, his mouth opening and closing, Sunqu's eyes plead for me to understand. "Please, Yakua, let me move on."

I glare at him. "Am I dead already?"

"No." He grips my arms, holding me in place, as if worried I'll run, rather than listen. "I think you thrive here, and I think this is where you're meant to be."

But not beside him, not Yakua, the daughter of Amoya Roca.

His emotions flow through me, a mixture of confusion and regret. For once, he doesn't flinch from my touch to cover them up, and it's me yanking out of his grip to sever the connection. Then I do something neither of us expects. Reaching up, I thread my hands through his hair and drag him toward me, kissing him the same way he kissed her. He falls to one knee as a slow burn travels up my back. He seizes my waist, draws me in, and thrusts me away.

"What are you doing?" he demands, eyes wide, hair even more crazed.

"Making sure I'm not forgotten," I say, following Pacay's path out the door without being asked, and without glancing back.

I didn't intend to kiss him when I arrived, but the image of her touching him awoke something in me. A realization, perhaps, that Sunqu and I belong together and even Pacay sees it, which is what made venturing here so fun for her.

Yes, Sunqu loves me, but I've loved him just as long, even if I didn't realize it.

Without Sunqu, I have no friends left.

Catching me by the shoulder, Sunqu flips me around as I descend his stairs, before I've made it past his well and the gorgeous mountain view I can no longer appreciate.

"What's wrong?" he demands.

My traitorously pale reflection stares back from his eyes. "Nothing." In fact, everything is fine. Or will be soon.

"Have you been chosen? Was an announcement made?"

"No."

I don't want to remember the sacrifice of the first princess, and I'd rather not let him pretend to care what happens to me when he's decided to give me up. "But it doesn't matter." Again, I wrench myself free of him, letting my words sink into the depths of his battered and blood-streaked chest—a result of playing too much Fidichi with the emperor.

His brow knits as he looks down at me. "What do you mean?"

Hurrying down the last few stairs, I motion with one arm that I'm done with this conversation, but Sunqu keeps up easily.

"Enough of this," he says. "Yakua, you can't afford to lose the only person on your side. Don't you realize that you're literally facing death if the emperor doesn't choose you?"

I turn on him, prodding his chest with my pointer finger. "I understand the danger I'm in, thank you."

This time, when I go, he lets me.

Sunqu and I are rocks and water, the sun and the darkest of caves, the moon and ocean currents. Opposites that belong together. Or at least, I thought we did.

Maybe it was as easy for him to forget me as it was for my father to forget my mother. Love is a choice, after all, and I'm not the type for someone like Sunqu to choose if he wants to stay bright.

Above me, giant Folqus glide on their massive wings and misty clouds wheel between mountain peaks. But all of Ma Hlocha's beauty and splendor is too distant to settle my flames.

CHAPTER SEVENTEEN

SITTING ON A POUF before a mirror made of obsidian with gold edging, I comb my hair until my fingers slide smoothly through as I contemplate my next move.

I need to solidify my relationship with the emperor, but I also need to forge deeper connections in the social system of Isul Urqu. With all the political weight the Huya clan holds with the emperor, they need to support me. But I don't know anything about them, not even names, and I can't ask Sunqu.

Digging a nail into my bottom lip, I push until the pain of it makes me stop.

Even the emperor's treacherous face is preferable to Sunqu's. What bothers me most is that I can't stop seeing the handprints Pacay left from touching Sunqu's Fidichi paint. Nor the press of his lips when I kissed him, even if it was a vengeful kiss.

I don't need him. I'll find support among the Huya clan without his help. I'll figure out how to survive the emperor's suspicions without another man's perspective.

Reaching out to Cuxy presents one option, except she has a strong relationship with the emperor, and he may not like my plans.

As much as Cuxy pretends to like me, I can't expect her loyalty.

Unlike the Chira Huya, the Isul Huya have little to no speaking relationship with the emperor. They avoid him if they can. But I can speak to Lina. The emperor would surely benefit if I restore the Isul Huya's good opinion. And if the emperor suspects me for having manipulative powers, he must see the benefit of having the support of the upper class, and the ability to influence them as well.

Irenti clears her throat as she folds the patchwork-striped fur of my Perja skins, peering over at me as she stacks them.

"What?" I don't mean for my voice to sound sharp, but it does.

"You've done nothing but pace around your room and brush your hair for hours. What happened? Did you see the emperor?"

I pick up my brush and bat the ends of my hair with it as she folds another blanket.

"No," I say. Unbidden, a question pops from my mouth. "Does Sunqu see other women often?"

Irenti's hands hover over her pile. "Why?"

"Nothing." Stroking the bristles of my brush with a finger, I refuse to meet her gaze. If I ask too many questions, she'll assume I like him.

Maybe I used to, but not right now.

After folding blankets with a speed I haven't seen in her, she stops, smooths them, and scans the room. "He sees Pacay from time to time. I told you that."

"You talked of visitors." Pacay isn't any visitor, she's a noblewoman who likes to entertain herself.

She eyes me. "He's seen her regularly almost since he arrived."

Almost?

"I see word gets around here," I say dryly.

I turn back to my brush, but most of the bristles lay scattered on my lap.

Sunqu has such soft hair. It slid easily between my fingertips.

Clenching my fists, I shake the stray bristles off my lap. The emotions circling my brain are unfamiliar, but clear enough for me to catch hold of them with my power and examine them.

Is it jealousy? Yes. Fear? Perhaps, but I receive no influx of energy because my life isn't in danger.

It's a fear of loss.

Irenti doesn't look up. "I hear Pacay Virimac is very interested in him, which is surprising to many. She's never stuck to one man before. He's a good man, at least." She studies me. "Are you sure you're feeling well, princess?"

I straighten my back. "Of course. I'm always well."

None of this matters if I die, so I might as well focus on more important things.

Rather than allow space for Irenti to ask more questions, I combat hers with a few of my own. "How did the giants come to be? Did the emperor create them like they say?" He created the tiny stone man right in front of me. Could he create them as large as the mesa cliffs, too?

She considers. "Yes, he did. He's a descendant of Mirchira, the god of creation. It's said that Mirchira created giants before he created mankind. They were his failed attempt. But he destroyed the giants quickly after he made them because they started eating the precious men he brought to life. The emperor has similar powers."

The stories of the gods always have such somber undertones, but I don't know if they hold any truth. If I must die in this city, I will choose the altar over getting eaten by a giant. Fortunately, the giants around the city are decorative and never move. The real ones fight wars elsewhere.

"What happens to you if I get sacrificed?" I ask.

Irenti's face pales a few shades. "Servants typically die with their mistresses." She turns to empty my washbasin.

My family, my kingdom, and Irenti. One more reason I can't fail, whether Sunqu still cares about me or not.

I force my chest to expand. "What do you know about Lina Il-lapu? Or any of the Isul Huya?"

"Rumors, mostly." Her plain brown robes billow around her ankles as she moves, bustling for another pile of cloth to fold.

"Do you know how I can convince them to support me?"

Out of skins and woven blankets to fold, Irenti resorts to twisting the fabric of her dress. "If you don't mind me asking… why?"

Because if the emperor decides against me, I want it to anger the Huya. I want them to resist. I want my political net woven with thicker ropes.

If he marries me, I want having the Huya's loyalty an added benefit, among others, and I want them united at my side. Essentially, I want to give him one more reason not to toss me aside.

I fully expect the Huya will resist knowing I have little to offer as a princess of a doomed country, but I have the power to manipulate both them and the emperor. If I prove I can control the emperor, would they support me? Or shrink away?

Instead of telling her this, I study her face. While I want to trust her because she has begun to feel like a friend when I have no one else to count on, I can't allow myself to be too open.

She bows her head. "Excuse me, princess. Your business is your own."

Grateful she understands, I drop my brush, cross the room to her, and grip both her hands. Apprehension envelops me as my magic absorbs her emotions. "What can you tell me about Lina?"

Irenti exhales. "She has two sons. One served in the army and he's looking for a wife. He nearly married once, but the woman he loved left him for his brother. I know Lina is at the top of the Huya clan and loves her sons very much. She was bitter when the Chira Huya came and replaced them as the most respected family in Isul Urqu. I believe she hopes the emperor will marry soon, so tensions between the Huya clans will dissipate and she won't have to worry for her sons' lives or fortunes. If the emperor dies without an heir, the throne could go to either the Illapu or the Chikankaray families. Not knowing which is a chilling problem for the empire to have."

Lina wants peace, but she also wants her power back.

If I offer to reinstate her family as they were before the Chira Huya came, I might make enemies among the Chira Huya, who have become powerful with the lands the emperor gave them.

But would they know I made these promises? They might never find out.

Irenti wriggles away from me, picks up her stack of blankets, and sets them down by the fireplace, adjusting the tops with long fingers. "Lina lives at the edge of the kingdom, close to the cliffs the family owns."

"Thank you," I say.

She meets my gaze. "If you plan to visit her, you should bring your guards."

Sighing inwardly, I admonish myself for thinking, even for a moment, that she might not be smart enough to guess my intentions, though I can't imagine a way to wriggle out of this situation. However, I could want to talk to Lina for any number of reasons, though I still don't want the emperor knowing I spoke to them in case he suspects something he shouldn't.

He's already suspicious of me.

"I don't need guards for a chat," I say. "She was kind to me when I spoke to her last and I haven't met a lot of kindness here. I'd like to see how she's doing."

Normal people do social calls, don't they?

I hope Irenti believes me.

She seems to because she nods with a sympathetic half-smile.

If I can't use Irenti, who can I trust to show me where these people live?

The flower mystic at the market comes to mind. She knew how to find Sunqu and may know how to find the others as well, but it's too late. Besides, why would I trust the mystic over Irenti? They're both, technically, in the emperor's employ.

"Let me take you to her," Irenti says.

"I would appreciate that," I say, feigning relief. For what else can I do?

Though I've accepted her help, my qualms still nag at me. How will I explain visiting the other Huya to her? If I avoid bringing her, that could arouse suspicion as well.

I'll have to think through these questions as we go.

Pushing aside the curtained door, Irenti follows me out, but as Irenti closes the curtain behind us, a recognizable figure makes my feet lock on the crispy grass.

The emperor leads a princess from her hut by the hand, the folds of his robes blowing in the wind. The princess smiles up at him as he speaks, his own smile slightly crooked.

Seeing him brings forward a myriad of bitter, angry emotions, but not as strong as the rage I felt at seeing Sunqu with Pacay. I hurry to push the anger back. It's distracting, and unhelpful, and I have better things to do than to think of either of them.

Neither the emperor nor the princess looks at me as they disappear down the hill into the village and I force my feet forward again until we reach a mesh of square stones that form the road into town, all tightly packed so I don't have to worry about my shoes getting stuck, though I wear leather sandals today instead of the glass slippers Sunqu made.

I'll never wear those slippers again.

"Who are the other powerful families of the Isul Huya?" I ask as we walk between huts, keeping beneath the thatched roofs for shade.

If I'm going to play a game of politics, I want it to be with the most influential families.

"The House of Isulasto. The Paqari, among others."

"I'd like to get to know them as well. If I marry the emperor and spend time in this city, I'd like to know the original residents. I want to feel at home here."

It's as good an explanation as any.

"Not all of them are kind, princess," Irenti says.

Her tone warns of something more, but rather than ask questions, I bite back my trepidation and let her think me unassuming, naïve, and hopeful to make friends.

"They'll be open to speaking to me."

"Of course," Irenti says. "The House of Isulasto is on the way. Shall I take you there first?"

"Yes."

Irenti clutches her hip like she struggles with a stitch as we climb another hill. Trickles of water slide down giant slabs of stones on our right, the carved channels in the rocks filling the city's water wells. Vines crawl up the sides of the houses and little buds sprout from stones.

I point to the wells. "Where does the water come from? The mountain?"

Irenti's face flushes with exertion as she takes a sucking breath. "There's a spring up the mountain that we call Esukya, or the Spring of the Gods. The water comes from deep within the earth and it's what inspired the founding of our kingdom. We wouldn't have been able to settle here without it. We use the stones to distribute water from that well to the rest of the city."

Impressed, I let my gaze linger on the stone slabs before tearing my eyes away.

We approach a house made of patchwork stones, each square engraved with images of the sun and sky. Spiked flowers grow on a vine around the door.

I lower my voice. "What should I know about the people here?"

Irenti stays close to my side. "The head of the Isulasto house is afraid of Mirchira taking over Isul's kingdom. His name is Hoq. They say he keeps hoards of Perja furs in his rooms in case Isul ends our eternal summer as punishment for abandoning him."

"Eternal?" After days of traveling in the freezing jungles, I noticed Isul Urqu attracts the heat of the sun as if it were a beacon, but I didn't know Isul Urqu has no seasons.

"Yes, we have no winter here, though ice and snow cover the surrounding mountains in the wintertime. The temperature is always mild. It's Isul's blessing on his kingdom. Hoq believes he should be High Priest instead of Ranu Achikoya. He thinks Ranu is going to lead the kingdom to destruction, especially if the gods return, and Isul sees the emperor assigned a new patron to his kingdom."

"If the gods do return, it's a legitimate concern." I can sway Hoq without touching him, with words, if I know enough about him. "Wait here," I tell her, because I don't want her to overhear our conversation.

She waits where I tell her to, obedient as always.

Stopping in front of their door, I knock. Scuffling comes from inside and the door creaks open to reveal a man in servant's loincloth. He shields his eyes. "May I ask who you are?"

"I'm Princess Nalia of Cochas. I came to request help from the Isulasto house."

He bows and moments after he disappears, a towering man of stiff sides and sharp edges emerges in the doorway, his eyes tight. A frown makes his chin jut out.

I take an involuntary step back.

"I'm Princess Nalia—"

He stops me with a hand.

"I know who you are. What I'd like to know is why, by the stones, I would help you."

I stand tall, fixing my face into what I hope is a confident, friendly-ish look, and not my usual glower. "I'm intended for the emperor and have heard of your plight. I want you to know I plan to reinstate you as High Priest as soon as I become empress. I support your worship of the sun god and am as fearful as you are of inciting the gods' wrath when they return to Hallja. Will you join me and ensure the safety of our kingdom? We can support each other."

I'm not lying. If the emperor refuses to allow it, I'll prod the emperor's emotions. Or I'll try, at least.

Hoq glowers down at me. "I don't know who you think you're fooling, but you will never become empress."

He has no reason to be cruel.

"I know you want the emperor to marry. Don't you want him to marry someone you support?"

A puff of air hits my face as he slams the door shut.

Turning to Irenti, I scan her face for her reaction. Did she expect this? Is she curious what our conversation was about? Or did she lie to me?

I was right in thinking I shouldn't bring Irenti, but we're here, and it's too late.

Irenti clasps her fingers in front of her, straightening her arms and raising her shoulders to her ears, the vines clinging to the walls behind her making her look sweet and innocent, even if I still can't trust her.

"Hoq has been through a lot this year, princess," she says, by way of explanation. "I believe he's entitled to whatever feelings he has. He lost his eldest daughter only a few months ago."

I force my voice to stay calm. "Fine."

Honestly, he's right. I have no way to know if I will become empress. In the end, it's up to the emperor. But I stare at the fine grain of his door and slam my fist against it before allowing myself to stand erect, my shoulders back.

The anger won't help me. I need to cast it aside.

"Princess?" Irenti asks in a soft voice.

Pulling in a calmness that steadies my feet, I turn on my heel and start down the road, Irenti scurrying after me.

"We find Lina," I say.

CHAPTER EIGHTEEN

PASSING THROUGH THE OUTPOSTS at the edge of the city, the guards let us through, their eyes following me as I descend a steep staircase that curves down the face of the cliff at the edge of the city.

"They let us through easy," I say to Irenti, huffing behind me.

"They know if you run, you'll freeze in the mountains. And I imagine there's someone tracking you as well," she says between breaths.

"Oh."

I'd be surprised if they weren't tracking me, though I hope the tracker can't get so close as to hear my conversations.

Descending to a hut that looks as if it slid down the side of the mountain and stuck in the middle, we arrive somewhere between the land of the living and Heliray's realm of the dead. Jungle plants grow around it, and elaborate carvings decorate each stone that forms the grand exterior.

The small form of Lina Illapu kneels by a row of garden beds squished against the cliffside and plucks weeds from the dirt. She looks up as we approach and folds her hands in her lap.

"Stay here," I say, and Irenti stops behind me.

As I come forward, Lina stands to brush off her dress. "Princess Nalia, I wasn't expecting you."

"I wanted to speak to you in private."

Her face remains open and unoffended, though she always looks that way. "About what?"

"The emperor needs an heir. I know that's why the princesses were forced to come here and why you hoped the emperor would marry. I want you to know that if I become empress, I will support your clan. I will give you an heir and promote your family back to its previous status."

Lina raises her eyebrows, which have long strands of gray in them, matching her hair. "Can you guarantee this?"

No, but she doesn't need to know that. "Yes."

"I'm not unaware of the effect you have on the emperor," she continues in a flat tone. "He plays Fidichi harder than I've ever seen him play and is, perhaps, mildly less suspicious of us than usual. He has certainly shown more interest in you than the others. But even you cannot control him. He won't allow what you're suggesting without force."

"What if I told you I have ways to sway him?" While I don't expect her to conclude that I have powers, I add, "He likes me," to ensure she doesn't.

Lina tilts her head, her expression unchanging. "Then I'd ask why you haven't done it already."

It's slow progress, and I've made mistakes, but she doesn't need to know that.

"He'll listen to me."

She narrows her eyes. "Forgive me, but I don't believe you. If you were able to sway him, I'm surprised no marriage announcement has yet been made."

I take a step back, stunned at her blunt statement, and how easily she bares my failures.

Lina's mouth stretches into a grim smile. "I appreciate you reaching out to me, Princess Nalia. Truly, I do. No other princess has bothered. But if I were you, I'd focus on keeping your emperor interested—for your own sake. I don't think it will be as easy as you hope."

She rubs her knuckles over her forehead as she faces her garden again.

She said she'll root for me in private, but that's only a small win and not enough. I step forward and touch her, using my magic to pull at her emotional threads, tweaking at her sympathies, prodding her to promise more.

Lina hesitates, her stern expression faltering. "These last few weeks must have been hard. I wish there was more I could do for you, truly. But this—" She gestures to her house. "Is all that's left to me. Everything has been taken, except my sons. I have little power, outside of my name, a fact the emperor flaunts. What would you have me do for you?"

As she says this, my hope withers and I let the emotion fade from the connection between us, the empathy vanishing from her expression as well.

While Lina isn't the kind fool I have the ability to turn her into, she truly can do nothing for me.

"I am happy to root for your success in private," Lina continues, her prior grimness back now that my influence has left her. "The Huya clan won't publicly support you unless you've given us what we want—which is an equal partnership with the emperor. Or no emperor at all. He has done nothing but shove us out and, unfortunately, even as empress, I doubt you can change that."

"I understand," I say instead, giving her a respectful bow. "Thank you for your time, Ma Lina. I will take my leave."

"Wait." She turns to me, almost as if changing her mind, but I know better.

"If you try to escape this city, you won't get far, but I'd be surprised if the emperor doesn't already know you're here. If he demands a reason, come up with a good one. People only look for allies when they intend to start a war. He'll be suspicious and you won't want to arouse distrust. No one is more distrustful than the emperor."

I shake myself free of the dread of her statement because knowing he's distrustful is enough, and I'm aware of that already.

I have no intention of starting wars.

After leaving Lina, I return to Irenti, still standing outside, waiting for me.

"How did it go?" Irenti's expression is optimistic. "Better than the last one?"

"Not really."

She joins me at my side, the hope sliding from her features as she matches my fast pace. "Then maybe you'll like the Paqari family, though I might have thought them the least likely to be a connection you'd favor."

"What do you mean?" I cast her a sharp look, nervous again that she guesses too much.

She wiggles her shoulders in a way that suggests she's unsure how to explain as she leads me to another set of stairs descending parallel to a waterfall.

Torrents crash down the mountainside from where the rivers meet the giants, down the side of the mesa.

Down, down, down.

"The Paqari family reign over the outposts and trails to the city."

Irenti points to the stone paths that lead toward the distant mountains, but I can't help but glance over my shoulder at the line of houses on the top of the cliff where Sunqu's house would be.

Flashes of hands in Sunqu's hair and the paint on his chest force its way into my brain.

You can't afford to lose the only person on your side.

I'm not done.

The waterfall merges into a river with snakes that slither through the crystal blue waters. A branch cracks and I whip around as a figure ducks behind a group of spindly trees—likely the tracker Irenti warned of. Though I expected to be followed, a knot of unease forms between my shoulder blades.

Soft musical notes calm the crisp air as we leave the heat of the mesa behind, a line of huts growing as we near, some larger than others. A man sits on a rock outside an open door, a pipe in his hand. He stops playing when he spots us, sets his pipe down, and pushes himself to his feet. Unkempt facial hair covers his chin and upper lip, one side of his hair expertly cropped short.

"You're not from here." He eyes my headdress. "You look very familiar. Are you one of the emperor's princesses?"

"I don't belong to the emperor," I say.

The huts behind him should be as grand as Lina's if they belong to an ancient Huya family, especially the well-known Paqari family. Instead, they have thinly thatched roofs pockmarked with holes.

"Can you point me in the direction of the household?"

He runs a hand through the half of his hair that isn't shaved. "You're looking at it. I'm Joachik, the eldest. My brother lives on the east side of the kingdom and my sister manages the south and west. It's just me here and those who choose to live with me." He gestures to the huts with his chin, then sweeps his eyes over me. "You're a pretty one, aren't you? I'm surprised the emperor manages to keep up this whole charade with you around. What are you doing here, anyway?"

His dirty tunic creates a steep "v" that reveals his collarbone. He's handsome enough, but too old to pretend youth.

I meet his gaze as it wanders too freely. "I'm looking for support. If you show me loyalty, I'll remember you when I'm queen."

"Done." He grins.

"Done?"

As I search his face for a smirk or a twitch of the lip that signals a laugh, he just smiles, and I don't like it. I check my dress for dirt, a loose thread, or even a hole. Nothing is out of place. "I haven't offered you anything."

I expected to need to influence him with my powers, to beg him. His smile grows. "I don't care."

A starved gleam in his eye forces me a few steps back, but he lurches forward and seizes my wrist, yanking me toward him. "I hope you survive," he says. "So I can see you again."

Mustering a flood of power, I channel it to calm the craving that bubbles up from his grip as I wriggle out of his grasp. I don't thank him, but leave, snatching Irenti's elbow as I go.

This isn't a man I want on my side.

"Don't leave me," I hiss into her ear as I drag her after me.

The weight of his eyes lingers on my calves until the river curves just enough into the hillside that it cloaks the hapless homes of Joachik Paqari.

We climb the stone stairs to the top of the mountain and board a boat to return to the palace, the water reflecting the twilight in streaks of gray. Even as night shrouds the city, dimming the colors, it's still more vibrant than any conversation I had with the Isul Huya.

Irenti glances sidelong at me as the boat knocks against the river-bank. "Do you want to visit another Huya house?" she asks.

"No."

She taps her fingers on the wood of her seat. "What were you hoping for, princess?"

Friends. Allies. Hope. Someone to fight for me.

I avoid her gaze.

"Princess, they expect you to die. Even if you don't die, they have no reason to care about you. They have no desire to get to know you."

She's right, but it doesn't change that I had to try. I can't sit around and wait for the emperor to decide I'm not trustworthy or capable of being an empress because I didn't enjoy his soup with the appropriate smile.

I don't need them, and I don't need Sunqu either.

But sitting here with Irenti, I miss home. I miss my mother.

When my mother was alive, she brought me everywhere with her. She held my hand as we walked from the market to the docks and stroked my hair as we sat on the wood planks and listened to waves crash. When the wind stole the warmth from my skin, she squeezed me tight. We sat in silence on principle. Only once did my mother speak as we watched the sunset, boats bobbing on either side of the docks.

The sea is beautiful, but don't go too deep or you'll find Uru Hlocha.

Now that Uru Hlocha has claimed her, there's no one left to comfort me. No one to teach me to use my powers. No one to give me advice.

The emperor is the only unknown left, and while I hoped to make use of the time sitting around, waiting for him, it's all I can do.

I look up, finally meeting Irenti's eyes. "Let's go home."

We disembark as the boat hits the riverbank, and then I follow

Irenti to our hut. She pushes the curtains aside and halts, so I must step around her to see what caused her to stop.

"What?"

Except she doesn't have to answer because I can see it plainly before me.

Ice shoots down to my toes, colder than the bitterest snow at the top of the mountain glaciers.

"By the stones," Irenti whispers.

Shredded strips from my bedding scatter the ground with jumbled rugs, pillows, and shattered vases. My breath catches between my ribs as my heart shrivels into a thousand flakes of dust, smaller than the remains of my blankets.

I dash to the bed skins, but the time it takes me to get there passes with eerie slowness. Tossing aside the pillows that cover my mother's necklace, only the soft fur meets my fingers as I sweep my hands across the rough floor.

I can't lose it. It's all that remains of her.

Ceramic shards bite my skin as I snatch up broken items and toss them aside, a silent fury pounding in my ears.

A gleam from above catches my eye where a knife protrudes from between two stones in the hut's wall. My mother's necklace dangles from the hilt, the emerald mount empty.

Someone stole the center stone.

A strangled gasp escapes my lips.

They ruined it. They want to ruin me. They desecrated the only possession I have that I care about.

Soft fingers touch my arm. "I'm sorry, princess." Irenti's voice hardly touches the sorrow that seeps through me.

"They hate me," I say in a deadly whisper.

"Who does?"

I gesture all around me. To the walls and beyond. "Everyone."

"They don't, Yakua," Irenti says.

I close my eyes. Maybe not everyone, but someone does.

Rather than let the cold fury consume me, I stand and go to my necklace, unpinning it from the knife on the wall. Putting the necklace on, I clasp the chain around my neck, so the silver snakes sit above my collarbone.

Whatever the people of Isul Urqu think, let them see me wear it.

Irenti squeezes my shoulder, but her silence fills the room more than her presence does.

CHAPTER NINETEEN

THEY STOLE MY CLOTHES, my headdresses, my jewelry, and they dared to touch my mother's necklace. The shells and unique stones I collected as offerings scatter the floor in every direction. I step on one and it flattens beneath my sandal with a crunch.

My mother is truly gone. I can't speak to her again. Whoever destroyed my hut—they took her from me.

"Princess—" Irenti pauses. "We can find you clothes. We can wash your dress tonight and have it ready for tomorrow. We can—" Her eyes go to my necklace and her shoulders jerk, as if she's never seen mutilated jewelry before and it strikes her as hard as a severed neck. "We can go to the market at first light tomorrow. I'll go and find you new dresses."

"I—" I don't have money, but I can't tell Irenti that. Instead, I lie. "They took my money too."

Her eyes sweep the floor. "We'll figure it out."

We won't.

"I'll wash myself and my dress in the river," I say.

This time, I don't need to pluck out any inhibiting feelings. Instead, the tides of emotion from discovering the necklace have overwhelmed my brain. They're still there, but my brain refuses to process them.

They don't affect me.

Swimming in my dress won't help to clean it much before appearing before the emperor tomorrow, but I want to escape the worried looks Irenti casts in my direction, so I leave for the river.

Trudging down the hill to the river that flows from Mira-Tamya, I plunge into the calm, rippling waters, though I didn't bring soaps or cloths to wash with. The water swallows my face and body, and I wish it would make me disappear altogether.

My lungs struggle for air until my head breaks the surface. Sputtering, I let droplets rain down my cheeks.

"Glad I'm not the only one who goes to the river to feel better."

I jerk at the sound of a feminine voice and swing around. The princess the emperor pays the most attention to sits on the riverbank with her toes in the water. She wasn't there before or I would have seen her. She has vibrant hazel eyes, and her hair drapes about her like a dainty blanket.

"Sorry to startle you. I was just behind that tree." She points. "I saw you run down here, and I haven't seen any royal throw herself into a river fully clothed before. You look pale. Did they make another announcement?"

"No." I turn my back to her.

She probably hopes my death is announced too.

I can ignore her, get out, and return to the mess of my hut, wash my dress in the basin and ask Irenti to bring water, but I'm disappointed to leave this place where I hoped to find solitude.

The woman nods. "That's good. We have a few weeks longer, I guess." She strips to her undergarments and drapes a towel over a rock. "Mind if I join you?" She doesn't wait for my answer but plunges into the water and reemerges to run her fingers through her hair and rub oils over her skin. "I grew up by the ocean too, you know. Frigelles isn't as close to the waves as Cochas, but we're close enough."

Keeping my back to her, I wade to the shore, unwilling to get to know her any more than the Huya care to get to know me. Why would I want to befriend my competition? Especially the one who's most likely to push me out of my place?

"I suppose you're right to ignore me," she says.

I face her, surprised by her saddened tone, my dress making sloshing sounds in the water.

"We don't remember the names of the deer we sacrifice," she says. "We don't look into the eyes of the pigs we kill. You're right not to talk to me. I had no intention of speaking to you either until I saw you running down here like you were already dead. I would have sooner killed you myself."

Staring, I let the truth of her words sink in.

Would I kill her too?

If I had to.

But as I look at her, a suspicion sneaks into being. She might have come to harass me, having chosen the perfect time to do so. We aren't far from my hut and she might be the one responsible for looting it, and she came to see my reaction. Which means she stole my mother's necklace out of spite.

"Give me back the stone to my mother's necklace." My voice comes out low and deadly.

She squeezes her hair so drops pelt the river's surface. "I really don't know what you're talking about."

I storm from the water and point an accusing finger at her nose. "In a few weeks, one or both of us will be dead, and I'll make sure it's you. When that happens, I'll get my stone back."

The princess emerges from the river and dries herself with a towel. "It was a nice talk, as short as it was. Thank you." She picks up her dress and prances, half-nude, up the hill to her hut.

My hands twinge and half-moons mark my palms as I open my fists.

After charging up the hill, I thrust aside the curtain of my tent. A servant with a shell necklace waits, Irenti beside him, the color drained from Irenti's cheeks.

He bows with a fist on his chest. "You are required to dine with the emperor and his guests tonight at sunset. He has an announcement to make." Bowing again, he shuffles down the path toward the palace, me glaring at his back as he goes.

I whirl on Irenti.

"He's going to kill me, isn't he?"

Irenti shakes her head. "I don't know what the announcement will be, but I found Sunqu when I went up the hill to ask the other servants if they knew of spare dresses. He said he has a friend who makes dresses for Lina Illapu and already has some made. He said he could bring them. If you must go to dinner tonight, you can't go with a wet dress."

Sunqu, the man I once called a friend. "You went to Sunqu?"

Irenti shrinks back. "Did I do something wrong?"

She didn't because I never told her what happened with Sunqu, nor does she know the whole history between us. All she knows is that I have no money, and he offered.

While I don't like being in debt to Sunqu, I'll find a way to repay him later, though my pride stings accepting this donation, the mortification almost too great to bear.

I level my voice. "It's fine, Irenti. Thank you." Though my voice sounds cold.

She bows, though a crease in her brow tells me she's still concerned that I didn't receive her help as gracefully as she expected.

Sitting on the floor in front of the obsidian mirror, I fold my legs. My hands shake as I pick up my brush and drag it through the coarse strands of my hair

Irenti stands behind me. "Can I help?" She holds a turquoise necklace grander than any the emperor has given me. It almost enlivens the color that died in my black eyes.

"Please."

When Sunqu arrives, he stands outside the curtain as Irenti fetches the dress, leaving before I have a chance to voice my gratitude, though I'm happy to escape the humiliation. Irenti helps me into a dress, and I study the mirror as she paints my lips with red stain. My nose and cheeks cast shadows over my face as the light in the room dims with the approaching sunset.

She faces me when she finishes. "Are you feeling well? I hear two of the other princesses are very sick."

I wonder at the reason. They might have drunk something foul in the water. It happened often enough in Cochas. Hopefully they recover soon.

"I'm fine, but thank you for your concern."

Pushing aside Irenti's hands, I stand and she watches me go as I head for the path outside my hut, down the hill, and in through the palace doors.

The guards don't speak as I pass, just stand aside, their spears raised in stiff attention.

A servant joins me, and the sound of his footsteps follows me down the halls. Pushing aside the thick, woven drapes into the banquet hall, I sit at the end of the table.

A few princesses away, a young man with dark, cropped hair and a square jawline sits with the women beside him, his smiles causing them to relax their stiff postures, though he wears the finest dyed wool, sewn with threads of gold and precious stones. His clothing reveals strong shoulders and arms, and a golden flush to his dark skin.

It's Sunqu, but not my Sunqu.

This Sunqu is broader, more muscular, and sharper around the edges. A scar stretches along his jaw and above his left eye while his nose healed crooked from when he broke it. He wears his wounds well. The biggest change, however, shows in his expressions. His smiles come in shorter bursts and are harder won, fading like the last embers of a fire once you've thrown water on them.

A princess flashes him a pretty smile. "I saw you practice Fidichi yesterday, Sunqu. The games have escalated since you joined the emperor's team."

"I assure you, the emperor's taste for danger has little to do with me, but I'm grateful for the chance to play at his side." He smooths his shirt, though there are no wrinkles.

"I hear you're an artist as well." She rests her chin on her palm, her elbow on the stone table. "I'd love to see what you're working on."

"My projects aren't far from here," he says. "If the emperor approves, I can take you."

The princess on his other side offers a plate of bread. She stares at him over her piece as she takes a bite, her cheeks a little pale, perhaps with a yellow tinge, and she wears powder as if trying to cover it up. But as Sunqu looks at her, she blushes pink.

I sip my wine slowly, though I haven't made my offering yet.

When he talks, his tone is light, the way he usually talks with me.

He thinks I need his help. Worse, I accepted it by wearing the dress he bought.

Folding my napkin on the table, I stare pointedly past Sunqu as the emperor enters the room, causing glasses to clink against the table as the attention in the room focuses on him. He sits and raises his cup.

"Guests, let me introduce you to our resident glassmaker, Sunqu. As you can see, he is a delight to everyone who meets him. I'm so glad you came to us, my friend. Your novel glass material will soon be the staple of Mirchira's empire. Even the heathen clans from the north will travel to Isul Urqu to witness the wonder of Mirchira's ice statues that don't melt, no matter how hot the sun blazes."

Sunqu dips his head. "On behalf of Cochas, I'm pleased to be of service to you."

"Ah yes, Cochas." The emperor touches his chin, as if he forgot there's a country on the southeastern side of Hallja. "You must express my gratitude to the previous king of Cochas for sending such a gift." His fierce eyes flick to me for a second, and I can't help but wonder why. Perhaps he makes the connection that I, too, am from Cochas.

At least he cares enough to remember.

He pours wine over the stone floor. "To the gods. May they live on in the stones of our table." His eyes wander toward me a second time. And a third.

Sweat trickles down my back.

Is this a bad sign?

A hand grasps my fingers and quickly lets go before my powers detect emotion from the touch. I turn toward the source, and the princess who spoke to Sunqu about Fidichi nods once. She wears the lightning belt of Ma Thala and either means to be kind or to laugh at me. I can never tell anymore.

The rugs shift as the princess I met at the river sits beside me, clutching her hands in her lap, her marvelous hair all around her like a shining mosquito net. The emperor stares at her with an eyebrow raised high.

She must notice me watching because she glances my way with a sneer. After running her fingers through her hair, she picks up a cup, takes a long, dainty sip, and smacks her lips together.

The emperor narrows his eyes, both fists on the table. "You're late, Princess Raysa. I assume you have a reason?"

Raysa's eyes dart to me and then back to him. "This princess," she points without looking at me, "ransacked my hut and broke several of your most exquisite vases. My servant saw her outside just before it happened. Fortunately, they were able to clean the mess up and all is as it was before."

My blood freezes. She doesn't just want to kill me; she wants the emperor to toss me off the cliffs so I can't make the same accusation.

But I can defend myself.

I clear my throat. "I did no such thing."

The emperor's face hardens. "Are you lying to me?"

"I don't lie." At least not in this case.

I'm already on treacherous standing with the emperor after our last outing together. This can't stand or I'm ruined.

The princess brushes her hair over her shoulder.

"But my room was destroyed too," I say. "And my servant can attest to it. I wouldn't destroy my own stuff."

Raysa's eyes narrow.

The emperor studies us both. "Enough. Princess Nalia, don't give me a reason to doubt your innocence again. You are not to visit any of the princesses' huts under any condition."

The emperor returns to his food and the conversation of the princess who sits beside him—the one who blushed over her bread at Sunqu—and I'm left reeling, wondering how much more of this I can take.

Princess Raysa bites off a piece of chicken, sets it on the table, and squashes it with her dining stone. "May the gods live on." Then she bites off a piece for herself. "If you touch my stuff again, Princess of Cochas," she says between bites. "I'll make certain the only ocean you see is the one behind your eyelids."

She fabricated the whole thing to make the emperor hate me. It's why she avoided looking in my direction when she listened to the emperor and Sunqu chat about monument plans for Mirchira.

The servants bring me sweet milk that warms my stomach as the room chills with sidelong glances and overeager humor, and my own apprehension. Then the emperor turns to me. "Princess Nalia, are you enjoying your meal?"

He hasn't spoken to me in days. "I am," I say, though I don't attempt a smile.

"Good."

I'm tired of this back and forth, weary of dissecting looks and words, of turning over every phrase, of looking ins and peering through outs. Of wondering and worrying. Of being me.

With one touch, I can remind the emperor of our previous connection on Mira-Tamya, but all I want is to go home. To leave and never see this city, nor the emperor again, even if it means I must wear rags and eat fish in Ma Cochira's temple every day for the rest of my life.

I want the waves knocking against pockmarked rocks. Cliffs that drop straight into the sea, no giants in sight.

I want a Sunqu who smiles because he's happy, not because he's forced to, waiting at the shoreline for me to swim back to him.

The emperor stands and motions to Sunqu. "I need to speak to you privately."

Without hesitation, Sunqu follows him from the room, and I can't find it in me to care what the emperor has to say. I just wish I could take him away from this place.

As the door closes behind Sunqu and the emperor, Drea, the older Huya woman who announced the name of the condemned princesses, walks in.

I should have known.

Drea coughs, clearing her throat before speaking. "Emperor Huamar has spent time with each princess he cared to spend time with this round. An announcement will be made tomorrow evening, after the emperor's Fidichi game, as was done before, and a new round will begin. You are all dismissed."

Outside of the singular question he asked, he hasn't spoken to me. I haven't had the chance to touch or influence him. He might be avoiding me. Or he looked so often in my direction because he planned to name me as the next sacrifice.

As soon as Drea finishes, she leaves, and the princesses go their separate ways. I return to my hut, change into a sleeping gown, and lay on my bed skins, my eyes wide open.

After a night spent tossing and turning, a servant wakes me up early in the morning, before the sun has risen, to announce that my presence has been requested at another Fidichi game, as expected.

I make my way to the arena alone, my vision bleary from lack of sleep.

After descending the steep stairs, my knees buckle, and I slump into the stone benches of the arena. The Fidichi game unfolds before me with thrown stones and shouting men, while the beat of my heart drowns out the noise.

Sweat glistens on my fingers and I dry them on my dress in case anyone notices. Forcing myself to count as I breathe, my heart races on, faster than the moving Fidichi stones.

I might as well be confined in a closed cave, with water filling the empty spaces around me. Every second, the air thins while the sun sets and the air cools.

I shift in my dress, the fabric clinging to my arms. The princess beside me wears powder, just as she did the day before, to cover the yellow in her cheeks. Today, her cheeks have turned a faint green. Shoulders slumped, sweat pours down the sides of her face and seeps into her tight dress. Her cracked lips have wrinkles white as chalk.

I haven't considered the nervous state of anyone else, but perhaps the green in her skin is more than nerves.

The princess on her other side holds her arm and tries to prop her up, but the sick princess only hunches further. Though I'm surprised at how friendly they are with each other, it's even more apparent that the sick princess needs herbs.

As I scan the stone benches for help, the men below clear the field, some hobbling behind, leaning on the shoulders of their comrades.

Drea stands slowly and approaches.

My mouth dries.

As she bows, her gaze passes over me. "Emperor Huamar has determined Princess Kuna of Joco unfit to rule at his side. When he tested her, she fell ill to the Cayuhu plant, which is a poison the ancients used to detect the bloodlines of the gods. If you don't have a strong enough tie to a god, you will eventually die from it. The emperor only wants an empress whose bloodline is worthy. As Princess Kuna is already on a path to death, she'll be sacrificed at the altar tonight, overseen by the High Priest and the emperor himself. You are all required to attend." She offers another shallow bow. "The Kingdom of Joco will build the next glass monument for Mirchira and is now absorbed into the new empire. For the next round, the emperor wishes you to know that he plans to determine who among you fully understands the hierarchy of power in this kingdom." She passes the watching Huya clan as she leaves, striding along the stone benches toward her own clan.

The sick princess, the same girl who blushed at Sunqu the day before, presses her hands to her haggard face and sobs.

The emperor put Cayuhu in my soup, too. He told me so. He must have known it might kill me. I am more directly descended from Ma Cochira than I thought, otherwise, I'd be dead.

I suppose it doesn't surprise me that the emperor has already tried killing me, without having the spine to do it properly.

Guards step forward and drag the princess away as more guards surround the rest of us. They escort us to the river and into the boats, just as they did when the last princess died. The boatman oars us to the edge of the city, where guards lead us up the stone stairs to another temple with the same cliffs and open ceiling.

We circle the altar.

At least I stand several steps before the altar, not beside it, but this isn't a win I can congratulate myself for. I didn't do anything to deserve life over Princess Kuna except eat soup and survive.

A line of sheep, cows, and deer enter and servants round them up in the corner. One by one, they bring livestock over. They must be properly drugged because the deer and sheep stumble over the stones, and don't resist.

"May the gods live on in the stones of this altar," the High Priest repeats as each animal lets out a dying whine and lays still.

A man grabs Kuna by the wrist, and she slumps as he drags her forward, still frail from the poison. It doesn't matter how many sacrifices I've seen; this is different. She doesn't have many servants, but the few she does have trail behind her, faces ashen.

The knife rises and, once again, the emperor turns away.

I study him as the metallic scent of her blood taints the air. When he turns back, he keeps his eyes averted, nose wrinkled, like he doesn't appreciate the stink she leaves behind.

The guards haul her body away, along with the bodies of her servants. The ground shakes and dust falls.

After everyone else leaves, I follow the trail of blood to the edge of the cliffs.

Wind tosses my dress and tangles my hair, but I stand as still as the giants below, which are just more rocks the cliffs sucked emotion from and leaves dry.

As I stare down, I can picture the princess's terrified eyes when she discovered her time had come. When I shut my eyes to black out the image, my own face appears on the backs of my eyelids instead of hers.

My magic fills my emptiness with a sudden influx of tangible strength. Fear tingles in my fingers, but it doesn't originate from me. Turning, I find Princess Raysa at my side, her face down-turned and her upper lip peeled back. "Don't fall," she says.

I step away from the edge.

"If I did, it would be because you pushed me."

My fingers itch to be the first to push. She would flail and topple, and I wouldn't have to worry about her again.

She shrugs. "I can't say I wasn't tempted, but while my first instinct is to survive, I have no blood on my hands. Even I have limits. If you die, it's because the emperor killed you, not because I did." The muscles in my back and neck tense as she passes, but she doesn't touch me.

She can say she won't hurt me as much as she wants, but I won't allow myself to be caught off guard by trusting someone who doesn't deserve it.

Folqus circle above the mountains with untouchable wings, at a vantage point only the gods experience. If only I can join them and understand the world as they do. See the emotions and the political moves from up above, rather than in the middle of it.

I'd have a much broader vision.

"Princess Nalia of Cochas?" I whirl around as Drea Chiki, the Huya matchmaker and spokesperson, approaches from behind in a long red dress, her expression stiff.

She bows, a fist over her heart. "Princess Nalia, Emperor Huamar would be honored if you would join him tomorrow morning for breakfast. Are you willing?"

I'm not sure why he wants to meet with me, but I'm grateful he hasn't cast me off yet.

"Yes."

He may want to see me and determine the truth of Raysa's accusation for himself, perhaps to deal out punishment. Or it's just another round.

Whatever the reason, this is a chance to influence the emperor.

Drea nods before surveying the cliff and my close proximity to it. She sniffs but heads off without a word.

CHAPTER TWENTY

DREA SAID I NEEDED to understand the hierarchy of power in the empire, but how will he test my belief in that hierarchy? Perhaps he wants to know if I respect him, or if I remember the gods.

I haven't gone to the temples as much as I planned.

Waiting outside my hut for the emperor, I cover the mess inside as he approaches. He looks disheveled than I've yet to see him, with his curly hair slightly ratted, and creases in his robes.

He stops abruptly a few feet from me, his hands behind his back, his face impassive. "There are eateries near here where they play music and dance, and we'll have a view of the mountains and jungles. Would that suit you?" Though I search for it, I can't find even a trace of enthusiasm in his voice.

But if I prod the emotion to life, will it come?

"It would." My response comes out disjointed as I struggle to add even the smallest inflection.

I can't afford to let him walk away.

"Come." He reaches for my hand, grasping it like he would a hammer, and pulls me down the hill to a boathouse on the river, but I don't sense elation from him with my magic, no affection. Just frost and barely contained anger.

It makes me jumpy as well.

We rent a reed boat with the head of a Perja and he sits with a few inches of space between us as the boat bobs down the river. Touching the backs of his fingers, I try to send him peace and contentment with my powers, but he snatches his hand away.

Rather than pester him more, I let the silence drive us further apart.

The knowledge that something is wrong coils inside me.

While the boat docks, he leads me into the door of a house that bursts with the smells of fresh food, the walls ringing with whistling pipes and pounding drums that remind me of that fateful festival months ago, when the summer began.

He leads me to a table where we listen to music, looking anywhere but at each other.

The place is lively and fun, but the atmosphere stops at us. "Is something wrong?"

He angles away from me, and silhouettes lengthen as couples dance across the floor. Attendants light candles and people gather to watch. Shadows play across the emperor's nose as muscles flex in his jawline, his hair growing more tangled as the night darkens and colors saturate the sky.

The longer he doesn't speak, the more my stomach turns.

They bring us food and he watches the crowd as he chews. He doesn't bother to do sacrifices either.

Another song ends, and he turns to me, his eyes hard as obsidian. "You and I need to talk."

I nod.

He wouldn't bring me to dinner if he planned to ignore me the whole time, but I wish he would state what upset him at the start, rather than make me sit with it for hours.

After tugging me outside, he leads me toward a cliff. I try to keep up with his quick footsteps until he halts a few feet from the edge. Sand tumbles off into a dark abyss until the wind picks up the dirt and billows it into the sky.

Peering over the edge, I catch my breath at the majesty of the giant standing as a motionless sentinel beneath me, tall as the mountain the city is perched on top of. Its craggy face creates a ledge for water to crash over.

Narrow stretches of land lead into the mountains and, far across those pointed peaks, Cochas nestles against the seashore. There, my family thinks me dead or a traitor and might never know the truth.

At this point, I'm too exhausted to care.

He touches my waist, and I reach to grasp his hand with one of mine, but he smacks my hand aside.

"What do you think?" he asks.

I think he plans to kill me. Perhaps right here, now. And why not? Who's going to care?

The truly terrifying part of this realization is that my powers don't respond to it, because I don't care either.

"It's so perfect it shouldn't be real," I lie, because nothing about this situation is perfect.

He won't let me touch him, and nothing I try works. My kingdom will fold. My family could lose their freedoms or even their lives, and there's nothing I can do.

His hands tighten their hold.

"You intend to sacrifice me, then? Is that why you're so cold?" I ask, and I'm proud of how calm I sound.

The emperor's eyes flicked between mine. "There is the potential for that."

I feign ignorance. "What do you mean?"

He paces back and forth like a cornered Perja. "The Princess Raysa accused you of ransacking her hut."

"I didn't—"

He raises a hand to stop me and presses on. "That's not all. Not even a little bit. I know you met with the Isul Huya. I know you're trying to build allies against me. Tell me, why would I make someone empress who bands with the very group I've sought to destroy? Though you're good at making me question my decisions, confronting you about what you did was the sole purpose of this round and why I chose to meet with you first before any other princess. Because I knew this round would be short."

No one knew I visited the Isul Huya except Irenti and the Huya clan members I met with. The Huya might have told him, or Irenti herself, but the Huya are more likely. They had little fondness for me.

I scramble for an explanation that could save me from his accusation. "Well, it's a good thing I did, because I found out Princess Raysa plans to steal your throne the moment you marry or kill you before then."

If I stretch the truth a little, it doesn't make her less guilty.

His eyes snap to mine. "Who told you this?" Like the gathering clouds of a storm, his brows converge over his nose. "Did she?"

Not quite, but she might as well have, though the darkness in his expression makes me wonder if I should rephrase my statement. "The Huya did," I lie, because I've gone this far already. "She bragged about it to them."

Tired of this whole charade, I just want it to end.

He flicks a hand and a servant with shells around his neck emerges from the shadow of a nearby tree. "Bachue', bring me Princess Raysa's handmaid."

I didn't know he had a servant following us.

Bachue' jogs off as Emperor Huamar stops pacing and grips my arms, a whirlwind of emotion flooding through me at his touch. I can almost pinpoint reds and oranges swirling with flaming tongues. "I knew it," he says, his eyes flashing. "They want my throne, whatever it takes. You're all the same."

His wrath far eclipses any I've experienced from anyone I've known, even the High Priest of Cochas, when I was arrested at the festival. It burrows into my soul, interlaced with tiny threads of fear and betrayal. I grip the fear tight and it spreads through me, but with the energy I recognize at the edge of a cliff, preparing to jump. If I pull, I can calm him, or I can redirect his anger.

Toward what? Me? He noticed the last time I tried.

I let the energy go and sway as it drains out my toes into the rocks.

His hands squeeze my forearms, but he scowls over my shoulder at the rolling roads that lead to the city. "We're staying right here until she comes. You have to see."

He probably means to question Princess Raysa's servant. If he does, the servant will attempt to protect her princess. Irenti would do the same for me. An emperor won't believe a servant over a princess, will he?

A soft buzz fills my ears and I blink to keep my eyes open, but the emperor still holds me upright, the strength of his grip sending tingles down to my fingertips.

His red robes billow over the ridges of his chest as his eyes acquire the hungry, predatory look I saw in him in the throne room the day I arrived at Isul Urqu. My vision blurs, but his fingers keep me alert.

The trampling of feet rumbles against the road and I force my eyes up. Several guards haul the limp shape of a woman between them.

"Your name?" the emperor demands.

The servant stumbles forward, bowing, her colorful dress ripped and smeared with dirt. "I'm Braeila of Frigelles, my emperor, servant of the Princess Raysa."

The emperor jerks his head toward the cliff. "Toss her. Your princess will join you soon enough."

Eyes wide, she hunches over as the guards seize her by the shoulders. Her legs flail, her heels kicking up dirt, her fingernails clawing hard at the arms of the men who hold her so rivulets of red drip from their elbows. Fabric shreds against the stones.

I lurch forward, lifting a hand as if to help, but I'm too far to do anything.

The guards' arms move as one and her shrieks shatter the twilight as they fling her off the cliff, the horror of it crystalizing my bones.

The ground shakes, pebbles skitter, and the green vines and flowers split apart. The emperor flings me backward as rocks plummet from beneath my feet, my own scream blending into the rumble.

He saved me from falling, but only just.

The whole world trembles, down to my bones, my very core, as the shape of a head detaches itself from the side of the mountain, followed by a torso and legs. The giant turns, lifts the broken body of Princess Raysa's servant, and stuffs her legs into its mouth. Bones crack and blood squirts from its rock teeth, dribbling down its chin. It grins and bits of hair stick out between its massive stone teeth.

"Here are the defenders of Isul Urqu, princess," the emperor says, his voice deadly calm. "The legends are true. I have complete control over them. But they do have to eat." He stands, though his headdress has fallen to the ground, his curly hair matted against one side of his head. "This is what happens to the people who try to take what is mine."

CHAPTER TWENTY-ONE

IT DIDN'T HAPPEN.

I want to believe I imagined the whole thing, but I can't ignore the chunk of missing cliff where the rocks fell. I blink, but the image of the servant crushed between the giant's teeth is still burned into my eyelids, her limp hair curling over the giant's lip and her blood spurting outward to paint the mountainside.

My stomach roils.

The emperor and his servants retreat down the road toward the palace as I vomit over the side of the cliff. They leave me like a sack of molding potatoes, though they could have tossed me over the cliff too.

Princess Raysa's servant died because of me.

Stumbling from the edge, I turn and stagger up the road.

It doesn't matter if Sunqu gave me up; I need him. I need him to tell me it will all be fine, that I will live through this, that the servant's death is Princess Raysa's fault, not mine. I need him to tell me I can fix this, even if no one fixes death.

I promised my father I would make everything right, and I promised myself I'd save my family and kingdom. It's not too late. It can't be.

Dragging my feet down the same road the emperor took back into the city, I veer right and take an uphill path that leads me to the houses that overlook the cliffs and rivers surrounding Isul Urqu.

After hurrying past Sunqu's well, I pound my fist on his door, but the door remains shut tight, without the sounds of clanking pots, murmuring, or movement from inside. My knees buckle and I slide to the ground.

He should be here.

I imagined my life as so much more than this. I never wanted to be the person whose lies sent innocent servants to their deaths. If Sunqu can't absolve me from what happened, who can? Maybe I can't be absolved, and I'm not sure I can face that truth.

While simply plucking the guilt out is something I have the ability to do, I don't, because it belongs there. I deserve it.

Shame rises as a burning sensation in my throat.

I have to get out of here.

Running down the road, I trip, pick myself up, and stumble on. My hands and knees sting, but I wipe them on my dress. Blood smears the gold threads and precious stones, but I would rip the whole dress in half and not mourn it.

The stones on the road pass in a blur. Vines. Flower beds. They all meld together into greens and browns, with the occasional shadow from the flying Folqus that cools my skin.

Somewhere, between these houses or beneath the hills, or at the end of the road, there must be an answer. The path curves, opening into the town square. Merchants stand behind tables of fresh herbs like the non-poisonous ones the emperor tossed in his soup. I hurry past, but the flap of the last tent reveals the emperor's mystic as she tends her flowers, standing beside the squat man I ignored before.

She ties the flap back and returns to pruning flower stems.

Veering toward her, I pick up my pace.

My breath comes in gusts when I stop in front of her cart, gulping several times to wet my throat.

She looks up and gasps. "Are you well, child?"

I snatch her wrist. Oddly enough, my powers sense no emotion from her, though I know she's surprised at seeing me.

"You're the emperor's mystic," I say. "You understand him as well as anyone. Help me."

Her lips close over her brilliant white teeth.

"He knows I went to the Isul Huya for help," I say. "He thinks I betrayed him. How can I prove myself trustworthy? And how do I stop him from killing anyone else?"

Comprehension dawns in her eyes. "I haven't known the emperor to give anyone a second chance."

I let go of her, bumping into another cart as I step back. I won't allow myself to fall into despair. There must be something I can do, though my brain fails to come up with a solution.

The squat little man who usually accompanies the mystic circles the cart, touching my elbow with a muddy finger. "Heliray, grant me power," he says in a low murmur.

My anguish seeps out of me, replaced, instead, by the calm of slow-moving rivers and untouched valleys.

Still touching me, he bows his head. "Be still, Ma Roca."

Here, again, is the title of respect the Dragunche gave me with my ancestral name.

The beaches of my youth pass before my eyes. The water that crashes on sand. The reds and pinks on the horizon. Mungacu slithering over the surf. I have only to stretch out my hands and lose myself in the serenity of those memories.

A stab of ice breaks through the calm, and I snatch my arm away. He used my own power against me.

"Who are you?" I demand.

He puts his bone pipe to his lips beneath his hooked nose and bites down on it, several dark holes showing where his front teeth fell out. Around his neck, he wears a necklace with horns on it. "I'm a friend. One of several, in fact. I can help you learn to use your power."

"I don't need your help."

He might be able to tap into powers like mine, but I own them, and they've been a part of me since birth.

"You do. You need to know how to defend yourself. Just as importantly, you need to know what to expect when you do. If you want to save yourself, your family, your kingdom, or anyone else, you must either marry the emperor and subdue him or find a way to remove him from the throne altogether."

My brain struggles to digest everything he's saying, and everything he's not saying. "Are you suggesting that I kill him?"

It's heresy. He could get us both killed.

Suddenly, I've gone from trying to make alliances to make myself the more attractive choice, to doing exactly what the emperor feared I would do. And it's because it's the best course of action.

It's what he would do in my place.

The man with the pipe eyes me with an eyebrow raised, as if surprised by my words. "He's afraid of you. When you use your power, you manipulate him, and he feels it. He knows something is wrong, and it leaves a void in its wake, which fills with the fear you feed on. The emperor is distrustful. When you toy with his emotions, you arouse his suspicion. He didn't consider what happened until afterward, but when he did, he became obsessed. When you went to the

Isul Huya, everything he feared was confirmed."

The mystic warned me back when this all started. She said I had more friends than I expected, but not in the places I looked.

While everything this man says holds truth, he knows more than he should. He doesn't feel like a friend. Instead, he makes my skin crawl. Though my skin was crawling before I got here. I must have lost my mind completely.

"Who are you?" I ask again. "Why should I trust you? Why would I have any reason to believe you?"

Because if there's anyone I shouldn't trust, it's the emperor's mystic and the man in rags that she associates with.

"You need to learn the bounds of your power," the man continues, as if I haven't spoken. "You need to learn how far you can prod without a person knowing. You stepped too far with the emperor, Yakua. There's nothing you can do to rectify it, except to understand the full breadth of your power so you don't do it unwittingly again." He takes a pull on his pipe and smoke envelopes his head as he exhales.

"He's a mystic from the mines of Hlos," the woman mystic cuts in, "and a refugee. One of many, actually. They're all here," she tilts her head to look at me out of the corner of her eye, "for you."

This man doesn't know me.

The emperor's mystic gives me an understanding half-smile. "Come back when you're ready, child. Think on your decision. We come here often. As for the emperor, I don't think he's able to forgive any more than he's capable of love, and it's not worth your time to search those avenues."

I scan her face for a sneer or any indication she means to hurt me, but she looks sincere.

"I'll think on it," I say in a voice close to a whisper, though I doubt I'll resort to allying myself in a war against the emperor with an impoverished refuge and a rogue mystic.

Outside of these two, I'm not completely friendless and, though I've almost forgotten her, I still have Irenti. While I haven't trusted her in the past, the emperor knows my every move already. There's nothing more to hide. Perhaps she might have a suggestion.

Stumbling toward the road, I hike my dress above my ankles and hurry toward the palace, climbing stairs to reach my hut on the other side. When I thrust aside the curtained door, Irenti sits on the floor, my ruined blankets spread across her lap. She holds a long, fibrous strand of thread between two fingertips, but fumbles it as she looks up. "Princess, what happened? What did you do to your dress?"

Reeling toward her, I grip both her hands in mine. "Irenti, you're the only person I know to ask. The emperor found out about me going to the Isul Huya. He threatened me. He threw a servant off the cliff and—" I gulp as the image of the woman falling returns, fresh to my mind. Then her scream and the crunch of her bones as the giant chewed on her broken body.

I shudder.

Irenti touches my hand, her own brow creasing with regret. "I know," she says. "Princess, the emperor is not a trusting man. He's ruthless when he feels threatened."

"How do I fix this?" I squeeze her fingers.

She purses her lips. "I think there's something you need to hear. Or something I should tell you. If I was a real friend to you, I'd have said it a long time ago. Maybe it will help you understand."

"What do you mean?"

"I'm from the mountains outside of Isul Urqu, but I've lived in Isul my whole life. In the wars before the original kingdom fell, Huamar's giants were ruthless. His general killed without mercy.

The king's family was taken and—" She chokes on her words. "The daughters were disposed of, the king brutally murdered. Many young girls from noble families were brought to the palace. Some became slaves. The families that kept their fortunes, lost their children."

Listening to Irenti recalls the original whispers I heard of the emperor that I dismissed after meeting him. It evokes the dread.

"I watched it happen," she says, pausing to take a shaky breath as the curtains of my hut swoosh open.

A panting servant stands in the doorway. "The emperor would like to make a last-minute announcement." He takes a deep breath. "You have been requested at the palace and are expected," another breath, "right now."

The emperor doesn't trust me. He barely even likes me. If he is to choose a princess to die on the fly, it will be me and no one else. The servant disappears and I lean against the wall, supporting my weight so I don't collapse.

I failed my kingdom.

I might as well have died from the Cayuhu.

Towing my feet forward to the palace, Irenti follows close behind, but not close enough to lend any comfort.

I can run, but I won't get far. The emperor watches with his spies. Besides, after this failure, I'm not sure I want to live, even if I could survive the treacherous journey through the mountains alone.

The guards open the palace door and stare straight ahead, past me, as if I'm a ghost already.

As I shuffle into the emperor's throne room, a servant with shells around his neck stops me with a hand. Apparently, they don't have time for stones of burden because the screen rises and reveals the emperor on his throne, glaring down at us, hands clenched tight. His eyes meet mine and his expression darkens further.

But then his eyes move to Princess Raysa.

"I've made my next choice and will make this announcement myself," he says. "I have heard a series of questionable accusations against Princess Raysa of Frigelles from multiple sources and have determined Princess Raysa the next to be sacrificed for Mirchira and the good of the empire."

My head turns against my better judgment toward Princess Raysa, the horror in her eyes stilling any relief I might have felt. My powers sense her fear as it emanates from her skin and charges my blood. Her bottom lip trembles, though she pins it with her teeth. She stands with her back straight, and for the first time since I've met her, a sliver of respect burrows beneath my skin.

Fatigue hits me as the energy I receive from her fear dwindles. My knees wobble and I lock them to stay upright as guards surround her, securing her arms behind her back. Her eyes meet mine and I go cold. Not because her expression is cruel, but because it isn't.

Though I don't consider what I said to the emperor a complete lie, Raysa will die because of what I told him.

But if she doesn't die, I'll be on the altar next. If her kingdom doesn't fall, mine will. If her family lives, mine won't see me or anyone else again.

Pressure rises inside me. It fills my ears.

The room empties except for two guards dressed in white robes with red sashes. They wait by the door, spears in hand as if they're concerned I might flee.

When I first came to Isul Urqu and saw the stone floors of the throne room, the same terrible fear didn't seep into my bones like it does now. Like it does every time his servants call me for another announcement.

Irenti pulls at my sleeve. "Princess, you have to go to the temple.

Do you need my assistance?"

They think me weak.

When I pull away, she continues gripping my arm, sliding a note into my hand, and closing my fist over it. "I was told to give this to you," she whispers, and slips toward the line of servants.

I grip the note tight. It could be anything: a comforting message or an accusation. Perhaps I deserve the second. Striding between the guards, I head down the hill to the river and step aboard another boat, but the sparkle of the water doesn't hold the charm it used to. The skies are too blue.

The guards watch us go from the shore. There will be more guards when we stop at the temple, or watchers who survey us wherever we float. But for now, the boat guide stares ahead, and the other princess looks out with a distant expression.

I unfold the note and smooth it over my leg, not knowing if I want to read it or not, but I must know what it says. The quick, frenzied writing addresses me in bold letters.

Princess Nalia,

The emperor killed my servant and I'm certain I will be next. Please, help me. I have a daughter they don't know about. My family won't protect her, so I had no choice but to bring her and my servant here. They look at my daughter as a disgrace. Zita was conceived when I was very young, and I've tried to keep her out of sight as much as possible. To everyone else, she is the daughter of my servant, who is now dead. My servant claimed her the day she was born. I want to leave her in your care. Keep her safe.

If anyone can win this contest, it's you. I never liked you, and I'm not asking you to save me. But please save my little girl.

She's waiting by the river—you know the one.

Raysa

A child, possibly as old as Naya.

I hunch over my knees and a hand pats my back—probably the princess beside me, but it only makes the guilt worse.

Raysa hates me. She shouldn't come to me, of all people.

I sentenced her to death and fed her young daughter to the same fate I faced as a child. Young Zita will be motherless and alone, just as I was. After her mother is sacrificed, I'll have to face her, or let her die too.

CHAPTER TWENTY-TWO

THE SIMPLE PATTERN OF the dress Sunqu gave me billows against my shins. In any other temple, the material would be stunning with its glossy silver threads. Yet no pretty fabric can take away the awful dread that cages my lungs as I step down the staircase into a wide circle of stones, the roof opening to a misted sky.

The mist isn't white or black, but a solid gray. So solid that even the gods must struggle to discern right or wrong in the midst of it. The altar is scrubbed so it shines an off-white, like no blood has ever marred it.

Princess Raysa sits on the ground with glazed eyes, her hair long enough to flow off her back onto the grass. She doesn't look up as I pass. Doesn't struggle or scream.

The priest stands behind the altar, preparing Mirchira's talismans while a line of people watch, including Sunqu, his cheeks stretched and pale, beside the emperor. The emperor doesn't move until I climb onto the ledge to sit beside him.

I have to try something. Raysa doesn't deserve to die this way. None of us do.

If I can spare her daughter the pain of losing a mother, I will.

Surely, the emperor can be reasoned with, or I can use my magic to temper him, and then convince him this is a mistake.

Picking up his hand, I try not to flinch as I kiss his knuckles.

When he turns toward me, the frown lines on his brow fade to smooth skin.

"My emperor." Touching his cheek, I'm relieved to sense that the anger he harbored before has gone. Though I'm not sure why he has allowed me a free pass, I'm grateful for it because it gives me an opening.

The priest opens his mouth, inhales, and chants as a servant leads a line of deer in and releases them by Raysa. She sits so still, even as one of the deer lays beside her, no sign of cognizance crossing her features.

Rubbing the back of the emperor's hand to tweak his emotional threads, I imagine Manco on my palanquin, his head bowed with shame; Irenti braiding my hair, on the verge of tears. I wish I could reach out to them the way I touch the emperor now. Instead, I release the compassion I felt into the emperor, but the emotion doesn't slide through the spiritual funnel that links us the way I want it to, so I push harder, despite the risk.

He clasps my hand in both of his.

"Emperor Huamar." I swallow hard. "I know what I told you about Princess Raysa, but I was misled. I have since discovered she is no danger to you and had no plans to steal your kingdom." I speak under my breath so no one else can hear. "There's no reason to sacrifice her today. I would be glad for Raysa's help as a maidservant. I feel terrible for my mistake. Could we not sacrifice the deer instead?"

The emperor stands. "Princess Nalia, walk with me."

He might ask me more questions and I'll have to think of answers. He'll want to know why I lied to him or where I got my information from, none of which I have solid answers for. Still, I follow him out of the temple, up to the higher tiers and into the thickest mists where I barely see my hands, much less breathe.

A short gust pushes the clouds aside so his shrewd face appears. "Princess, you surprise me."

I fight the urge to cover my face and instead raise my chin.

"Please, emperor, let her go. She's innocent."

"She would have died, anyway."

I wind my fingers through his. "Why though? Why does she need to die? Why do any of them need to die?"

A muscle in his jaw flexes. "The gods take whom they will."

Pulling in my power, I push compassion into him again. "The gods can't take what they aren't given. Show her mercy. What could her death do for you?"

He gives me a sharp look. "Her death proves to the Huya that they should fear me. That I can take life as easily as I give it. That if I don't want love, I won't have it. It shows her kingdom and the king who leads it that they are at my disposal. And that I will dispose of them if I choose to." His hands tighten their grip. "You don't know what it is, Nalia, to be afraid at every moment that you might not wake up in the morning. I'm sure your family loves you. My mother and father loved me too until they discovered I could take the throne."

He might live in fear, but so do the princesses he brought to his doorstep.

"Do you not see how incredibly cruel you're being?" I ask.

And then, too late, the implications of what I've said strikes me.

But as I look at the fiery, unyielding expression in those green and brown eyes, I don't care what becomes of me, or what I must do. Or what anyone thinks when I've left the empire in ruins.

I came for my family—to prove I deserve to be among them. To prove I belong on the rug at their table. But as much as I want to belong, I can't tear another family apart. I can't live with what I pretend to be. If he stripped off the layers I built around myself to please everyone, what will be left of me? I won't know myself.

"I do," he says. "But does it matter?"

I change tactics. If he doesn't care about being cruel, he certainly cares about power.

"But why not give life rather than take it? Would that not make you more powerful? Utilize your strength at its greatest potential by using your power for what it was meant to be used for."

"I'll decide how my power is meant to be used, not you." His hand touches the small of my back without warmth. "It's time to go, or we'll miss it. You're the only one who truly watches. So, of course, you must be there."

I don't want to go. I want to run all the way to Cochas. Or to Sunqu's house, to hide behind his beautiful well and hope no one finds me.

Either that, or I want to find the closest dagger.

He tugs me down the stairs as the priest slices the neck of the last sheep. It lets out a dying bleat and lays limp on the stone until they roll it to the side. Then a man picks up Princess Raysa and carries her to where the sheep's blood is still stuck to the altar.

She meets my gaze, eyes pleading.

"May the gods live on in the stones of our altars by the blood of our people." The haunting words of the High Priest ring out.

The emperor diverts his eyes.

With one slice of the High Priest's knife, the skin of her neck rips open, and blood spatters over the top of the altar, the harsh crimson vivid against the flat gray of the stone. The princess makes a gurgling sound, twitches, and lays still as her beautiful, wavy hair fans to the floor.

I stagger down the final stair and the emperor grabs my arm.

Across the room, Sunqu stands, but he's too far to do anything.

Shoving the emperor away, I turn and throw up on the walls of the temple.

The emperor exhales loudly as I lean my forehead against the cool stones.

"You may go," he says. As he motions to his servants, they drag the bodies of Raysa and the deer over the edge of the mountainside, probably to be eaten like Raysa's servant. The mountain trembles and they're gone, as if they never existed. As if Princess Raysa's daughter never had a mother at all.

After we're dismissed, I take the first boat back to my hut from the outskirts of the city and sit on the edge of the wooden seat.

The only future worse than dying like Raysa did is one where I must marry the emperor and wake up every morning beside him. I'll have to overlook the neglect he throws my way and crouch in his shadow for the rest of my life as the princess he let live and the princess he took because he could.

Princess Asari, the last remaining princess beside myself, gazes with sad eyes at the slow-moving water, an arm's length across from me. If I can't figure out how to rise against the emperor, I'll have to send her to her death too, and learn to live with it.

She moves closer, wraps an arm around me, and rests her forehead on my shoulder. "I know how you feel," she says.

Normally, I'd scoff. How could she? I don't like being touched by anyone, especially someone I don't know or want to know. But the muscles in my back release and I can't keep myself upright anymore, least of all retreat to the bitter loneliness I've known since I came here.

Asari squeezes my arm. "It's not your fault."

But it is.

For a princess, failure isn't a failure for one, it's a failure for thousands. This princess wouldn't be so kind without a reason, and there are far too many reasons to pick from. For now, I want to forget them all.

I try to give her a reassuring smile, but my cheek only twitches. If she knew the news I have to deliver to a child who prays without hope for her mother's return, she won't bother comforting me.

As the boat knocks against the dock, the boatman offers his hand and helps me out. I leave the other princess behind as I traverse the path to the river where I spoke to Raysa after the gem from my necklace was stolen, my legs heavier with each step. The trees part and a small form sitting on a rock stands taller.

She faces me. As I approach, her big eyes fill with tears. She must be younger than Naya, but her expression holds a maturity and sadness Naya doesn't have.

If I'm here, it means her mother won't return. She must know that. I could say a few words, or her name at least. But a guilty lump lodges in my throat as she falls to her knees and buries her face in her hands.

Nothing I say will change anything. I can't comfort her, can't offer hope.

Time mends all wounds. That's what the healer told my father the night my mother left us forever. *Move on with your life, Father Roca. Let her memory die and be happy.*

He moved on, but I never forgot.

CHAPTER TWENTY-THREE

THEY TOLD ME MY MOTHER was sick. The healer came to our door the night she fell ill and warned my father she wouldn't make it. My father didn't believe him. Nothing ever stood against my mother, especially not a stomachache. But the next day, my mother didn't rise from her bed, and I cupped her cold, stiff fingers in my hands.

I wouldn't be able to ask her advice again. She couldn't arrange my marriage. She wouldn't hear from my teachers how well I kept track of the names of the gods or see the rugs I weaved with more intricate patterns than I ever attempted before.

And now Zita will know that feeling.

Despite the heat outside, a chill spreads down my arms and legs every time I glance at little Zita curled up in the corner of my hut. She has refused to speak to me in the short weeks since we met, but now she won't look at me, and I deserve it.

I didn't save her mother and I, alone, am responsible for her mother's and caretaker's deaths. If she can't ask her mother for advice again, no one else can carry the blame. I will carry it to my grave.

Irenti tidies the skins and blankets, washes the linens, and avoids my eyes. Maybe she's disappointed in me. Or angry I brought Zita here, but I haven't brought up the subject. However Irenti feels, Zita will stay, though it's only a matter of time before the emperor finds out she's here.

I want to trust Irenti, and I don't think she's capable of sending a child to her death. But I need to find Zita a safer place in case I'm wrong.

Light creeps through the curtains of my hut. Rather than wash my face and let Irenti change me, I push the curtains aside and leave without a destination. I can't face Zita's silence anymore. I haven't slept in days because every time I close my eyes, I see my family in chains and my throat on the altar. I see Raysa's neck as the High Priest slices it open.

Meandering down the path that circles the palace, I swerve into the trees, heading to the waterfall, but hesitate at the fork.

A month ago, I would have hiked to the bridge, ready to jump, thinking I held a few plays, not realizing I had nothing to support me, and forgetting the rocks at the bottom.

The emperor enjoyed when I played a fool.

The rocks beneath my sandals press into my heels, through the stiff leather, as I turn around. I won't come here again.

Facing the palace, I pick up my pace. I have to marry the emperor for my kingdom, for my family, and for my own survival, but my mother's voice rings in my head.

Be with someone you respect, Yakua.

She regretted marrying my father. I sensed it in the way she spoke to him and in every bit of advice she gave me when he turned his back. Despite his faults, my father is a good man. My mother said to marry someone I respected, but she missed an important part. I want to be with someone who respects me too.

Though I must save my kingdom, I can't marry the emperor, so I'll find another way.

"Princess?"

Jerking to a stop, I look up. I've come close to the huts again, but they're empty now, except for one occupied by the last princess I have to beat if I want to live.

She followed me.

With long eyelashes and a sweet smile, she doesn't belong in this grim mesa of a city. Especially not after everything we've faced. "I'm Princess Asari of the Kingdom Thalas. I'm sorry I didn't say much to you before, but I've watched you walk up here and down by the river many times. I know what's bothering you. But you couldn't have done anything to prevent what happened to Princess Raysa. You weren't the one who ordered her death."

Not wanting to hear why I don't deserve my guilt when she doesn't know the full story, I turn away, but she snatches my wrist.

"Princess, please."

Compassion, fear, and anger emanate from her fingertips, the emotions tingling in my arm. "I didn't mean to scare you. I know how wary you are. But you need to know that the emperor is watching you. He's watching me too, especially now. You must be careful."

I should wrench my arm away. I have every reason to distrust her over everyone else. If I live, she'll die, but I was wrong about Princess Raysa. I've been wrong about a lot of things.

Asari dips her head and reaches into a shallow pocket in her dress. "My servant found this," she withdraws a fist, "in the dirt outside Princess Kuna's hut." She opens her hand and an emerald rolls over her open palm. "Is it yours?"

I lurch forward, snatching it from her and clutching it to my chest beneath the broken necklace I now wear. A momentary relief sweeps through me, emotion burning the corners of my eyes. "Thank you." She can't know how much it means to me.

She drops her hand, flushing. "I believe it was another of the emperor's tests. One of his servants convinced the Princess of Joco that rampaging our huts and destroying our things would put her ahead. Princess Kuna was scared, and the emperor wanted to see how we would react. It's a game, Nalia. Just a game. And I don't want to play anymore."

The relief fades to a nasty lump of cold, hard anger in my gut. "How did you discover this?"

"Servants talk, including mine. This stone didn't belong to me, and Princess Raysa said it wasn't hers either. I figured it had to belong to you."

We are rivals. This woman has no reason to be kind. It makes everything worse, like there are cliffs I failed to scale and new heights I might have reached if I hadn't hiked alone.

Princess Asari meets my eyes, unflinching beneath my gaze. "The emperor has done this before with the daughters of the Isul Huya. It's why they hate him so much. He wants to prove himself right—that we're as small and selfish as he makes us out to be. He has no intention of marrying any of us. He wants everyone to know how little power we have against him."

If she speaks the truth, the King of Cochas sent me to fail. To die.

Because I was the one person who might have been able to make a difference and was also disposable. If I died, I would live on as a traitor in Cochas, and the king and high priest would say I deserved it because of who my mother was.

The injustice of this reality stings, and I bite my lip until it bleeds to hold the anger in.

But I'm not helpless. I have my powers.

"I don't expect either of us will survive this," she continues. "But if you do survive, I want you to know I don't blame you for any of this." She clears her throat and blinks several times. "Whether I live or die, there's nothing to forgive."

She expects to be killed, but here she stands, telling me not to worry.

"Why give me back my mother's stone, then? Why bother?"

Her mouth twitches. "Because the gods live on in the stones. And in us too."

After she leaves, I return to my hut with quick steps. I must speak to Zita, whether she wants me to or not. If the emperor has no intention of marrying me, I have a deadline for her care and safety.

I kneel beside the bed skins where she sits with her head bowed and wet my lips.

"Zita?" I ask.

She shifts her toes but doesn't look at me.

"I want you to know—" My voice breaks. She needs to hear hope in my voice, so I try again. "I want you to know I'll do everything I can to protect you. I'm sorry for the terrible things that have happened to you. It's my fault—more than you can possibly know. I promise I'll do everything in my power to—" To what? I can't set things right. I can't bring her mother back. "To be whatever you need. I know I can never replace them, but I'll be here for you. As much as I can be."

Zita's shoulders shake and I freeze. She won't like me watching. I start to stand but hesitate. When my mother died, Sunqu sat beside me. While he often doesn't say the right thing, he's always willing to listen when I need him to. I sit down again and wrap my arms around my knees, a silent presence at her side. She doesn't lean into me, but she doesn't ask me to leave either. She just cries.

A cough comes from the doorway. A servant in the white and red uniform, wearing the seashell necklace of the emperor, bows. "Princess, I'm here to announce that the emperor has decided on the last round. It will be announced by Ma Drea at breakfast. Please be punctual." He bows himself out and the curtain flaps shut.

When I squeeze Zita's shoulders tight, the fear doesn't come. I can face this last round of the princess contest. I can save myself, my kingdom, and Princess Asari. Though my powers haven't worked against the emperor's stubborn anger, I can harness my magic at the level my mother was known to use it—if I can figure out how she did it.

But my future can still be the altar and I won't allow Zita to follow me, not if I can save at least one person if I fail everyone else.

I exhale. "Zita, follow me."

Her cheeks pale a few shades further, but she trails behind me as I touch my mother's necklace, the center stone back where it belongs on my neck. I lead Zita out of my hut, down the hill, into the village, and through the winding streets past the marketplace. As we hurry up another hill to Sunqu's home, footsteps scatter pebbles down the road and Sunqu himself strides toward us.

His pace quickens as he nears. His hair, which has grown longer in the last few weeks, flutters in a determined breeze. Exertion colors his cheeks and sharpens his gaze.

"What's wrong?" he asks, out of breath.

Too overwhelmed to speak, I don't slow, but crash into him, wrapping my arms around his waist, and holding him tight. I wish I could rewind time to the last night we spent in the mountains together and live it on repeat.

He folds into me, his face in my hair. "You're right to hate me, Yakua."

I pull away so I can see his face, the dimple in his chin, the wave in his hair. "I never hated you."

But he shakes his head. "I lied the day you came to my hut."

The gap between us widens as he drags his thumb down the length of my jaw to my chin. "I came to Isul Urqu to be worthy of you, to gain a name and reputation you'd want to be part of." He lets go. "I hoped to return a new man. But everything changed when the King of Cochas sent you with me. I realized I had to put myself in the best position I could to keep you out of harm's way. But I gave up, Yakua. You seem so well suited to this life and didn't need me in it, so I tried to move on."

He reaches for my hand, and I grip it tight, holding to his words.

I never imagined our time together having an expiration date.

"No matter what I did," he continues, "I couldn't forget you. Your courage, your drive, and determination inspire me every single day."

He came for me, stayed for me.

But I can't forget what I came to Sunqu for.

I grasp Zita's hand behind me. "Sunqu, I—"

Unaware of Zita, he keeps talking. "We can run away from this. Perhaps among the clans northward, I can give you the life you always wanted."

"Sunqu," I repeat, stopping him.

He blinks, his eyes bouncing between mine, wanting to understand.

I want to run away, to live the life in Cochas we should have had together, even if it means decaying floors, thatched roofs, and a clan who curses my name. I might have been happy with him. It only makes my answer harder.

"Listen to me," I say.

His face falls as he sees my refusal written in my expression. "I can't watch you die," he says, shaking his head. "Don't make me. This is not a time where I'll sit on the beach while you jump."

Clutching his wrist so he doesn't draw away, I pull Zita gently forward.

"My decision has nothing to do with you, but has everything to do with the people I'm accountable for. My duty to our kingdom hasn't changed. Besides, the emperor wouldn't let me go. He'll send his guards and giants after us. Please understand, Sunqu. I won't be able to live with myself if I left."

His eyes fill with dismay.

"I have a plan. Even if the chance of it working is slim, I have to try it."

"Let me help you," he pleads.

I unpeel myself from him and his hands drop to his sides. "I have something more important to ask of you. I need you to meet someone." Drawing Zita to my side, I introduce her to him. "This is Princess Raysa's daughter, Zita."

His gaze falls on the little girl.

"I need you to protect her," I say. "If I die, she dies with me, but I promised I would keep her safe. I want you to leave just as you planned, Sunqu, but without me. I want you to take Zita instead."

"You won't come with us?"

"No. Please trust that I know what I'm doing."

The muscles in his neck and shoulders tense, but he nods. After rearranging his face and wiping away the pain, he faces the girl and bows. "I'm sorry, little one. I didn't mean to ignore you." He offers her his hand. "I'll do my best to protect you. I give you my word."

Zita lowers her gaze to the ground as he takes her small hand from mine. His forearms flex as he squeezes it.

"She's packed and ready," I say. "You need to leave now. Don't come back. Get our families and take them as far from Cochas as possible. Take them to the north, or to a free territory. Take them somewhere safe."

"I will."

"Take care of Naya for me. Tell her I love her." I take a step back, though my heart wants to go with them and experience Cochas and my family again alongside Sunqu and Zita. I want to see the ocean again and look out at the horizon knowing that it doesn't matter who in the village despises me. Because the world is big, and I know who I am within it.

He smiles with sad eyes. "I'm proud of you, Yakua."

I don't know how long I've waited to hear those words, or why I want them so much, but I can't recall ever having heard them before, and they fill empty spaces I didn't know I had.

And yet they're not enough, because I need them from myself first.

I must carry the weight of a kingdom, just as a princess would. As much as I wish I could bottle the memories of Isul Urqu and toss them away, they have forced me to grow. I wouldn't give them up for anything.

If I come out of this alive, I'll have to thank the emperor because he showed me what I'm made of.

"I've loved you my whole life, too, Sunqu. I'm sorry I didn't show it like I should have." It doesn't change anything now, but he should know.

He only draws Zita closer.

CHAPTER TWENTY-FOUR

AFTER LEAVING SUNQU, I HURRY through town, checking over my shoulder for pursuers as I head to the village center where traders from surrounding kingdoms gather to sell their wares. The mystic from Mira-Tamya sells flowers from her usual cart, her gray hair braided with beads, her floral-engraved staff at her side.

Her wrinkled business partner sits with his legs folded, pipe in hand. As I near, the man's features grow distinct, his nose hooked, beads dangling from his hat, his robes layered, and horns that hang from a necklace around his neck.

My determination ebbs at the sight of him and I pause before I can command my legs to continue. I've already made the decision to do this. I can't turn back now.

A group of customers enter the tent and the mystic who sells flowers hurries to assist them, but the man with the horned necklace looks past the new customers at me.

He winks.

Gulping down an acrid taste, I force my legs forward, folding my arms to hide my unease as I stop in front of him.

The flower mystic trusts him, so I should too, even if I don't like it.

"I'm ready to learn about my powers."

His smile grows. "Are you?"

"I am. You promised you could help."

"That's right." He sucks on his pipe. "I'm happy to teach you, but we must go somewhere private," he takes the pipe from between his teeth and uses it to point to the tent behind me, "as you're being followed."

As I flip around, the shadow of a man ducks behind a tent. I thought I was careful, but sneaking isn't on my list of first-rate abilities.

The man offers me his pipe when I face him again. "Take a puff," he says.

Shoving it aside, I pull a face. "I don't smoke." I didn't come to relax and laugh my worries away. That won't help anyone.

One of the mystic's customers inspects the flowers at the stand beside me. The man with the pipe motions for me to follow him toward the corner of the tent, offering the pipe again. "You really do need to take a puff. Unlike you, I rely on herbs and rituals to do magic. This herb will connect you to your spirit and release your hold on the physical world. It will allow me to lead you away unseen."

The hollowed bone handle looks creepier than my mother's necklace, but I came all this way to trust him, and I don't have alternatives. I take the pipe, inhale, and cough.

He steadies me with a firm grip. "You'll get used to it."

Shoving the pipe back into his hands, I wipe my own hands on my dress. I don't want to touch that thing again.

"This way." He checks over his shoulder as he leads me out of the square, past rows of smaller, more worn houses and shops, and down into a ravine. The river that cuts through the steep hills churns with foul, black water. Burial graves, like the one they dug for my mother by the river, pockmark the sides of the hills. It looks like they've been re-dug and robbed.

I point to the holes. "Are we going through those?"

"No, we're going down the river a ways, that's all. We're very close." He vaults over a set of rocks, as lightly as a man half his age, while the horns hanging from his neck dance across his chest.

A group of people, young and old, huddle at the river's side where it bends and changes direction. They all wear layered robes, just like the man with the pipe, and have similar horned necklaces and emerald jewelry with snakes, much like the necklace around my own neck.

The man beside me pulls an oval emerald from his pocket—exactly like the one in my mother's necklace. "I have one too," he says, guessing my thoughts.

My mother kept a lot of secrets.

She must have been a part of this group, or worshipped the same goddess, though I haven't seen any of these people in my life before coming to this city.

"Who are you?" I ask the man leading me.

He bows with his fist over his heart. "My name is Amaru. I'm the head of Heliray's mystic clan. We used to worship her in the mines of Hlos but were evicted when the emperor took over. We came here, to the capital, where no one knows who we are. We can hide here in plain sight, because there are enough people in the city to make our presence unremarkable. Especially if we look like beggars. No one dares approach us."

Associating with the mystics of the god of death will be the final demise of my reputation. My kingdom hates me, my father already thinks me a traitor, but they all depend on me, including Sunqu and

Zita. If I can influence the emperor at the same level my mother could, I can manipulate him into marrying me and either lock him up or make him a puppet. If I do, I'll be stuck at his side for the rest of my life. But I can save the empire, my kingdom, my family, and servants like Irentl. I can give the kingdoms back their thrones and undo the damage wrought by Emperor Huamar's fear and greed.

I choose my words carefully. "How are you associated with my mother?"

The clan told me she persuaded people and deceived them. She had a way of convincing them to do things they wouldn't have done on their own. She made friendly connections in Cochas with the Caya clan, the family of the king. She even convinced one of the emperor's close cousins to invite her to their home. A few weeks later, his son found him lifeless on the floor. My father confronted her, but she denied any association. A few months later, she died too.

Amaru inclined his head toward the sitting crowd. "Come, we will speak more with my clan. Though none of us are related to you or your mother, we knew your mother well. We used to worship together."

I should be excited to meet people who knew my mother in her younger years, but my disquiet outweighs my curiosity. Nothing he can say will make me want to be here.

A woman stands, lighting a fire in the center of the gathering, and then a man flings a plant into the flames. Smoke spirals upward as if the gray coverage is more important than warmth.

I fold my legs and sit on the ground as they do, Amaru settling beside me, his shoulders hunching. Again, he offers his pipe. "You'll need a bit more."

I try not to look as I take another puff, my chest compressing with unease. The pipe feels wrong, the crowd of people too silent.

Several of them watch me closely, their expressions empty. "What are we doing? What's the point of this?"

He points to the sky. "We're summoning a Folqu."

"A Folqu? Why?" I cough on smoke as it billows.

My chest expands and my muscles relax like they haven't done in weeks, like I can walk out of my skin and go anywhere or be anyone. I can shed all the warnings, advice, and scolding I carry from my mother, yet be closer to her than I've been in my life.

My stomach flips and pain shoots through my abdomen. I clutch my waist and fold over, prepared to retch but unable to, and slump to the ground instead.

A hand touches my back. "The Folqu will take you where you need to go. They only come if you're close to death, so we have to bring you to the brink. The herbs enable us to do this. Don't be afraid."

Despite his assurance, a muted horror freezes my insides, down to my fingertips.

I'm dying?

He's literally killing me on purpose.

A cool shadow falls over my skin, followed by the cry of a bird and the flapping of wings. As the sounds grow louder, I strain to look up. Then a pair of feathered wings with intricate gray designs swallow the blue of the sky. Its chest dangles with a shredded netting of veins and sinews, a black velvet beak snapping shut as it stares with beady red eyes.

Claws clamp my arms painfully tight. My navel jerks and my feet lift from the ground.

My own scream resounds through my ears as the fire and all the people around it shrink. The Folqu carries me upward, my body limp in its grasp. The world spins while blues and greens mix with black. I close my eyes until my toes brush dirt and the claws let go.

I'm not by the river anymore, nor in the sky. The Folqu took me somewhere unnatural.

I'm standing in musty darkness, cold and still like the caverns beneath the cliffs in Cochas, rot and mildew pressing in from all sides. Everywhere I turn, black emptiness stretches on.

The lightheadedness in my head fades the longer I stand still. The Folqus are known for carrying the dying to the land of the dead. If the legends are true, the mystics of Heliray must have trapped me in Uru Hlocha.

Rushing to the stone walls, I run my fingers along lines of sharp ridges. As the wall goes on, I run alongside it, dragging my fingers until my skin breaks. Still, I continue, because there must be a way out.

I shouldn't have been so foolish as to trust the man with the pipe when every instinct, except my own desperation, warned me not to. But what choice did I have? What else could I have done?

I did the right thing, wherever it landed me. I must hold on to that thread or lose my sanity.

The sun doesn't penetrate the caverns of Uru Hlocha, according to the stories of the gods. I might never enjoy the warmth of the sun on my skin again.

They say that at the beginning of time, there were three gods. The god of the sun, Isul, the goddess of the earth, Hlocha, and the goddess of the moon. In those days, the moon was as beautiful as the earth, and the gods looked at the moon in envy.

Isul and Hlocha met in secret and formed new gods to enrich their worlds and rival the moon, but when they created Mirchira, he formed his own creations out of rock and made the first giants, and then the first humans.

But the humans died, and there was no god willing to rule them.

Thus, Isul and Hlocha turned to Heliray, goddess of the moon, and begged her to relinquish her celestial throne for one beneath the earth. They promised her the power of persuasion to control the mortals under her care and, for whatever reason, she accepted. When she abandoned the moon, the moon lost its splendor and became a wasteland, a mirror of the underworld.

I'm in her realm now, the realm beneath the earth, and there's no way out because there was never meant to be one. Not unless the goddess herself lets me go, or the Folqu comes back to find me. But the goddess of death is gone, just like the rest of the gods.

The wall I follow curves and circles around until I hit a dead end.

Slumping, I press my back against the rough stones, more jagged than the rocks in Cochas, or even the stones that form the walls of the palace in Isul Urqu. The Folqu trapped me far from that familiarity.

I can examine the other end of the cavern, if that will do any good, so I push myself upright, preparing to try.

As I stretch out my hand, I'm about to let the wall guide me, but as my breathing quiets, I sense many auras with the same absences of emotion that I sensed once in the mountains before descending into the valley around Isul Urqu.

Straining to make sense of it, I startle when a subtle clack of shoes alerts me to a new presence, though any hope of it being someone who can help me escape drains before taking root.

It can't be anyone or anything good.

The room brightens, not with any source of light, but with tendrils of smoke that creep into the room as a woman emerges. She wears boots with a red fringe, a gold breastplate, and a golden headdress with feathers and horns. Though her face is gaunt, she has beautiful high cheekbones.

She stops a few short strides away, the mist folding in like a cape behind her.

Sizing me up with a sharp gaze, she speaks in a nasal voice that grinds against my bones. "Yakua Roca, daughter of Amoya, you came at last."

I suppress a flinch. "Who are you?"

"I'm your grandmother." She smirks. "Heliray, the goddess of death."

CHAPTER TWENTY-FIVE

ALARM PIERCES MY CHEST as I hurry to bow. While I am very much at her mercy, I can't accept her claim.

My family has lived in Cochas for generations...on my father's side. I love the sea. My mother manipulates people, yes, and power like hers hasn't been seen in generations. But demigods like the emperor have risen out of the same diluted blood.

"I'm a descendant of the goddess Ma Cochira, not you." I shouldn't speak to a goddess so disrespectfully, but I can't allow her assumption to stand without contest.

Her smile stays fixed, though it's not a happy one. "You are, it's true. But you're also my descendant and my blood is stronger in you. You have the purest demigod blood that remains in any of the realms since the gods left your people. Their lines run thin, but not mine. Your mother is my daughter, and that heritage is the source of your power. I know you came here to learn about yourself, and accepting this fact will enable you to tune into your abilities.

"You are a political strategy among gods, that is all," she continues. "Demi-gods are politics and have been since the dawn of time."

My mother worshipped Heliray. Both the Dragunche and Amaru called me "Ma Roca," as if they considered me someone significant. Only a demon would consider a daughter of Heliray worth their reverence. On top of that, I manipulate people with my magic. What's more characteristic of Heliray than my power?

Heliray lowers her voice. "First, I want to understand why you came to me now when you could have done it weeks ago when my priest first approached you." She waits, lips pressed into a thin line.

She's right. I should have made this choice a long time ago. I didn't understand enough when I arrived, or when I saw Amaru for the first time. "I was afraid of him." I can't describe Amaru in any better light.

"Why didn't you run from the emperor? Why did you stay?"

The answer to that question is simple. "I have to protect my kingdom. If I don't, no one else will."

She studies my face. "They'll hate you either way."

The people who thought me a monster will continue to curse my name. My parents won't know the difference. My entire clan thought I died a traitor. Even Sunqu, the only person who knows the truth, begged me to run.

"You're probably right."

Her words take me back to the day I stood at the edge of a cliff, when Sunqu told me I didn't have to jump. He was teasing, but he had a point.

My answer hasn't changed, but my reason to stand here has.

I raise my chin. "I plan to do it, anyway."

Tattoos down the woman's neck glisten as she takes off her headdress and sets it slowly on the ground. "However foolish your reason," she says. "I'm glad you came. You have a lot of potential. If you want to tap into the same powers your mother had, I'll teach you to use them." She gestures to the empty cavern as if a crowd watches—

perhaps the Heliray worshippers still sit around an invisible fire. "My priests and I will teach you."

With the use of my power, I will become the woman my father chooses not to remember. I'll become my mother.

The notion fills me with dread.

"Just help me save my kingdom," I say.

"Ah, you see," Heliray holds up a finger, "I want to help you, but I don't care about your kingdom. In fact, if they all die, either from being overworked in the mines or in the wealthy homes of Isul Urqu, they will become part of my kingdom. I see no tragedy in that."

She brought me here for a reason, though.

"And yet you still want to help?" I ask.

"I do." Her grim smile widens, and it makes me grateful I don't smile because her twisted, dark smile is much worse than the lack of one. "I want a human kingdom. It's what I was promised. While all of the other gods fall one by one to Mirchira, he doesn't deserve it. He's not even good at creating anything. It's my turn to reign over the realms. The empire belongs to me and I'll do a better job ruling it. Right now, I rule the greatest kingdom beneath the earth. I want to rule the one above it, too, bigger than any of the kingdoms have been before. I will rule what the moon should have been."

She might have shoved me with the point of a knife against the edge of the cliff. If I take a step forward, I'll die. If I step back, I'll fall. If I don't move, someone else will find me and they won't give me options.

Worse, my refusal means I'm trapped alive in Uru Hlocha

I should have known this is what Heliray would want, but if it means I can remove Emperor Huamar from the throne, I'll take my chances, though my decision weighs heavy, especially as I sense another strange aura of no-emotion press closer.

Yet something about the presence clicks in my head, igniting a new, fiery anger.

Leveling my gaze with hers, I glare at her. "The Dragunche was yours, wasn't it?"

Heliray only looks at me.

"Your little minion killed my servants in the mountain. Why?"

She takes her time before answering. "It was keeping watch for me, ensuring no one goes through those passes without my permission. I didn't anticipate your arrival. In fact, I didn't know of your existence until my Dragunche informed me. Your mother hid you well, and never brought you to my temples."

She was a goddess that even my mother wanted to protect me from. Worse, I should despise her for what she did, for killing innocent people who defended me.

Heliray might make an even more evil ruler than our current conqueror, but I can deal with that when the time comes. If the giants wipe out my people, it won't matter who sits on the throne.

I hate myself for it but nod my head once in unhappy agreement.

"Don't make that mistake again," I say, my voice low and seething.

Heliray folds her arms, her grin flickering at the corners of her mouth. "Our lesson begins now." She folds her legs and sits before me.

I hesitate, still fuming, before allowing myself to kneel, watching her warily as she presses her palms together.

"I created your mother as an experiment. She was to be my champion and found my new kingdom among the living. Instead, she married your father." Heliray grimaces. "I hope she loved him because she threw away everything I gave her. I'll explain your powers as I explained them to her and can only hope you'll be smarter than she was."

Despite knowing they married against the clan's wishes, I can't imagine my parents in love, though I've been told it was the case many times.

"First," Heliray says, "you must understand that every object has a physical presence and two spirits. One spirit to create it and one to animate it. Having a tie to a god will give you a stronger connection to one or both of these two spirits. The emperor is powerful because he can create and, by creating, can imbue loyalty in his stone giants, though his control over the giants is founded entirely on the loyalty he created in them.

"You, however, are the opposite of the emperor. He is life, as we have seen with the giants he created. You are death. Your power over creation is minimal, but you have a stronger influence over the animation spirit. You can persuade, just as your mother did. But there is also a difference between subtle manipulation and total control. I can show you how to control the emperor, as I'm sure you have planned. That's why you came, is it not?"

"Yes."

There's no need to hide what she's smart enough to see as my only option. My mother taught me about the spirits when she taught me how the gods' power works.

"I've noticed," she adds, "that you're wearing your mother's necklace."

I finger the stone, a stone of Heliray, tempted to rip it off, though I've only just restored it. I don't though, because it was my mother's too.

Heliray displays her usual smile without warmth. "There are a few more rules you need to know. Your power is stronger when you're touching someone. However, if you wear your mother's necklace, the gem broadens and hones your power. Fear makes you stronger. It also enables you to control without touch. But remember: if you don't use the fear that fuels your power, it has the opposite effect. It makes you weaker.

"The emperor uses energy when he creates. I believe he mentioned this to you. While you use energy when you tweak emotions, you lose a lot more when you refrain from consuming fear. When you feed on fear, you are at your strongest. It's what you're meant to do.

"I'm sure you've also noticed that when you alter people's emotions, they sense it. This is because if you push too hard, you replace their emotions with fear and that fear is often directed toward you. It can be a good thing if you take advantage of it, but it also exposes you."

It's as I always suspected. I'm a monster at my core.

"Emotion is finicky," Heliray continues. "It must be coerced, moved, and shuffled around. You're quite adept at this for not having had a teacher. But to take over and control someone, you must reach in and grab the strings. You can't be timid."

She bares her teeth. "Make them bend their knees."

Though Heliray's words bring only disgust, I can't back away from them.

Heliray stretches out a hand and grasps my wrist. My back arches and a flood of emotions fill me to the brim, spilling out. My vision fogs and my muscles tense. When she releases me, I'm lying flat on my stomach with my knees folded beneath me in a bow.

Scrambling to my feet, I scour my thoughts for an explanation. She did it so fast, so easily, and I lost control completely. "What did you do?"

"I controlled you." She holds out her own hand, palm up, fresh blood oozing from an open wound. Subtle hints of gold swim in the red.

An awful dread courses through me, and I understand for the first time why a doe hates a mountain lion, and why my village hates me.

"The more you fear me, the easier you are to manipulate. I can sense it, just like you can. I can feel that you're afraid right now."

I don't want to give her the satisfaction of knowing she's right, so I bury my fear beneath my focus.

"That's better."

Though I dislike the casual way she belittles me, I stifle my irritation too.

Raising a shard of glass, she displays the edges so they glint in the dim light.

"Glass is like stone," she explains, "in that it contains the life and souls of the gods the way stones do. But you can see through glass. You can reach out and grasp the worlds on the other side like you're connected to them. But if you break glass, it becomes harsh and jagged, and you can use it to sever connections, like the connections to spirits. But that kind of power requires a sacrifice. A blood sacrifice. When this is done, you must wield the severed spirits with a firm and ready grip, or lose them.

"Try it."

Hating the idea of unnecessary sacrifices, and what those would entail, I take the shard of glass with slight hesitation and hold it over my hand.

"You have to want it. You have to want to control me. You have to want to be worshipped. Let go of everything else that might distract you from that one desire. Let it overwhelm you. Be ready to take charge of the spirits when you reach for them."

Without giving myself time to think, I slice my wrist and reach for the spirits the way I used to reach for emotional threads, but as Heliray warned, they slip away and Heliray grips my fingers so hard I cry out and dance back.

"It's not enough. You have little time to figure this out, Yakua."

I try again, pressure mounting inside my head as the knife bites into my skin.

"No, no, no." Heliray shoves my chest with a single finger. "Be quick. Be agile."

I try again and again, I fail.

She studies me. "Go on."

I try for what feels like hours, but the spirits flee every time I reach out. Even as I snatch the tail of one, it slides away, like trying to cling to the memory of a memory.

Heliray watches her finger twitch with interest. "Again," she repeats as if no accomplishment was made.

I'm never able to replicate it, and her other four fingers refuse to abide by my increasingly desperate commands, until Heliray waves for me to stop.

"Enough."

Blood drips down the length of my arm, and my head whirls from the loss of blood as I strain to focus on her.

"Let's try something else." She strokes her chin with a finger. "Can you change my mind about death?"

Though my head still spins, I sigh with relief.

While I don't have the energy to keep trying to control her, prodding emotions is something I learned as a child, when my mother asked me to help her hope again, though she begged me to conceal my powers from my father.

I could show Heliray the crippling fear of the unknown, of pain, and of the finality of death as the Dragunche stared at me from across my tent. I could reveal the nightmares that plagued me every night since that time, the fear that consumed me from the time the emperor announced I might be sacrificed to the gods. But with her knowledge of the afterlife, the unknowns any human would feel will be lost on her.

Instead, her statement about forgetting Cochas and all its value hooks into me.

What if I showed her the value of human life?

Naya as she clutched my waist and thanked me for her dress, my mother when she held my hands by the docks, Sunqu when he pushed aside my sandcastles, as he gave me a pair of glass slippers, as he stared wide-eyed at the Mungacu, as we danced together and he stumbled, when he carried my bags across the emperor's throne room. When I let him go.

His face consumes my thoughts.

Heliray jerks and I stare down at my fingers over her forearm, yanking my hand back.

I didn't mean to touch her.

She blinks and her cold expression dissolves briefly until she pushes herself upright and brushes the dirt off her boots. I can't tell if I changed her opinion, but she picks up her headdress and sets it firmly on her head, takes a few steps back, and clears her throat.

"I can see you've used your power before," she says, "but you should have come to me sooner, Yakua. You need far more training than I can give tonight. I only hope this is enough to aid you. Controlling the spirits requires more practice than you've had, and you've been taught to be afraid of yourself for far too long."

The emperor doesn't know I have the ability to manipulate animation spirits. If nothing else, I can surprise him. I must try. "Thank you."

"If you choose to stay in the city of Isul Urqu, it's on you. If you do stay and somehow live through this, you will find no support from the people here. You'll need me, Yakua, and you'll need more mentoring than what I've been able to provide in this short time. When that time comes, I expect the kingdoms of Hallja to worship Heliray."

If I live.

"And Yakua?"

I keep my face neutral. "Yes?"

"You were never meant to be liked. You are meant to be feared."

Before I can open my mouth to respond, the creeping, black-robed figures of several Dragunche emerge from further down the cave, appearing as if from vapor, circling me. The temperature plummets, sliding Dread's ghostly fingers across my skin.

Heliray snaps her fingers and the air stirs. Claws clasp my arms again. I blink and, instead of the Dragunche, a circle of mystics stares at me from across the flames of their bonfire.

Amaru touches my arm and I flinch away.

"Yakua Roca," he says, "it is time. The emperor plans to announce the final round very soon."

CHAPTER TWENTY-SIX

IF MY POWERS DON'T FAIL ME, and if I don't end up on the altar myself, no one will question my claim to the throne after I force the emperor to marry me as there's no one else to pass the throne to, but once I bend the emperor, the nobles will see it, and they'll be suspicious.

I'll have antagonism wherever I turn.

A servant wearing a necklace of seashells waits outside my hut, bowing in front of the door, his face stretched and colorless. "Princess," he says. "You have been invited to the Fidichi field for the final round announcement."

"Thank you."

He inclines his head. "I'm to wait here until you're ready. He wants you to look your best."

The emperor must have a reason for sending his servant to escort me when I have my own. Glancing at Irenti over my shoulder, she stands in the corner, her eyes lowered.

"Wait here then," I say to her.

Heliray can't help me. Neither can Sunqu nor my mother. My mother may have been wrong about a lot of things, but she wanted me to live to my full potential.

I drag a finger over the emerald on my necklace, the part of her I carry with me because she's a part of me. Perhaps I need to remember her as the imperfect woman who loves me, not as someone others disdain. Not as a shard everyone wants me to pluck out, but as history to learn from.

Whatever happens, I can't postpone the inescapable. I set the headdress Sunqu bought me over my hair, adjust my dress, and slip the glass slippers he made over my feet, wearing them for the first time since our fight.

My obsidian mirror reflects the straight strands of black hair that tormented me in Cochas. Here, in Isul Urqu, the physical characteristics vary, but I tried to fit in other ways. After this, I won't fit anywhere. I'll stand apart.

"I'm ready."

Guards in gold breastplates wait with spears in their hands as I walk between them. They join me on either side, keeping pace as the servant with a seashell necklace follows close behind.

A line of four women I don't recognize cross the grass from the palace. They separate, each wearing headdresses and extravagant gowns as they head for the doors of huts that used to be empty because the princess who lived there died.

The emperor has already replaced us.

I'm sorry for them, and I'm sorry for myself too.

The servants push me forward and we continue on to the stone tiers of the massive Fidichi stadium. I expected the throne room, but maybe the emperor and his friends want to play first, as they often do before an announcement, though I don't care to sit through another game.

The emperor, however, stands by his throne near where the Huya clan typically watches games, fully clothed and without the characteristic Fidichi paint. Ma Drea stands at his side, her lips pursed so tight they pale against her skin.

Princess Asari halts with a few feet between us. She glances at me, attempting a comforting smile.

Everything about the field—how we stand in the midst of it and before the throne—feels wrong. Unease lodges in my throat, especially with the new princesses arriving at the palace making it uncertain whether anyone will survive this round.

The emperor steps forward, the red sash around his waist dangling in the subtle breeze. Above, the Folqus circle, casting shadows.

"Today," the emperor begins, "I will speak my own announcements and assign my own rules. And I will witness the results.

"Many of you don't know the story of how I bested my brother before I took the throne. My father and mother demanded that we prove which of us was more powerful and which they should take to the capital. There could only be one emperor.

"They gave us each a knife, and the winner became their favored child, while the loser died. I'll leave it up to you to imagine what happened. We will do the same today. Our empress should have the skills to keep her throne. The final round begins now."

The guards and servants around us back away, though two stay to drag Asari and I apart. They lay two knives on the ground by our feet.

I can't see Asari's face at this distance to know if she plans to kill me and I won't blame her if she tries, but my hand trembles as I pick up my knife, tossing it so the blade glints in the sun.

While I can't control the emperor from this range, I have to survive long enough to get to him. Surveying the stands, I pick out a line of guards separating me from him. Even with a knife, I won't get far.

Princess Asari stoops and picks up her own knife, striding toward me with quick, determined steps, never faltering. With each beat of my heart, she prowls closer.

The incessant pounding of my blood echoes in my ears as she cocks her arm. I take an involuntary step back. The Princess Asari who sought me out to speak to me alone wouldn't kill me.

Would she?

She slices her dagger toward me in graceful arcs that show she's proficient with her blade, that she has received lessons when I've had none.

I cry out and dart back, holding my dagger like a bludgeon.

Is fighting with a knife normal tutelage for a princess?

She jabs again, barely missing my jaw. Once more, I dart to the side, dancing away, afraid to return her strikes with a strike of my own, and terrified not to.

Combat isn't what I'm good at, and I scramble to focus on the fear that pours into me, making me powerful. Latching onto Princess Asari's emotional waves, I sense her determination, preparing to shove empathy toward her to convince her not to kill me.

Until I stumble.

Princess Asari's aim grazes my arm, and I recover in time to save myself from another blow.

I'm panting, my heart quivering, ready to drop my knife on the stones, but I need to breathe and don't have time to.

Sweat trickles down Princess Asari's face. She's watching me, not in the predatory way the emperor watches, but in a calculating way, as if she's measuring how quickly I tire.

Again, I reach for my powers, but trip over a loose stone as I dodge another of Asari's thrusts.

"By the stones," I curse, swinging back to my feet, dust clouding around my ankles, each breath coming in short gasps.

Again, I dance back, avoiding another close shave by my waist.

Asari twirls, changes direction, and cuts, nearly slicing my leg, but I catch the hilt of her blade on my knife, my hand shaking with the impact. Pulling her arm back, she jabs. I catch her again, but this time, I drop my blade, my fingers too weak to clutch it.

As I dive to retrieve it, Asari's eyes flash and she hurls her dagger. I flinch, preparing for pain, waiting for my chest to tear open, but the thud doesn't come. The knife doesn't strike.

Instead, the emperor grunts.

I look over my shoulder to find that Asari battled me into the corner closest to the emperor himself, trapping me with his throne overhead. The dagger she threw quivers, blade first, in the emperor's shoulder, right where his heart should be. Or above where his heart should be.

She missed, but barely.

Asari faces the emperor, eyes narrowed. "I won't play your mind games, Huamar. You cannot make me less than I am."

The emperor growls, pulls out the dagger, and rips fabric from his cape to press to his wound. As he motions to the guards, they step forward, spears raised. "You forfeit," he says in a gruff voice that barely masks the pain. "Take her to the sacred temple of Mira-Tamya."

Asari doesn't fight them but locks her gaze on the emperor. The shadows of the Folqus grow larger, thicker, as if they sense impending death. I stand frozen, my blood sluggish and cold. The guards seize Asari's arms and yank her backward. Silent screams echo through my skull as they drag her up the stone steps toward the palace.

Guards surround me, their hands grasping my arms. Someone jabs my shoulder blade with a sharp point, and I stumble forward. They lead me up the stairs and over the grassy hills, past the palace toward the mountain, and onto the same trail I took with the emperor on our first outing together.

Asari's fierce scowl lives on in my thoughts as I put one foot in front of the other. I'm so proud of her and more frightened for her. She doesn't know the full meaning of her sacrifice. She doesn't know her body will be fed to the giants rather than buried by the riverbank with honor like her ancestors before her.

We cross the bridge of Mira-Tamya to the other side, the path continuing through the trees. I used to consider the bridge a stunning destination. I stood close to the emperor on those same wooden boards and ropes. Back then, I didn't think about what could lie on the other side or that the emperor might have a temple at the heart of his city. I suppose the emperor and his game blocked my view of a lot of things.

Keeping my eyes straight ahead, I avoid looking over the edge at the turbulence of the falls hitting the stones at the bottom, though the sound ricochets off the mountainside. I won't forget the overwhelming pull of the water as it dragged me down. Or the streaks of red that trailed down my bleeding arm.

Slipping while I trudge up slick rocks, a guard clutches my arm. As my headdress clatters down the steps, the servant who walks behind me snatches it up and hands it back. I nod my thanks.

How many other highborn women have they escorted up this mountain? It's strange that the serenity of Mira-Tamya will lead to the place where a priest cuts throats and spills blood over an altar, and then feeds bodies to stone giants for breakfast.

The trees thin and the tips of the palace emerge at the edge of the jungle below, sprawling against the hillside and towering over the city that stretches out almost as far as the horizon until it stops on the edge of a precipice.

Isul Urqu only has one mountain on the vast mesa, the one beneath my feet and at the center of the city.

This might be the last time I'll see any of it.

"Princess, you have to keep moving." The servant prods my arm.

Before giving him an answer, I let the air fill my lungs. "I'm going."

We crest the peak and dip down into a tiny valley, as if the god of mountains, Skapu, knocked off the tip. Water erupts from a hole in the ground and flows into another waterfall as the stone path descends deeper into the valley to the temple. This temple has the same open ceiling as the others, but the walls end with an altar at the edge of another drop-off.

At this temple, the emperor doesn't hide what happens to those he sacrifices.

I walk inside, the guards filing in behind me.

Faded red stains mark the pristine white altar in the center of the room as if the gods haven't absorbed their last sacrifice and are still hungry.

The emperor perches at the front of the room, surrounded by the Huya clan. When I hurry toward him, a guard grasps my shoulder and spins me around. If I can't touch the emperor, I won't be able to sway him, let alone control him, and the fear in the room is latent, smothered by monotonous routine. It isn't strong enough to grasp.

The guard pushes me so I stand where the princesses once lined up, but now there's only me. Alone, surrounded by the living and memories of the dead.

Princess Asari sweeps through the door, her wrists bound, as two guards trail behind, their expressions perplexed. She kneels before the altar and lifts her chin to meet the emperor's gaze.

He eyes her with one eyebrow raised, but she relaxes her shoulders.

Princess Asari's previous words shake me.

There's nothing to forgive.

The High Priest's sleeves billow as he picks up his knife from a woven cushion and raises it. The obsidian hilt flashes in the light. Pressure builds in my chest as the emperor turns his face away until the force bursts into a single word.

"Stop!"

If I can't touch the emperor and control him the way I want to, I'll influence him from afar.

I force myself to meet his gaze as his veins protrude from his wrists. If this is who I must become to be empress, I don't want it. Rather than watch this happen again, I'll do something to prevent it. Princess Asari might forgive me for her death, but I'll never forgive myself and I'll never forgive the emperor either.

The eyes of the Huya fix on me and the emperor's mouth twitches, though he holds up a hand.

The High Priest pauses, holding his knife aloft, while Irenti stays still, her head bowed, waiting for the end.

"What did you say?" the emperor whispers.

Heat replaces the acid in my stomach.

I can barely bring myself to look at him, but I have to, because I can't let him escape me.

"I know you suffered as a child, often at the hands of the wealthy, but we're not all the same, emperor. We're not dolls for you to play with. Your vengeance won't restore the childhood you think we've stolen."

While I'm not a princess, I've unconsciously grouped myself with them.

"What you're doing is murder," I continue, "not sacrifice. You forget that your ancestor is the god of life and creation, not death."

His upper lip curls. "I don't think you realize, princess, that I'm the one in power here. Even your servant, Irenti, is in my control." He grips the sides of his throne, his knuckles white. "She has been spying on you for weeks. I knew every step you've ever made, every word you spoke. And all along, you thought you'd made a friend." He chuckles. "You are a doll, princess, and I'll do what I like with you."

Clutching his arms, Emperor Huamar's expression becomes as stormy as the late summer hurricanes in Cochas, while the circle of Huya on my right look on with impassive masks for faces. They've seen so many young women die that they've allowed callouses to grow around their hearts.

He motions for the priest to continue. "Give her what she wants. Kill them both."

A renewed sense of urgency makes me straighten as my brain combs for the best way to awaken the Huya's resentment for the emperor. I need them to be afraid if I want to touch them emotionally without a physical bridge.

The emperor spreads his arms, leaning on his palms. "You were supposed to be better than the rest," he says, "princess."

I meet his gaze. "At least you can admit to being wrong."

I'm not better. I'm far worse.

The priest motions for a guard, who approaches, spears in hand. Behind him, a line of women emerge from the side of the building, dressed in gowns finer than mine, their faces just as pale—the same women I saw arrive earlier.

They won't deter me.

I turn to the members of the Huya clan gathered in the room as the guard grabs my arms, twisting my skin and gripping tighter than necessary. "You don't know anything about me—"

The guard drags me forward, but the emperor stops him by raising a hand again. "No, I want to hear what she has to say. I want her to see how little it matters. Continue, princess."

I force myself to ignore him, surveying the room instead.

"You don't know me, except that I'm a princess who came from a far-off land with odd traditions, creatures, climates, and people who choose a different patron god than you worship. But I want you to know that I feel the same feelings you do and have more flaws than any of you. Like you, I know this man who presumes to rule over us is corrupt and cruel. So long as he keeps his crown and power, he is happy. Whatever happens to the rest of us—friend, Huya, or stranger—we're the same to him. He doesn't trust anyone. You can end my life here today, but your mothers, daughters, and nieces will be next." I look at each of them down the rows and they avoid my gaze, even Hoq, the man who lost his daughter. They won't help, and I don't expect them to, but I can soften the callouses they have formed to protect themselves. The room spikes with fear and I breathe it in, power rippling through my blood.

Reaching for the strings of the emperor's emotions, they aren't readily accessible beneath my fingers, but my power senses tendrils of dread. Blowing a song through them, I twist it with the rawest emotions I have. I imagine standing close to the cliff's edge with Sunqu calling me back, the terror that clawed my chest when the Dragunche appeared in the doorway of my tent amidst the slaughtering of my servants, the revulsion in myself when I realized I'd been the cause of a child losing her mother in an even more horrible way than I lost mine. Then I take those emotions, experiences, and people that taught me to view the world in a new way and fling them outward to everyone within my reach.

Grabbing hold of the emotional strings that lead back to the emperor, I fasten my focus on him and yank with my magic as hard as I can. The fear that stems from him is rooted in distrust—a darker fear than self-preservation.

With a jarring thrust of my foot, I smash the heel of my glass shoe into the stone floor of the temple. Once, twice, three times before the heel cracks. Then I pick up the glass shard and slice my hand, cutting the threads that lead to the emperor and reach for his animation spirits to control him.

But the spirits flee too fast, just as before. And as I try to sway his emotions, I fail in that too. Despite his fear, his anger boils through my grasp, complicated by many layers of other emotions and reasons for being in place. The emperor's inflexibility breaks my song. No emotion I send outward can touch a heart so torn and broken.

Sunqu and Zita's faces flicker at the corners of my vision.

Naya, Zarrill, my father, Stellya.

My chest heaves and I stumble into the altar. Pushing me forward, the priest binds my hands as I fall on top of it. Then he forces me upright.

Despair threatens to drown me in "what if's."

Heliray was right and I need more practice. I should have gone to her a long time ago.

The emperor folds his arms. "Say what you want, Princess Nalia, but I control these people. You aren't a threat to my command. A few months after you're gone, they'll have forgotten you. Your name will join the dozens of other princesses that died on this mountain. But don't worry, you won't die alone." He motions to the guards, who disappear behind a doorway and reappear with a taller young man, a woman, and a child, their hands bound together behind their backs. The guards shove them, and they stumble sideways, collapsing on the stones beside Asari and the altar.

I grow roots so deep I couldn't move if I wanted to. The young man on his knees hunches so his nose touches the ground, but when he raises his head, Sunqu's brown eyes meet mine. "I'm sorry, Yakua—" Servants tie cloth around each of their mouths and muffle Sunqu's voice.

I lurch forward but the High Priest digs his fingers into my shoulder and holds me back.

I'm dreaming, dying, drowning, and I can't wake up.

I can't allow Asari, Sunqu, Irenti, and Zita to die here with me. Failure was never an option, but now the consequences are immediate. I failed the one time it counted and I'm not sure my soul will survive.

The emperor smirks. "Yes, I found them. I watch all the people who come to my castle and noticed you visited Sunqu often. What a surprise it was to see him abandon me after all I've done for him. And then to discover he had your child! I don't know what you two were planning, but the empire will thank me soon enough for getting rid of you."

Irenti hides her face from me, but her bindings don't allow her to hide the seashell tattoo that marks her wrist—a symbol of the origin of the nations, and of Mirchira, not Isul, her patron god. It's the tattoo of a slave.

I didn't notice it before. I suspected she might be working for the emperor all along, though I hoped it was the Huya that told the emperor I visited them, not her. While I don't blame her for protecting herself, I'm not surprised, just disappointed.

The top of Zita's head faces me, but I didn't need to see her to recognize her. I wish it was anyone else.

Rather than have my neck sliced at the altar, I want to sink and become one with it, to never think or feel again, to be remembered and thought of as little as the stones that form the base.

The emperor clicks his tongue and regards me without the smallest trace of pity. "When people get too close, they hurt you. It's better to gain loyalty through obligation and fear. Turning my followers and the Huya clan against me couldn't have worked. Don't you see why? The giants are everywhere. They're as chiseled into people's thoughts as they are into the cliffs and even this mountainside, and only I control them. I rarely have to use them because the knowledge of what they can do is enough."

Just over the emperor's shoulder, beside her sons, Lina Illapu shifts and averts her gaze.

The emperor is right. His inner circle of friends revere him as the man who gave them an opportunity and protected them from the dangers of opposing him. The Huya clan have their own agendas, but in the end, they're afraid and I don't matter enough.

The emperor's eyes don't leave me but burn with a mockery that chars my skin from my cheeks all the way down to my toes.

To the emperor, winning means life and death, and he likes it that way.

Emperor Huamar creates and controls giants, just as he boasts to everyone present, but while Mirchira, his patron god, controls the creation spirit, the descendants of Heliray have a stronger influence over the animation spirit.

Where I struggle to use my powers on the complex mind of a human, perhaps, like the emperor, I will have more luck starting with something simpler, or with a simpler mind.

In our legends, Mirchira created giants before he created humans. It took Mirchira, a full-fledged god, at least two tries to master his craft.

The emperor motions to the High Priest. "Show them what happens when you lie to your emperor and plot to take his throne."

The guard forces me to my knees beside Asari, who glances my way, eyes shining, and I yearn to set her free.

"Forget Asari," comes the emperor's voice.

The priest raises his knife as he approaches, but turns it to its side and presses it against my throat, letting it bite into my skin. I grit my teeth to keep from crying out and probe the mountain with my mind for foreign spirits.

"Not yet."

Blood tickles my skin as I open my eyes.

The emperor gestures to Sunqu, Irenti, and Zita. "Kill the child first. And then Sunqu. I want her to watch."

I can't save Sunqu and Zita by yelling, as much as the emperor deserves it, but it takes considerable concentration to keep my mouth shut.

"I'm going to kill you and toss you off the cliffs you love so much, princess. But only after you've watched your loved ones die. Take heart it wasn't them who tried to kill you."

Sunqu struggles against his bindings as the High Priest unties Zita and hauls her toward me. She digs her heels into the ground and arches her back, but the priest kicks her and she goes limp.

"Please," I whisper, squeezing my eyes shut. "Heliray, help me." Emotions too dull to be human brush my consciousness, just at the edge of my own fear. I pry them open and boredom swells within me. A pair of giants press their backs against the mountainside, right beneath my feet, just as the emperor reminded me. Waves of curiosity replace the boredom, rippling toward me, soft as the wind.

The animation spirits of the giants hover lazily at the edge of my consciousness, already severed from my earlier blood sacrifice and unable to refasten while my palm still oozes.

I snatch the spirits and hold fast.

"Come." I force obedience and the whole of my fear into a single word, as well as the desire for approval I felt on the cliffs months ago, when I lived and breathed to restore my family name and position in the clan. The emotions flood into the mountain and into the spirits of the emperor's precious giants.

The simple brains receive them, lapping the emotions up like empty sponges.

Pebbles scatter. Dirt dances across the altar. Trees shake and topple to their sides. The stone seats the nobles sit on crack and people scream as they spring to their feet. Lina Illapu clutches the arms of her grown sons and stares around, wide-eyed, as the High Priest scrambles back.

The emperor's face blanches. "What have you done?"

Exhilaration fills me as the power I so often neglect burns in my fingertips, expanding in my chest. I don't know these giants. Their thoughts aren't familiar. I don't know what they're capable of, but I did what I needed to, and it worked.

Pebbles tumble into deep fissures that snake down the mountainside. The walls of the temple shiver as a horrible creaking sound fills my ears, followed by another crack.

The Huya in the crowd scramble over each other to get out of the way, their screams slicing through my ears as they flee up the mountainside.

More rocks tumble off the cliff. The altar trembles, slowly sliding with the High Priest in tow. He flails his arms and shrieks as his form disappears behind an avalanche of dirt and rocks. Zita, Asari, and Sunqu scramble, their arms still bound, as dirt shifts beneath them. I throw myself forward and reach for Zita's cloak, but the fabric slips through my fingers.

It doesn't matter if I won, or if the giants obey me over the emperor, if I lose the only people I care about.

My feet slide as I scramble after them. "Help me!"

I don't know if the giants can hear or if they're smart enough to react in time, but a head appears over the cliff's edge and revolves to face me. Then it raises an arm and stops the cascade of dirt just before Asari, Sunqu, and Zita topple over the edge. Grabbing them around their waists, I drag them. Sunqu helps me get them to the staircase that leads to the peak. I slice their bindings at the base.

"Run!" I yell, pointing up.

Sunqu seizes Zita's hand and yanks her up the stairs, Asari following close behind. They stumble alongside dozens of Huya nobles, but they're safe.

I try to run after them and stumble on my broken shoe. Shaking it from my foot, I leave the beautiful glass that Sunqu made me behind.

Pain lances through my scalp as someone grabs a fistful of my hair, yanking my head back.

"Who are you?" The scent of dust mixed with incense envelops me as the emperor hisses into my ear. His chest presses into my back, rising and falling as he pants. When I don't answer, he pushes a blade to my throat and pain bites my skin. As I gulp in air, the sharp hilt presses deeper.

Suddenly, his chest stiffens. He shrieks and his grip relaxes. As I bite down on his wrist, the knife drops to the grass, and I spin around to see the emperor held immobile by my giant, who grabbed him by the back and pinched him until his eyes bulged. He can barely move to look at me.

Stooping to pick up his knife, I cock my arm and plunge it deep into his chest. He screams as I twist it, my eyes on his face the whole time. A metallic scent fills my nostrils and blood splatters onto my glass shoes, but I push the knife harder.

I make a better villain than he does.

The giant lets him go, and he stumbles toward the cliff's edge, blood oozing from the corners of his mouth.

Huamar deserves every second of pain for each princess he killed, for planning to harm Sunqu and Zita, for challenging the heir of death on her own playing field.

I press my lips to his and let my mouth linger an inch from his skin. "Am I not everything you wanted in your empress?"

I don't wait for an answer but release the knife.

His jaw slackens as he sways, his weight carrying him backward, the life in his eyes flickering out like a candle's flame. His cape spreads with his arms and he drops.

The giant catches him in the air and, with a vacant expression, tosses Huamar's limp form into his mouth with a crunch.

Fear flows across the mountainside and ripples through me. It swirls in my chest and penetrates my bones.

I can do so much with these giants. I can conquer kingdoms and force the Huya to fear me. I can be the name people whisper amongst themselves in awe and reverence. I can be known across empires.

No one will dare to toy with me. Who my mother was will cease to matter, except to entrench that fear deeper than any knife can cut.

I can, but I don't want to.

Instead, I turn to my giant. "Protect my kingdom."

CHAPTER TWENTY-SEVEN

A S I SHOVE THE PALACE doors open and stride down the hallways, my single glass slipper clacks against the patchwork stones. Light brightens the rooms, illuminating the carvings of the gods. Even the air I breathe is clearer, and more crisp.

The giants will return to their posts in the mountainside and the empire will go on as before, except with me leading it.

Lines of servants bow as I pass. Fear rises and fills my lungs as more people enter. Members of the Huya file through the doors, their eyes wide and their faces pallid.

My steps falter as the throne rises before me. If I don't sit there, who will? A member of the Huya? I know none of them well enough to trust them. If I want to protect Zita and Sunqu as well as the kingdoms, I must control the empire's guards and armies. I can't shirk that power now.

Straightening my shoulders, I sit on the emperor's throne, rubbing the armrests with my fingertips. The King of Cochas once sat before me on a throne less grand than this one. I couldn't have imagined this day then.

A servant hovers at my side and smooths her dress.

I wait, staring until the silence echoes. "Yes?"

She nods, giving me a jerky bow as she eyes the necklace I wear. Strange to be neither liked nor supported, but followed without question. Moments ago, she would have killed me on the emperor's orders.

Refusing to show how much her fear bothers me, I give my first order. "Bring me the glassmaker and the girl who's with him."

They can't be far. The last I saw them, they were running into the hills with the Huya. That must have been less than an hour ago.

Bowing again, the servant scurries out the doors.

Lina Illapu pushes away from the lineup of ashen-faced Huya, hesitates, and then takes several quick steps forward, bowing so low to the floor that her nose almost touches it.

Some time ago, I stood where Lina stands now, my token burden slung over my back, waiting for marriage. The emperor wouldn't look at me. Now he's dead and I sit in his place.

Whatever comes, I'll revere the memories of the princesses who came before me, whether they sat on this throne or not. Whether they were as kind as Princess Asari or not, I'll leave shell offerings in their names.

Refusing to break the silence, I let it fester until Lina straightens.

She looks up at me, her graying hair smooth, despite the dust on her shoulders, evidence of running from the crumbling cliffs. "Now that the emperor is dead, and you have stepped forward to lay your own claim to the throne, you must marry one of my sons to become a legitimate ruler. My family is next in line. You promised to ally with us."

The soft light in the room dims as the doors open again. Sun-qu enters with Zita and Princess Asari beside him, Zita's worn dress ripped in several places and her expression as ravaged as the day her mother died. Asari, on the other hand, holds herself with quiet pride despite the dirt covering her dress.

Sunqu's brow furrows.

I look at him and not at Lina. "I will not."

Lina's voice rises. "Then we, the Huya of Isul Uruq, cannot support you. You aren't our empress."

This time, I face her, both impressed by her challenge and unwilling to bend to it. "I gave you a chance to support me," I say in a quiet voice. "If you weren't courageous enough to stand with me then, why should I let you stand with me now?"

Fear spirals, my blood pumping it through my veins. If I used it, they couldn't defy me. "Do what you like, Lina, but you couldn't remove me from this throne if you tried. Not even with the Chira Huya behind you."

I scan each of the faces of the Huya, some more somber than others, and point to the door. "It's time to leave." The sounds of their feet scraping the floor fill the stone-walled room, before the room quiets in the wake of their absence.

They should be happy the emperor is dead, but I don't care that they aren't. I'll be the queen I want to be—which is the queen the empire needs, even if it isn't the queen the Huya or the people of Isul Urqu want.

The door closes and I slump into the throne as the energy from their fear drains into the gold beneath my fingers.

Sunqu walks slowly across the court and stops in front of me.

Zita stays back, though the fear has faded from her eyes and expression. Meanwhile, Irenti keeps her face turned away, her head bowed.

"Zita needs glass slippers too," I say, though I can barely mumble the words. "You never made her any."

Sunqu doesn't smile.

I turn to the servant closest to me. "Take Zita to the finest rooms this palace has and ensure she's safe. If anything happens to her, by the stones, I'll send my giants after you. Do you understand?"

The servant bows and Zita follows her.

Ignoring Irenti, I turn to Princess Asari. "Do you wish to stay?" I ask.

She studies me, her kind, round face more contemplative than calculating. "I want to go home."

After many months of yearning for Cochas, I understand, and expect this response. "I will send an escort home with you, so you may travel safely through the mountain passes."

"When?" she asks.

"As soon as one can be assembled."

Princess Asari nods. "Then I will pack my things."

She inclines her head, turns, and strides for the door, leaving Irenti behind.

When Irenti looks up, she shifts beneath my gaze.

"I'm sorry," she says in a whisper, hanging her head, her thick brown hair covering her eyes.

"I know." I won't give her the satisfaction of accepting her apology any more than those two words, though she did what she had to do to free herself from the emperor's grasp. I'd have done the same in her position.

She nods several times as if she doesn't know what else to do. "I'll leave the city. You won't have to see me again." As she shuffles back, I stop her with a gesture.

"You'll stay," I say. "And you won't lie to me or betray me again."

Her lips tighten, but she gives me another curt nod. After a moment's hesitation, she leaves, the sun straying into the room and marking the floors as the servants let her out. When they shut the doors after her, the floor regains its prior shine.

Sunqu takes a step closer. I forgot he stood beside me, but his close proximity heightens my awareness. "Can we have a moment alone?" He glances at the guards, and I wave them away, admiring how natural it is to command them. They file out without hesitation as if my presence chases them off.

The doors close with a click, soft as a sigh.

"Yes?"

He gestures to the carved stone walls and tapestries depicting Huamar in all his beautiful youth. "You'll be a better leader."

As long as I rule in my own way, with more wisdom than the day before, I will be satisfied. "I'll be the best leader I can be." Only the gods know how much I still have to learn.

Sunqu runs a hand through his hair, mussing it. "You pushed him off the cliff?"

"Yes."

I watch his expression, waiting for a reaction. Will I find horror written there? Disgust?

He simply grins a bright Sunqu grin. "Fitting," he says.

"You still love me after this? After everything I've done? I'm a descendant of the goddess of death." I forgot to tell him that part. "I killed him, and I enjoyed it."

As the shock of my last statement settles in, so does the truth of it.

"A demi-god of death? That explains a lot, actually," he teases, cupping my chin. "But you're still Yakua, and you'll still be the girl who makes my life difficult." He kisses me lightly on my bottom lip. "I suppose I love that about you. You push me to do more, be more. But what I love about you most is that it doesn't matter what people expect from you, what they call you, or who they say you are, you define your own version of good, bad, and evil."

I thread my hands through his hair and kiss him back, the taste of him salty on my tongue, like home. I won't let him go again. "I love you too, Sunqu," I whisper. "But I love that I make your life difficult even more."

He chuckles and tucks my hair behind my ear.

And I smile.

GLOSSARY

Amaru (ah-mah-roo): Priest of Heliray.

Amoya Roca (ah-moy-ah row-kah): Yakua's mother, a demigod who was hated in Cochas.

Animation spirit: Spirit that is manipulated when using the magic of the gods.

Bachue' (Batch-hu-way): The emperor's servant.

Braeila of Frigelles (breh-EE-lah): Princess Raysa's handmaid.

Caya clan: Family of the king.

Cayuhu spice (kay-OO-hoo): Poison said to kill those with diluted and unworthy blood.

Chiki Clan (cheeky clan): Old house of the original Huya clan of Isul Urqu. They oversaw conveying important information across the kingdom, especially in times of war.

Chira: Southern Kingdom of Hallja with the patron god of Mirchira.

CoccoInta Illapu (coco-in-ta Ill-lap-OO): Son of Lina Illapu.

Cochas: Southeastern Kingdom of Hallja with the patron goddess of Ma Cochira.

Cochmayu river (co-ch-may-oo): River that flows from Cochas, past Paria, to the Jocalyna Sea.

Creation spirit: Spirit that is manipulated when using the magic of the gods.

Cuxy Pa: Wife to Opo-Mayta Pa. Brought from impoverished Chira and given lands to become a Huya in Isul Urqu.

Darhi (dar-hee): Priest of Cochas.

Dokas (doe-k-has): Eastern Kingdom of Hallja. Patron god of Ma Dokara. Many of the kingdoms rely of Dokas for food imports distributed through mountain passes or by ship through Kiani Bay.

Dragunche (drag-un-ch-ay): A demon of Heliray, known for its whistle of death.

Drea Chiki: Head of the Chiki Clan and chosen to announce the princesses as they are sacrificed.

Emperor Huamar (who-uh-mar): Originally a peasant from Chira and now the conqueror of Isul Urqu. Demi-god of Mirchira. Feared for the giants he controls, and for his mercilessness in war.

Esukya (es-oo-k-yah): Spring of the gods.

Father Tiawa: Built a temple on the mountain to honor Ma Cochira for saving him from a storm.

Fidichi: Sport played by throwing heavy stones through hoops.

Folqu (full-kew): Giant birds that feed on dead flesh and carry the weight of dying souls to Heliray in the afterlife. They were attracted to Isul Urqu by the carnage the giants left behind.

Frigelles (free-guh-el-less): Western kingdom with the patron goddess of Ma Frigello.

Gothlu: High Priest of Cochas.

Hallja (hall-huh): Lands containing Isul Urqu, Dokas, Joco, Cochas, Paria, Ragua, Thalas, Chira, Frigelles, Jaspa, and Skarag.

Hanup: Constellation symbolizing the power of the gods.

Heliray (hell-EE-ray): Goddess of death with powers of manipulation, though the goddess' power is limited to the underworld and minions of the underworld where she reigns. Once the goddess of the moon.

Holya (hole-yah): Island on the southwest coast of Cochas, known for its lush plants. Mother island to Tarya. Flat landscape.

Hoq Isulasto (hawk EE-sul-ahs-toe): The head of the Isulasto house. He is afraid of Mirchira taking over Isul's kingdom and hoards Perja furs in case Isul ends the eternal summer.

House Illapu: Oldest house of the original Huya clan of Isul Urqu. Their family would have inherited the throne after the previous King, had he not been dethroned.

House Isulasto (EE-sul-ahs-toe): Of the original Huya clan of Isul Urqu. This family was originally in charge of sacrifices for Isul, and of ordaining the next priest, until Isul was removed as the patron god of Isul Urqu.

House Paqari (pah-car-EE): Old house of the original Huya clan of Isul Urqu. They oversee guarding the kingdom's borders and have huts stationed at each of the four known mountain trails.

Huya (who-yah): Noble clans.

Ichu Illapu (each-oo ill-ah-poo): Son of Lina Illapu.

Irenti: Yakua's handmaid while in Isul Urqu.
Iro Roca: Yakua's father.

Isul (EE-soul): God of the sun. The previous patron god of Isul Urqu.

Isul Urqu (EE-soul irk-OO): Once the kingdom of the god Isul, and now the capital of the new empire. This city is built on a massive mesa with a small mountain at the center. The city has been blessed with eternal summer and gets its water from Esukya, the spring of the gods.

Isul-Fuyu (EE-soul foo-you): The old name of Mira-Tamya, before Isul Urqu was conquered. The waterfall was once dedicated to Isul.

Jaspa: Western kingdom with the patron goddess of Ma Jaspu.

Joachik Paqari (joe-ah-cheek pah-car-EE): Manages the northern mountain trails of Isul Urqu.

Joco (joke-oh): Eastern kingdom with the patron goddess of Ma Jocoya.

Kiani Bay (key-ah-knee): Where the gods first landed with the demigods to found the kingdoms of Hallja——the lands of all the kingdoms, south of the wild clans. Now has its own pier and is used to trade food across the kingdoms of Cochas, Thalas, Chira, and Joco.

King Kunica (kooh-knee-kah): King of Cochas.

Kurku (kirk-OO): Star that foretells amusing sport.

Lamuna clan: Yakua's father's clan. While it's typical for couples to join the woman's clan after marriage, Amoya and Iro Roca join Iro's clan because Amoya doesn't have family.

Lina Illapu (EE-lap-OO): Head of the Illapu House. Her sons are

Ichu and CoccoInta.

Luthuya (luth-OO-yah): Constellation symbolizing the fertility of the land.

Ma Cochira (co-ch-ear-ah): Goddess of the sea.

Ma Dokara (doh-car-ah): Goddess of plants, symbol is grain.

Ma Frigello (free-guh-el-oh): Goddess of crafts. Taught the first demi-gods and humans the art of spinning.

Ma Hlocha (hole-oh-cha): Goddess of the earth.

Ma Jaspu (jah-sp-OO): Goddess of young girls, represented by a woman holding a golden rod.

Ma Jocoya (joke-oh-yah): The goddess of health and happiness, represented by the tea leaf.

Ma Thala (thall-ah): Goddess of weather, represented by lightening.

Manco (man-coh): Yakua's servant through the mountain passes to Isul Urqu.

Master of the Docks: Person in charge of the docks and maintenance of boats. In Yakau's Cochean village, this is a highly coveted position.

Mines of Hlos (h-low-SS): Because the goddess, Heliray, doesn't have her own kingdom, her worshippers gather in the mines of Hlos.

During the wars of the giants, they moved to Isul Urqu for refuge. The mines of Hlos are located in the Kia mountains, north of Dokas.

Mira-Tamya (mirr-ah-tam-yah): Spring dedicated to Mirchira in Isul Urqu.

Mirchira (mirr-cheer-ah): God of creation. Known for first creating giants, and then creating humans.

Mungacu (moon-gawk-OO): Sea serpent.

Naya: Yakua's half-sister.

Oci (oh-see): Yakua's favorite student.

Opo-Mayta Pa (oh-poh my-tah pah): The emperor's general. Brought from impoverished Chira and given lands to become a Huya in Isul Urqu.

Pacay Virimac (pah-kay veer-EE-mack): Brought from impoverished Chira and given lands to become a Huya in Isul Urqu. Bored with her small circle of friends and cowed enemies in Isul Urqu.

Paria (par-EE-ah): The city of the priests, known for its rainbow sands, founded by Parifalko.

Parifalko (par-EE-falk-oh): God of water and rainstorms.

Perja (purge-ah): Half human and half cat, they were created by the gods to carve ice sculptures in the mountains to remember them.

Known for their claws that they use to carve the ice, and for killing people who get too close.

Phaqcha clan (pack-cha): Clan that departed from the first clans of Ma Cochira and settled along the cliffs. Since that time, other clans have joined them.

Princess Asari: Princess of the Kingdom of Thalas and skilled knife fighter.

Princess Nalia: The former princess of Cochas and Yakua's pseudonym.

Princess Raysa: Princess of Frigelles and Yakua's nemesis.

Princess Tullu: Princess of Dokas.

Qori Mountains (kori): Mountain range in Cochas.

Ragua (rag-OO-ah): Kingdom north of Paria and east of the Isul Mountain Range, with the patron god of Raguary.

Raguary (rag-OO-ar-EE): The god of metals and treasure.

Ranu Achikoya (ran-oo ah-ch-ee-koh-yah): The current High Priest of Isul Urqu.

Roca (row-kah): Yakua's family name through her mother's side.

Skapu (sk-ah-poo): God of mountains.

Skarag (sk-ar-ah-g): Northwestern kingdom with the patron god of Skapu.

Stellya (s-tell-yah): Yakua's step-mother.

Sunqu Sua (sun-coo sew-yah): Yakua's best friend.

Tarya (tar-yah): Daughter island to Holya. Thought to once be the baby of Skapu, god of the mountains, and Holya, until Holya threw her baby into the sea to escape the gods. Being a child of the god of mountains, Holya is more mountainous than Tarya.

Thalas (th-all-as): Southern kingdom, just northeast of Chira, with the patron goddess of Ma Thala.

The four worlds: The four worlds include Uru Hlocha, the underworld, Valhanen, the upper world, Hallja, the world we know, and the world that was once the moon, though its name has been forgotten.

Uru Hlocha (oo-rew hh-low-cha): Lower or under world.

Valhanen (val-han-nen): Upper world.

Yakua (yah-kew-ah): Main character and daughter of Amoya Roca.

Zarrill (zah-reel): Yakua's step-sister.

Zita (zeet-ah): Princess Raysa's illegitimate daughter.

LET'S BE FRIENDS

brookeclonts.com/subscribe

@brookeclonts

@brookeclonts

@brookeclontsauthor

LEAVE A REVIEW!

If you *loved* this book, the best way you can support me is to *leave a review*. This helps me find readers and get my books into conferences. Reviews are invaluable!

Do this quickly here: brookeclonts.com/leave-empire-a-review

ACKNOWLEDGMENTS

Thank you to Tami Mandarino, Chase Davies, Karlie Dalton, Santana Saunders, Caryn Larrinaga, James Nicholas Adams, Mary Celeste Ricks, and Sarah Jensen for beta reading my book before its release and for giving me the feedback that brought it to its final draft. And thank you to Kelley Riegert, Karie Crawford, Katherine Petersen, my editors, for polishing the first edition. And to Fiona McLaren and Sharon Stogner for helping me edit and improve the second edition. Thanks to Ben Dougal for the most amazing cover! To Jenna Evans Welch and A.K. Wilder for taking the time to read and endorse my book. And to my family, especially my husband, Tyler, for believing in me, and Des, for rereading this book to make sure it was ready.

I appreciate and love you all.

ABOUT THE AUTHOR

Brooke Clonts was born in Salt Lake City, Utah. Her passion for writing started as a kid when she spent most of her time hiding in her bedroom with a book. Her cousin recommended she try writing and it became her obsession. She has a degree in exercise science she's never used, is a self-taught software engineer, left her job as a software engineering manager for Adobe to run her own business, and is a wife and mom to the most beautiful boys in the world. She often writes late at night after her sons go to bed. But her stories follow her all day long.

Brooke writes no-spice fantasy with relatable characters. Her goal is to deliver themes with positive messages that uplift and resonate with teens.

You'll find Brooke terrifying her husband at the edge of cliffs, jumping on trampolines, hiking mountains, wake surfing, reading, collecting ridiculous amounts of Halloween decor, pretending to be a good dancer, and just being awkward and nerdy in all the best ways.

SECOND
STAR PRESS

www.ingramcontent.com/pod-product-compliance
Lightning Source LLC
Chambersburg PA
CBHW021220310726
48971CB00006B/1628